"I've changed, Annabeth."

Although he spoke very deliberately, with his jaw tight, it wasn't hostility she saw in his eyes but some sort of murky promise, something that went beyond words, something personal and solely between them.

"Hunter." She sucked in a hard breath. "I don't think—"

"Stop, Annabeth. Stop arguing with me and let me finish." With a move so swift she didn't see it coming, he took hold of her hand.

His touch was somehow comforting.

He rubbed the pad of his thumb across her knuckles. Warmth spread up her arm.

"I'm not going to hurt Sarah." He moved closer, too close, and added, "Or you."

She snatched her hand free, her fingers curling into a fist. "Words, Hunter. Those are just words."

"Then here are some more words for you to consider. No matter your motivation, I won't let you stand between my daughter and me."

Books by Renee Ryan

Love Inspired Historical

The Marshal Takes a Bride
Hannah's Beau
  Heartland Wedding
Loving Bella
  Dangerous Allies
The Lawman Claims His Bride
  Courting the Enemy
  Mistaken Bride
Charity House Courtship
The Outlaw's Redemption

Love Inspired

Homecoming Hero

*Charity House

RENEE RYAN

grew up in a small Florida beach town. To entertain herself during countless hours of "lying out," she read all the classics. It wasn't until the summer between her sophomore and junior years at Florida State University that she read her first romance novel. Hooked from page one, she spent hours consuming one book after another while working on the best (and last!) tan of her life.

Two years later, armed with a degree in economics and religion, she explored various career opportunities, including stints at a Florida theme park, a modeling agency and a cosmetics conglomerate. She moved on to teach high-school economics, American government and Latin while coaching award-winning cheerleading teams. Several years later, with an eclectic cast of characters swimming around in her head, she began seriously pursuing a writing career. She lives in Savannah, Georgia, with her own hero-husband and a large fluffy cat many have mistaken for a small bear.

The Outlaw's Redemption

RENEE RYAN

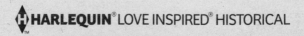

HARLEQUIN® LOVE INSPIRED® HISTORICAL

Recycling programs
for this product may
not exist in your area.

™ LOVE INSPIRED BOOKS

ISBN-13: 978-0-373-82971-2

THE OUTLAW'S REDEMPTION

www.LoveInspiredBooks.com

Printed in U.S.A.

And He said unto me, "My grace is sufficient for thee: for My strength is made perfect in weakness."
—*2 Corinthians* 12:9

To my older brothers, Bill, Bob and Noot,
for teaching me how to hold my own in a family
full of alpha males. I'll never know how to throw
a punch (thanks for sparing me from that), but
I certainly know how to rely on someone who can.
I love each of you with all my heart.

Chapter One

Denver, Colorado, 1890

Hunter Mitchell was a free man. After two years of hard labor and endless nights of soul-searching, he'd paid his debt to society. His life was once again his own. Countless possibilities awaited him.

And yet, here he stood but a stone's throw away from where his downward spiral had first begun.

Long before the judge had sentenced him to prison, Hunter had vowed never to return to this house of sin owned by the notorious Mattie Silks. Two years ago he'd made an exception, to take another man's life.

So much regret. So much hurt.

Just when he thought the worst was behind him, and would stay that way, his past had caught up with him again.

Lips pressed into a hard, flat line, Hunter rolled his shoulders and considered his next move. The most obvious course of action would be to storm through those ridiculously ornate doors and demand what was his. *Take* what was his.

He had the right. No one would argue that. But Hunter had learned to be a cautious man.

Mattie could have lied to him in her letter. She'd done so before. For no other reason than to see how far she could push a man. What the surly madam didn't realize was that Hunter was no longer susceptible to her games. He knew Mattie's well-guarded secret, a secret he wouldn't hesitate to use against her if she tried to toy with him.

Red-hot determination coiled in his gut. Hunter would get the truth out of the woman tonight.

No mistakes.

No loss of control.

Calm. Cool. Careful.

Melting into the shadows, he blew into his cupped palms. The air had taken on a cold, nasty bite. Hunter couldn't help but feel he was being watched, a remnant of his former life when he had to look over his shoulder wherever he went. But those days were over, the members of his former gang either dead or living in Mexico.

His breath formed a fine mist around his head, adding a sinister feel to what he'd come here to do.

And yet, *and yet,* he felt a sliver of hope building inside him. Hope for the future, hope that he could become the godly man he'd once been. And maybe capture some stability along the way.

He lowered his hands and stepped in the direction of the brothel's threshold. The physical act of moving brought the rest of the world into focus. Sights, sounds, the smells of stale liquor and wet horse flooded his senses.

Music drifted out of the brothel's open windows. The bawdy songs suited the raucous laughter and coarse shouts. Golden light called to Hunter, the soft glow promising warmth from the cold and a momentary respite from the constant loneliness that plagued him.

An illusion. Nothing but pain and regret followed a night with one of Mattie's girls.

And Hunter had stalled long enough.

With single-minded focus, he shoved away his dark thoughts, then took the steps two at a time. As he shouldered into the vine-covered building, a sickening dread crept through his stomach.

Nothing had changed. Not the hideous decor. Not the musky odor of cigar smoke mingled with cheap perfume. Not the seedy clientele. The brothel wasn't as bad as he remembered. It was much worse.

Mattie Silks was nothing if not obvious.

The gaudy red velvet furniture stood in stark contrast to the gold filigree wallpaper. Tasteless rugs with bold, floral prints covered the wood flooring. Vulgar paintings hung on the walls. Their vivid colors and shocking themes gave Hunter a new perspective on past sins.

Only recently back in the habit of praying, he lifted up a silent request.

Forgive me, Lord.

A simple prayer, born from a lifetime of bad choices and wrong living. Shaking free of the thought, Hunter stepped deeper into the brothel and caught sight of Mattie's right-hand man striding toward him, a scowl on his mean, ugly face.

"Jack." Hunter took in the big brute's broad shoulders, flat nose and bad attitude. "Still the ever faithful servant, I see."

Jack smiled in response, not a real smile, more a baring of teeth. "You were told to come by tomorrow."

"Yeah, well." Hunter stuffed his hands in his pockets and rocked back on his heels. "I'm here now."

"Nevertheless." Jack crossed his arms over his massive chest. "Miss Silks isn't expecting you."

"I say we let Mattie decide if she'll see me tonight."

Eyes locked with his, the big man dug in his heels. "She won't like that you've come during business hours."

Of course she wouldn't like it. Neither did Hunter. But he wanted answers more than he wanted to appease a difficult woman like Mattie Silks. "Either you inform her I'm here, or I tell her myself."

Finished with the standoff, Hunter started forward.

Jack stepped into his path. "Wait here."

"Whatever you say."

Frowning, Jack disappeared into the crowd.

Left to cool his heels, Hunter shifted out of the main traffic area and looked around. Business was booming.

He heaved a heavy sigh. The curvy blondes, willowy brunettes and pouty redheads perpetuated the cycle of sin and degradation. All had similar expressions on their faces, blank, distant, slightly separated from the moment, as if they'd given up hope a long time ago.

Hunter understood such brokenness, such pain. Understood all too well.

A small commotion broke out near the back of the room, saving him from further reflection. Low, excited murmurs filled the air, followed by a quick straightening of female shoulders, a widening of male eyes. All heads turned. A beat passed. And then…

Mattie made her entrance.

Dressed in a blue silk dress with layers of cream-colored, frothy lace, the infamous madam sauntered through the main parlor of her brothel like a queen lording it over her realm. She ignored everyone but Hunter.

With a half smile on her lips, she took her time crossing the room, striking a pose every fifth or sixth step. She carried a flute of champagne in her hand. A prop, nothing more. Mattie never indulged in alcohol, especially not during peak business hours.

Her head was always the clearest in the room, and the reason she'd been able to run her business for the past thirty years with alarming success.

Hips swaying, her face overly painted, Mattie stopped her approach inches shy of running into Hunter, close enough for him to get a whiff of her cloying perfume.

"Hunter, darling." She struck a final, dramatic pose—one hand on her hip, glass poised at shoulder-level, eyes lowered to half-mast. "What a surprise."

"A pleasant one, I hope."

"Time will tell." She angled her head to the side. "Greet me properly, you rogue, and maybe I won't hold your impertinence against you."

"But of course." He leaned down and touched his lips to the plumped, curved cheek she offered. "Hello, Mattie."

"Hunter." She pulled back and studied him with narrow-eyed precision. "Now. Let me look at you."

Having been through this routine before, he stood completely still, eyes cast forward. Her gaze traveled from the top of his head, down to his toes and back up again.

"The years have been kind to you," she decided, then reached up and ran her fingers along his jaw. "It's really unfair, you know, that you should look this handsome when you are so decidedly in need of a shave."

Without waiting for a response, she continued her scrutiny, seemingly oblivious to his tense shoulders and stiff smile. He worked to contain his need to speed things along. This was Mattie Silks, after all. The woman had her own set of rules. If he wanted answers, he had to play her game. For now.

"If memory serves," he said in a low, confidential tone, "you like your men a little scruffy."

"Oh, I do." She circled around to his other side and plucked at his sleeve. "I really, really, really do."

Hunter watched the madam out of the corner of his eye. "You're as pretty as ever, Mattie. I must say, you don't look a day over twenty-nine."

She laughed in delight, then leaned in closer, her hand clutching at his arm. "You always were a silver-tongued brute. Is it any wonder I like you better than that holier-than-thou brother of yours?"

Of course she liked Hunter better than Logan. Hunter had spent most of his adult years on the wrong side of the law. While his brother was a former U.S. marshal, a man bent on seeking justice by legal means only. Hunter had no such compunction, as evidenced by his two-year stint in prison. An eye for an eye, a life for a life.

"Tell me, Hunter, my dear boy—"

"Boy?" He gave a humorless laugh. He hadn't been a boy for a very long time.

Grinning at his reaction, Mattie walked her fingertips up his arm, squeezed his biceps. He swallowed his distaste. *All part of the ritual,* he reminded himself.

"To what do I owe the pleasure of your company this fine evening? Dare I hope you've returned to your old ways?" She looked him over yet again, this time with obvious intent in her heavy-lidded gaze. "Shall I order you a bath, a shave, a friendly chat with one of my girls?"

Hunter stiffened. *Enough.* "You know why I've come."

"Yes, well." She dropped her hand and sighed in disappointment. "A girl can always hope a big, handsome man such as yourself hasn't turned completely good."

Games. The woman couldn't help playing her games. "Let's not forget you summoned me, with quite a convoluted tale."

Her chin jutted out. "Not a tale. The truth."

"So you claim."

Breaking eye contact, Mattie tracked her gaze through

the room. As if she'd only just become aware of the interested stares, her entire demeanor changed. The tiny lines of worry around her mouth were impossible to miss. Interesting.

"Perhaps we should continue our conversation in private."

Unexpected. And yet, he realized, greatly appreciated. "A sensible suggestion."

"Follow me."

Spine stiff, head high, she led him through the main parlor toward the back of the brothel. Hunter knew the way, for all the wrong reasons. He kept his eyes on Mattie and his senses trained on the activity around him. The air of forced revelry was palpable, depressing. Sounds and bodies moved past him in a whirl, sometimes brushing against him, sometimes steering clear. Some of the patrons knew him, a few too many feared him.

He'd once cultivated that reaction. Now he wondered if his past would ever be forgotten.

He sighed.

In uncharacteristic silence, Mattie bypassed the kitchen and directed Hunter down a darkened corridor that ran along the southern perimeter of the first floor. A few more twists and turns, then, at last, she stopped in front of a nondescript door and indicated he take the lead.

Reaching around her, he opened the door then stepped inside the room. He had to blink furiously to accustom his eyes to the burst of light. Memories of the last time he'd been in this room warred with his attempt to remain outwardly calm.

The decor was different in here, at complete odds with the rest of the brothel. Homier, full of plush, comfortable furniture and a pleasant, floral scent.

Mattie had redecorated in the past two years.

With leaden feet, Hunter made his way to the mantel-piece on his right. Despite his efforts to stay in the present, his vision tunneled down for an alarming moment where all he could see was the past.

Gritting his teeth, he dug his toe in a small groove along the edge of the stone hearth. Just over two years ago he'd faced off with Cole Kincaid on this very spot, at nearly this exact hour of the night. Cole had proved soulless and without mercy, even in that final showdown. Ultimately, Hunter had prevailed in the ensuing struggle.

At the cost of his freedom.

He had no remorse. Cole had deserved to die after he'd murdered Hunter's beloved Jane in cold blood. She'd been so young, so full of God's goodness. Knowing her had made him a better man.

Losing her had nearly destroyed him.

An eye for an eye, a life for a life.

He couldn't change the past. But could he start anew? Could he become the man Jane had thought him to be, a man worthy of raising a child?

Not a child, he reminded himself. *His* child.

Maybe.

If Mattie was to be believed, Hunter had a nine-year-old daughter as a result of his brief first marriage to Maria Bradley. Their union had been a disastrous, impetuous mistake on both their parts. But where Hunter had been utterly captivated and painfully naive, barely two weeks off the ranch, Maria had been three years into her profession as a prostitute and had married him for the thrill of corrupting an innocent.

She'd succeeded beyond her wildest expectations.

He swallowed back a wave of bitterness. "Tell me about the child."

Mattie set down her glass and moved to the other side

of the room. She dragged her fingertips across the top of a wingback chair. "Her name is Sarah."

Sarah. Pretty. Biblical. Had Maria named her, or someone else? "All right, then. Tell me about…Sarah."

"As I said in my letter, she recently celebrated her ninth birthday."

For the hundredth time since discovering he had a daughter, Hunter did a mental calculation. The numbers added up. The timing was right. Sarah could very well be his child. That didn't mean she was. Maria had "officially" returned to her chosen profession less than a year after their wedding, but she hadn't been faithful for months prior to that. Any number of men could be Sarah's father.

But if the child was his, Hunter would…

What? What would he do with the knowledge?

One step at a time.

"…a pretty child." Apparently, Mattie had continued talking while Hunter had been lost in thought. "She has your unusual golden-amber eyes and her mother's dark, Mexican coloring."

Something passed in the madam's gaze as she spoke, something not altogether kind. Was she threatened by Sarah, a mere child?

That made no sense. Except…maybe it did.

Maybe this was as personal for Mattie as it was for Hunter, if in a far different way.

"You say the girl has my eyes. I want to see for myself." He strode across the room, stopped within inches of Mattie and used his superior size to make his point. "Get her."

Mattie blinked up at him. "She isn't here."

"Where is she?"

"Charity House."

Sudden, unexpected relief buckled his knees. He had to reach out to steady himself on a nearby chair. Hunter knew all about Charity House, the orphanage Marc and Laney Dupree had created for the abandoned boys and girls no other institution would touch. Because of the Duprees' noble efforts, children of prostitutes were welcomed into a loving, safe home without question. And given a solid, Christian upbringing.

Some of the bitterness Hunter had harbored toward his first wife released its brutal hold on his heart. Maria might have left Hunter for her former life and died less than a year later. She might have kept the knowledge of his child from him. But she'd had the sense to provide a good, Christian home for Sarah at Charity House.

He should be grateful.

And he was, on one level. But he was also confused. Why was Mattie Silks involving herself in the matter?

Surely not out of the goodness of her heart. Mattie had always hated Maria. That much Hunter remembered. As the illegitimate daughter of Mattie's bitter rival and the outlaw she'd once considered her man, Maria had been a physical reminder of Mattie's folly. Of the madam's mistaken belief she'd found a man to take her away from this life.

"What could you possibly hope to gain by telling me about the child?" he wondered aloud.

But deep down he knew. The situation just turned a lot more complicated.

"Now, Hunter, darling, I'm a traditional woman at heart."

"Of course you are."

"Don't be snide." She brushed aside his sarcasm with a dismissive wave of her hand. "I believe families should be together whenever possible."

"Except when it comes to your own."

Her gaze narrowed to two mean slits.

Hunter remained unmoved. "Don't forget, Mattie. I know your secret."

"You have no right to pass judgment on me."

No, he didn't. His list of past sins was a long one. "You're right." He inclined his head. "Forgive me."

"Yes, yes. Now, where were we?" Not quite meeting his gaze, she redirected the conversation back on its original course. "Maria was wrong to keep your own child a secret from you. She should never have—"

The door swung open with a loud bang, sufficiently cutting off the rest of her little speech.

"How could you, Mattie? This time you've gone too far." A whirlwind of tangled skirts and angry female rushed into the room. "You have no right to interfere in my life, or in Sar—

"Oh." The woman's pursuit ground to a halt. "I didn't realize you were…entertaining." Her gaze settled on Hunter for a fraction of a second, swept past him, then returned with lightning speed, widening in shocked recognition.

His sentiments exactly.

Feeling as if he'd just been smacked in the head with a board, Hunter fell back a step. Beneath his skin, his muscles twitched and tightened.

Memories took hold, memories of another woman with the same startling blue eyes, the same Mexican heritage.

But this wasn't Maria blinking up at him in obvious shock. This had to be her half sister, Annabeth. The last time he'd seen her had been at Maria's funeral. But she was a woman now, no longer a girl.

Pieces fell into place in his mind.

Mattie's unusually timed letter. Her interference in a matter that had nothing to do with her.

Except, it did have to do with her. Indirectly, at least.

"You…" Long, silky eyelashes fluttered rapidly as Annabeth's small, plump mouth tightened. "I thought you were in prison."

"I served my time."

The initial shock in her pale blue eyes turned to something else, something resembling alarm. Tinged with fear.

More pieces fell into place.

"I…don't know what to say," she admitted, her voice cracking over the words, her gaze chasing around the room.

"*Good evening, Hunter* would be a nice place to start."

"Yes, of course." She twisted her hands together in front of her waist. "I… Good evening, Hunter."

"Good evening, Annabeth. Or would you prefer a more formal address? Perhaps I should call you…" He paused, making sure he had both women's attention before continuing. "Miss Silks."

Chapter Two

*M*iss Silks.

Miss. Silks. Two simple words, spoken in that gravelly, deliberate tone and the carefully constructed life Annabeth had provided for Sarah and herself imploded. All because Hunter Mitchell knew her name. Her real name.

He knew she was Mattie's daughter.

An avalanche of emotion crowded inside her. She could hardly breathe, could hardly make sense of the moment.

She wanted to pray—*needed to pray*—but the words refused to form in her mind.

Shivering, Annabeth lowered her gaze and stared at her entwined fingers.

She shouldn't have come here tonight, shouldn't have risked being seen in her mother's brothel at such an hour. She'd made a mistake that could ruin everything.

If a man recently out of prison knew about her connection to Mattie, it was only a matter of time before the rest of Denver discovered the truth. Everything would change then, just as it had a year ago, when Annabeth had been released from her position at Miss Lindsey's Select School for Girls.

The good people of Denver would know her private

shame. Then what? No godly, moral man would want Annabeth as his wife, not when her mother was the most celebrated madam in town. She didn't care so much for herself; she'd given up hope for a respectable marriage at this point in her life. But Sarah. Poor, dear, beautiful Sarah.

"You may call me Annabeth." She shifted from one foot to the other. "Annabeth Smith."

"Smith." The silky, ironic tone had a dangerous note underneath. "Not very inventive."

Annabeth stared straight into Hunter's glittering eyes. His expression had grown fierce, ruthless even. A man on a mission, determined to get answers by any means necessary.

She forced herself to think fast, to sort through every possible solution to the threat he presented to her and the child she loved as her own.

What if he wanted to take Sarah away?

A chill ran up her spine.

There had to be a way to forestall the inevitable. But Annabeth couldn't make her mind work properly, not with Hunter's gaze locked so securely with hers, waiting, measuring, gauging her every reaction.

He stood over six feet, all broad-shouldered and lean-hipped. And those eyes. Piercing, intense, full of suspicion.

His lips curved at an ironic angle. "Finished with your inspection?"

"I..." She jerked her chin at him. "Almost."

For a split second, humor filled his gaze. Then he gave her a slow, mocking perusal of his own. "You are looking well, Miss...Smith."

He was intentionally trying to throw her off balance. Sadly, he was succeeding.

If only he wasn't so handsome, so masculine, so rugged, so...so...*handsome.*

"Thank you, Hunter." She resisted touching her hair, smoothing down the riot of curls she'd not bothered to tame before leaving Charity House. Another mistake on her part. Her desperation had made her careless. All she could do now was grasp for some semblance of control. "You, too, are looking well."

His big shoulders shifted, flexed and then went still. Dangerously still. She should take care. She knew what Hunter Mitchell was capable of doing when pushed. If even half the stories were to be believed, the man was deadly. Yet beneath the day-old stubble, his chiseled features looked entirely too wholesome for a man who had spent two years in prison for manslaughter.

Could he be trusted?

Was his life of sin behind him?

So many unknowns. Too many to allow her guard to slip.

Why, oh why, had Mattie followed through with her threat to contact him? Why had she ignored Annabeth's pleas to stay out of the matter?

Her mother would answer for her interference. Later.

For now, Annabeth had a very determined man to appease. No matter what happened next, he could not be allowed to take Sarah away with him.

He's her father. The thought whispered through Annabeth's head, filling her with renewed guilt. She'd come here tonight determined to do whatever it took to hide his child from him.

What did that say about her?

That she was cautious? Protective? Or simply selfish?

Silence grew thick in the room, making the air feel heavy, stifling. Even Mattie seemed to be rendered momentarily speechless, her gaze darting between Annabeth and Hunter.

More seconds ticked by. And still, Annabeth couldn't stop looking into Hunter's mesmerizing eyes. The impact of all that concentration directed solely on her was like a physical blow. And not entirely unpleasant.

For a brief moment, he looked as agonized as she felt. She wanted to soothe his anguish, to offer him comfort, to—

What was wrong with her?

Hunter was an unsafe man, one who knew her secret. He could ruin everything she'd built in the past year.

"It's been a while since we last met," he said, breaking the silence with his deep, velvety voice.

She nodded. "At least eight years."

Mattie sprang back to attention, snapping her head from one to the other. "You two have met before?"

"Yes, Mattie." A slow smile spread across Hunter's mouth, making him far too appealing. "I am acquainted with your daughter."

"But…" Mattie released a hiss, the sound equal parts hostility and warning. "That's impossible."

Annabeth understood her mother's shock. Through the years, Mattie had shielded her from men like Hunter.

"How…how did you two meet?" Mattie didn't bother hiding her horror at such a prospect, or her outrage. "Where? When? I demand to know every detail."

A sigh leaked out of Annabeth. "Does it matter now?"

"Yes." That one word, spoken through clenched teeth, said so much. "It matters a great deal, Annabeth."

She supposed so, at least from Mattie's perspective. Her mother had worked very hard to protect Annabeth, sending her far away to school where she could learn the precepts of Christian charity and proper behavior. No drinking allowed. No gambling. And definitely no friendly acquaintances with gunslingers recently released from prison.

Bad character corrupts good morals.

A noble ideal, to be sure, straight from the Bible.

But life at Miss Lindsey's had proved just as hazardous as the one Annabeth would have had in Denver, the people just as unforgiving once the truth had come out about her mother. She'd been guilty by association. Her dream of respectability gone, gone, gone. Her reputation not quite in tatters, but close enough to warrant leaving Boston for good.

"Annabeth." Mattie crossed her arms over her chest and glared. "I am waiting for an answer. Where did you meet this man?"

Despite the tension of the moment, Annabeth had to fight back a smile. Now he was *this man*.

Oh, the irony. Hunter Mitchell wouldn't even be in this room if Mattie hadn't contacted him.

Annabeth cast a quick glance in his direction. The expression in his eyes was kind now, encouraging, reminding her of the first time they'd met. She'd been more than a little dazzled by the attractive, broad-shouldered rancher her sister had married so impetuously. He'd been twenty-one at the time, more man than boy, full of charm and humor and determined to save Maria from herself.

Much had changed since then. Everything had changed.

"Annabeth. Stop staring at the man this very instant, and answer my question."

She sighed again. "We've met twice before tonight. The first time, a few days after he married Maria." He'd taken them shopping and had been so patient, so generous, even to her. "We met again at Maria's funeral."

"Her funeral?" Mattie's stunned expression precipitated her sinking into a nearby chair. "I forbade you to go."

Annabeth remembered the day well. She'd been fifteen at the time, home from school on holiday, and saddened over her sister's death, a sister she'd hardly known, who'd been born the daughter of Mattie's bitter rival, Emma Bradley. Her mother had been adamant Annabeth stay away from the funeral.

She'd gone, anyway.

"Maria deserved to have family present."

She'd been glad she'd gone, too. Only one other person had attended the funeral besides Annabeth. Maria's estranged husband, Hunter.

"Family?" Mattie spat out the word in derision. "She was that horrible woman's daughter."

"She was my sister."

"Your half sister. She had no relation to me."

"Regardless, Maria was always good to *me,*" Annabeth defended. "She was my blood kin. I loved her and she loved me." Turning to look at Hunter, she added, "She loved you, too."

He showed no reaction to the declaration, other than a careful narrowing of his eyes. "Did you know about the child when we met at the funeral?"

The question brought them back to the real issue at hand. Hunter might have been kind to her, once, long ago, when they were both much younger. But she knew what sort of man he'd become since then. Lawless, tough, a member of a ruthless gang.

Tread carefully, Annabeth.

"No, I didn't know about Sarah at the time," she answered truthfully. "Maria kept her existence a secret from me, too."

"I find that hard to believe."

So had Annabeth. She'd been terribly hurt when she'd discovered the truth. But that hadn't stopped her from building a life with Sarah once she'd discovered her niece's existence. A safe, respectable existence now threatened by this man's inopportune arrival.

How had matters gotten so quickly out of hand?

"Who knows what was in Maria's head at the time of her death." Annabeth closed her eyes against the image of the last time she'd seen her sister alive. Her beauty gone, the sunken cheeks and eyes, the despair. "She was sick, Hunter, and delirious most of the time in her final days."

"Yet she was lucid enough to send the child to Charity House instead of telling me about her." Hunter's voice cut through the room like a dagger. "I wonder why."

Didn't he know? "She was protecting Sarah, from you."

"From me." He spoke softly, his amber eyes lit with raw emotion.

"By the time she became ill you weren't exactly a model of good behavior."

"True."

Annabeth sighed at the regret in his voice, and the remorse. Such remorse. Had he changed?

Dare she hope?

"I understand why Maria didn't tell me about the child, but why didn't she tell you?"

Annabeth lifted a shoulder. "Perhaps she was protecting Sarah from me, too."

"You? No." He shook his head. "I don't believe that."

"What could I have done for her at the time? I was a child myself, spoiled and selfish and—"

"I don't remember you that way."

He didn't? How did he remember her? Had he thought of her through the years like she'd thought of him? Did he…

No. Oh, no. She could not let down her guard like this. "I was certainly too young to raise a child by myself."

"Perhaps." He fell silent then.

So did Annabeth.

Mattie eyed them both, gave a little sigh, then entered the conversational void with gusto. "Hunter, you must know it's not too late to change the situation. You can retrieve your daughter from Charity House and start fresh. You can—"

He raised a hand to silence her. "Stay out of this, Mattie."

She scowled. "I'm only trying to help."

"Yes, yes." He tossed a dismissive flick of his fingers in her direction. "Now hush. I need a moment to think."

"Of course." Mattie pressed her lips tightly together and, surprisingly, didn't speak again.

The groove between Hunter's eyes dug deep, his mind clearly working through the various revelations of the past few moments.

Maybe, when he thought the matter through to the end, he wouldn't want the responsibility of a child.

Oh, Lord, please. Let him walk away tonight.

Spearing his fingers through his hair, Hunter paced the room with hard, clipped steps. Back and forth he went, moving with the lethal grace of a large, menacing cat. Every few steps his hands clenched into fists, as though he were trying to control his pent-up emotions.

Understandable.

While he continued walking off his thoughts, Annabeth followed his progress with her eyes.

He'd changed since she'd seen him last and none of the changes were for the worse. His lean, long-legged body had filled out with the muscles of a man used to physical labor. His skin was a little weathered, and his hair had darkened to a rich, sandy-blond, the tips burnished by the sun.

He was dressed in stark black from head to toe. And even without a pair of six-shooters strapped to his hips, he had the swagger of a gunslinger. His square jaw, defined features and the shadow of a beard made him look threatening.

A formidable foe under any circumstance.

Her rebel heart found that bit of insight beyond exciting. Not that she'd actually *choose* to pursue a relationship with a man like him, but she could certainly allow her mind to…wonder. Perhaps she had a little more of her mother in her than she cared to admit.

A hideous discovery that couldn't possibly be true.

Unused to giving up control of a situation for long, Mattie rose from her chair and stepped into Hunter's direct path. "Yes, well, facts are facts. You have a daughter. You must take on the responsibility of raising her and—"

"No." Annabeth rushed forward, moving in front of her mother, fighting desperately for the right words to steer Hunter away from what Mattie suggested. "You can't just show up and claim Sarah as your child. She doesn't even know you."

"An oversight I plan to rectify immediately."

"But—" *Think, Annabeth, think.* "She's happy at Charity House. It's the only home she's ever known. She has friends there, people who love her, people who care for her."

"People like you?"

"Yes. People like me. Please, Hunter." She reached for his arm, then pulled her hand back before making contact. "Think this through. Now is not the time for hasty decisions."

"No. It's not." He looked torn, confused and maybe— dare she hope?—ready to concede.

Could it be this easy?

Annabeth pressed her advantage. "What can a man like you offer a nine-year-old little girl?"

"Family," he whispered after a long pause. "I can give her a real family."

Of course.

Of course.

Annabeth shut her eyes against a surge of panic. She'd forgotten who this man really was, and where he came from.

Regardless of his lawless ways and time spent in prison, Hunter was a member of a prosperous ranching family that included both parents, loads of brothers and sisters and a former U.S. marshal thrown in for good measure. The Mitchells personified respectability and, better yet, were a close-knit group. They would welcome Sarah into their midst without question. And love her unconditionally.

An ideal solution from any angle.

Unless, of course, Hunter chose not to return to his family's ranch. Unless he took Sarah to some unknown destination, to live among unknown people.

Annabeth couldn't take that risk. "You don't even know she's yours."

She was grasping for any argument now. She knew that, felt the shame of it. But Sarah's future was at stake. And Annabeth was desperate to protect her niece as best she could. She owed that much to the sister she'd lost before truly knowing her.

"Not mine? That's easy enough to determine." He pushed past her and headed toward the exit, seemingly convinced one look at Sarah would settle the matter.

Which, of course, it would.

"Wait. Just wait." She caught his arm and was stunned at the strength of the hard muscles beneath her fingertips, like a rock, solid and unyielding.

"Let go, Annabeth."

She released him at once. "You can't possibly think to see her tonight."

Brows lifted, voice low and rough, he said, "Because?"

She really had to spell it out? That alone proved how ill prepared he was to take care of Sarah on his own. "Because it's nearly midnight." She swept her hand toward the clock on the mantelpiece to make her point. "She's been asleep for hours."

"Asleep for hours." He cracked a smile, as if amused by his mistake. *Glory.* Annabeth couldn't deny the man was devastatingly attractive when he smiled like that.

She almost sighed. Almost. There was too much at stake to show weakness now.

"Oh, honestly, you two are acting worse than children. Step aside, Hunter."

His big shoulders shifted and then Mattie appeared from behind him. When Hunter didn't move completely out of her way she shoved and pushed for position. Satisfied at last, she slapped her hands on her hips and scowled at them both.

"You—" she pointed her finger at Annabeth "—will not stand in this man's way."

Annabeth opened her mouth to argue, but Mattie had already spun around to face Hunter. "And you—" she poked him in the chest "—will wait until morning to go to Charity House. It's the polite thing to do."

"You're right." He conceded quickly, graciously. "I will follow your advice and wait until tomorrow to meet my daughter."

A momentary glimmer of pleasure flashed in his eyes, sending another burst of panic through Annabeth.

What if he wanted to do right by Sarah? Could she stop him? *Should* she stop him?

He represented everything she distrusted in a man. He

was a former outlaw, a gunslinger, and had spent two years in prison for killing a man. By no stretch of the imagination could he be considered respectable.

Then again, he'd served his sentence. Didn't that mean he deserved a second chance? How could Annabeth claim to be a Christian and not wish for Hunter to have a fresh start?

She studied his face, searching his gaze for something that would ease her mind.

He looked tired, ready to drop on his feet.

Clearly, he needed rest. And maybe someone to care, someone to understand what he'd endured these past two years. No condemnation. No judgment.

A portion of her trepidation subsided, replaced with something softer and far more complicated. Perhaps Hunter would turn out to be a decent man, after all. Wasn't that more important than something as tenuous as respectability?

His appearance in their lives might be a good thing.

Faith. Annabeth just needed to have faith that all would turn out well.

"You will stay here, tonight, Hunter, free of charge. I'll accept no argument on the matter." Mattie pulled him toward the door leading into her brothel. "We'll set you up with a hot bath first. Then I'll send one of my girls to—"

"No." His refusal was immediate, too immediate to be questioned. "I appreciate the offer, Mattie." He smiled down at her, even as he extricated himself from her hold. "But I'll find my own accommodations for the evening."

"If you change your mind—"

"I won't." He inclined his head. "Thank you for telling me about my daughter."

"How could I not?" Mattie's gaze traveled to Annabeth and stuck. "It was the right thing to do."

Annabeth swallowed back a retort. They both knew Mattie hadn't written Hunter out of the goodness of her heart. She'd done so to protect Annabeth, unwittingly endangering Sarah in the process.

How could Mattie have been so shortsighted? So reckless?

They didn't know Hunter Mitchell, not really. He could turn out to be a hard, cruel man bent on destroying himself and those around him.

The responsibility of protecting her niece had never felt so heavy. Whatever it took, no matter what she had to do, Annabeth *would* protect Sarah. Even if that meant keeping the child from her own father.

Chapter Three

Hunter watched the steady stream of emotions advance across Annabeth's expressive face. He was able to track her thoughts easily enough. She didn't trust him to take care of his own daughter. Not that he blamed her. He wasn't sure he trusted himself.

How many times had he almost broken free of his past, only to be dragged back, sometimes willingly, sometimes not?

This time would be different.

Because this time he wanted something new, something within reach, something he'd never really wanted before—stability. Not only for himself, but for his daughter, as well.

I have a daughter.

Tenderness filled him, followed by an unbearable churning of the most terrifying emotion of all. Hope. That dangerous, slippery belief that all would turn out well in the end.

Perhaps, for once, it would. Hunter simply had to believe. He had to do his part, then let go and trust the Lord with the details.

His biggest obstacle was blinking up at him with those large, round eyes. Annabeth's gaze had turned a startling shade of lavender in the muted light and Hunter's gut clenched with…what? What was this feeling? Anticipation? An awakening?

Something far less pure?

A distraction he didn't need right now.

Ignoring her for the moment, he turned his attention on Mattie. She smiled up at him, the gesture full of warmth. Few people knew this softer side of Mattie Silks. He smiled back, grateful she'd taken the time to contact him. He knew she'd done so for her own purposes, but the result was the same.

Partially to see what she would do, and partially out of impulse, he yanked the ornery woman into a hug so tight her feet lifted off the floor.

"You rogue." She twisted and tugged and came up sputtering. "Put me down this instant."

Grinning at her reaction, he set her back on her feet. "I'll be seeing you soon, Mattie." He tapped her on the nose. "You may count on it."

"Yes, yes." Cheeks flushed, she dismissed him with a curt shake of her head. "Go on with you now."

Satisfied in the knowledge that he'd finally found a way to disconcert the unflappable Mattie Silks, he gave her a formal bow. Politeness personified, with a hint of mockery around the edges.

The woman deserved to lose some of her prideful composure. She'd contacted him in a letter, with the shocking news he had a nine-year-old daughter, leaving him to wonder for a full month what to do with the information.

He still wasn't sure.

What he did know was that Mattie had insinuated herself in the matter for a very personal reason. Her daughter, Annabeth. Sarah's aunt.

Hunter turned his attention back to the girl.

No. Not a girl, he reminded himself, a full-grown woman, one with a delicate bone structure, soft curves and a rich, throaty voice. Something about her calmed his soul. Even Jane hadn't been able to do that, not for want of trying.

Blinking at the betraying thought, he ran a hand over his face. He was bone-tired, and surely that explained the disturbing direction his mind had taken.

As if somehow sensing his agitation, Annabeth touched his arm. "Come, Hunter." He felt himself relax beneath her soft voice. "Let me walk you out."

When had she developed that confidence in her manner? The last time he'd seen her she'd barely looked him in the eye.

Now she held his gaze with conviction.

"All right," he said, realizing she still had something to say to him, something she didn't want her mother to hear.

Hunter found himself intrigued.

Walking into the hallway ahead of him, Annabeth stopped short and looked over her shoulder. "I'll only be a moment," she said to her mother. "When I return, we'll... talk."

"I'll be right here, darling." Mattie Silks in an accommodating mood?

Curious.

"This way, Hunter." Without waiting to see if he followed, Annabeth headed out. She directed him along a narrow corridor, past a row of closed doors and out into the moonlit night.

He drew in a lungful of fresh air, looked to his right then to his left. They were standing on the deserted street directly behind the brothel. A sense of foreboding took hold. Again, he felt eyes on him as if someone was silently tracking him, biding their time before pouncing.

He'd made enemies, but most were either serving their own prison sentences, or too busy watching their own backs to come looking for him.

A low-level hum of chatter, music and laughter flowed from somewhere in the near distance, probably from one of saloons down the lane, or a rival brothel. Another quick check of the surrounding area and Hunter relaxed, slightly. Other than a stray dog pawing at the ground, they were completely alone. No one was waiting for him, nor were there prying eyes to misunderstand this late-night meeting.

Clearly, Annabeth didn't want anyone to see them together. Not that Hunter could blame her. With a mother like Mattie Silks and an outlaw father known as one of the meanest cutthroats in the territory, the woman had a lot to hide from the world. Cavorting with an ex-convict, no matter the reason, wouldn't do her reputation a lick of good.

He looked down at his companion, noted how her troubled gaze went through a series of minor contortions. At the sight of her obvious worry, he felt an unfamiliar need to offer comfort, to let her know he wasn't here to hurt her.

He touched her arm. "Annabeth."

She took her time looking up at him. The ethereal beauty of her upturned face took his breath away. Leached of color in the silky moonlight, her exquisite features could have been carved from marble.

He could hardly bear to hold her gaze. He wanted to smooth away her concerns. But he didn't know what they were, not entirely, and as he'd never been a gentle man, he knew nothing of tenderness or affection.

Perhaps she was concerned he would reveal her personal connection to Mattie to the rest of Denver. In that, at least, he could ease her mind. "Annabeth, I—"

"Hunter, I—"

They both fell silent.

"You first," he said.

She took a quick, shallow breath and forged ahead. "I meant what I said earlier. Sarah has a good life at Charity House, safe and respectable. With me living there as well and teaching at the school, she's not on her own. She's…"

Her words trailed off, as though she wasn't sure how much more to reveal.

Hunter smiled at her, the gesture inviting her to continue.

She did not.

He waited her out, taking note of how the soft glow from the streetlamp brushed her dark hair with golden light. For a long, tense moment, her eyes flickered over him, too, her expression unreadable. She wasn't frightened of him, that much was evident, but she was wary.

For the first time since she'd barged into Mattie's private rooms unannounced Hunter considered what his presence meant to Annabeth. How involved was she in Sarah's day-to-day life?

With me living there and teaching at the school…

"How long have you been at Charity House?"

"Almost a year."

She had more to say, but he saw her hesitation as she pulled her bottom lip between her teeth.

"Go on, Annabeth." He gentled his voice to a mere whisper. "Say your piece."

"About tomorrow. I…don't want you upsetting Sarah. I…" Not quite meeting his gaze, she drew to her full height before continuing. "What I mean to say is that she isn't expecting you."

Easy enough to put right. "Then you'll tell her I'm coming."

"No, you don't understand." Her chin shot up, her gaze

full of challenge, the pose reminiscent of her notorious mother. "The situation is more complicated than that."

At a loss for a reason behind her hostile tone, he eyed her closely. "Then maybe you should explain *the situation* to me."

She braided her fingers together at her waist, a gesture Hunter was coming to recognize as a nervous habit, one that reared whenever she had something unpleasant to say.

He braced himself.

"Sarah doesn't know she has a father."

"You haven't told her about me?" His voice was raw in his own ears. He hadn't expected this, wasn't sure how he felt about this new bit of information. Angry?

No. Disappointed.

"Try to understand. I didn't want to disrupt her life, or give her false hope, in case you didn't—" she spread her hands in a helpless gesture "—you know, want her."

Now he was angry. The hot burst of emotion made his breath come in fast, hard spurts. He forced himself to speak slowly, to remember Annabeth didn't know anything about the man he'd become since the judge had sentenced him to prison. "What made you think I wouldn't want her?"

She looked pained and stressed. "It wouldn't be the first time a father didn't claim responsibility for a child living at Charity House."

Was she speaking only for the children now, or was she thinking of herself, as well? Her own father had been a Mexican outlaw that hadn't been known to stick in one place, or remain loyal to one woman, for long.

Hunter's anger dissipated, turning into something close to sympathy. Considering her past, Annabeth's reasoning made sense. But this wasn't about her father. This was about Hunter, and whether or not he would make the moral choice. "Would you have told me about Sarah if Mattie hadn't done so?"

"I don't know." Annabeth lowered her head. "I'm sorry, Hunter. I'd like to think that I would have, eventually, but I just don't know for certain."

Appreciating her honesty, Hunter absorbed her words. For all intents and purposes, Annabeth had conspired to keep his daughter a secret from him and would have done so indefinitely if not for her mother's interference. Did he blame her?

No, he didn't. He knew countless men who'd walked away from far less responsibility than a child. At one point in his life, Hunter had been one of them.

That was then. This was now.

A swell of emotion spread through him, seeping into the darkest corners of his soul. After all he'd lost, dare he hope for this new beginning, this second chance to get it right?

He had to try, had to go at this logically, rationally. Anything was possible with God. Or as his mother was fond of saying: *We can't out-sin the Lord's grace, or His forgiveness.*

A good reminder.

Hunter needed to be alone, to think, to plan, to work through the particulars of what came next. "I'll call at Charity House first thing in the morning."

"Better make it after school," she said. "Say, four o'clock?"

"Good enough."

He turned to go.

"Hunter, wait."

He stopped, but didn't pivot back around.

"I think it best we don't tell Sarah who you are, at least not at first."

It was a good idea, a wise suggestion, all things considered. However, a part of him rebelled. He'd spent the past two years being told when to wake, when to work, when to eat. He'd had enough. "I'll make that decision when I see the child for myself."

"Hunter, please." She hurried around him. "You can't just show up out of the blue, claim a daughter you never knew you had and then make promises you can't be sure to keep."

He bristled at her unwarranted accusation. Hunter never made promises he couldn't keep. Except once. Two people had ended up dead, one an innocent, one a very bad man.

Beneath his calm exterior, Hunter burned with remembered rage.

This time would be different, he told himself. Because *he* was different.

No more death, no more loss, no more bad decisions. "I didn't say anything about making promises."

"But—"

"One step at a time, Annabeth." He flexed his fingers, stopped short of making a fist. "We'll take this one step at a time."

"One step at a time." She repeated his words through tight lips. "Yes, that sounds like a good plan."

He moved a fraction closer, inexplicably drawn to her despite the tension flowing between them.

Chin high, she held her ground. For three long seconds. Then, she scrambled backward. One step. Two.

Hunter had seen that same look in many gazes through the years, some he'd deliberately cultivated. Annabeth thought him a threat.

She was right.

If Sarah was his daughter, no one—not even her devoted aunt—would keep him from claiming her as his own.

* * *

Heart in her throat, pulse beating wildly through her veins, Annabeth watched Hunter disappear around the corner of her mother's brothel. Nothing had prepared her for her first encounter with the man after all these years. She'd expected to meet a hardened criminal, an outlaw who'd earned his place in prison.

Annabeth had been wrong.

Ice-cold dread shivered across her skin. Hunter Mitchell was a man full of remorse. And hope. Yes, she'd seen the hope in him. It was that particular emotion that made her the most troubled. Ruthless and cruel, she could handle.

But a man with a desire to do the right thing?

How did she fight against that?

Was she supposed to even try?

She shivered, and not merely because Hunter could take Sarah away from her. In the depth of his eyes Annabeth had seen an aching loneliness that had called to her, one human to another, two lost souls searching for their place in a world that had dealt them cruel blows.

Now she was being fanciful.

Annabeth was never fanciful. She was practical, down to the bone. In that, at least, she was her mother's daughter.

Speaking of Mattie…

Annabeth spun on her heel. Retracing her steps, she paced through the darkened corridors of the brothel, back into Mattie's private suite of rooms. She drew in a soothing pull of air and then shut the door behind her with a controlled snap.

One more calming breath and Annabeth turned to face her mother.

Mattie had moved from her earlier position by the bookshelves. She now stood next to the fireplace. Her stance was deceptively casual, while her gaze remained sharp and unwavering. She had the attitude of a woman whose high opinion of herself far outweighed her place in the community. That regal bearing, along with her business acumen, had kept her at the top of her chosen profession for thirty years.

Annabeth resisted the urge to sigh. If only Mattie had used her many talents for legitimate purposes, maybe then Annabeth's shame at having a madam for a mother would not exist. Nor, perhaps, would she crave respectability so desperately, to the point of setting aside all her other hopes and dreams.

A familiar ache tugged at her heart.

Oh, she knew Mattie loved her, without question or reservation. It was that knowledge that turned Annabeth's shame back on herself.

The Bible taught that she should be sympathetic and love as Christ loved, to be compassionate and think of others before herself. That included her mother.

"Did Hunter get off all right?"

"Yes, fine." And not at all the point. "How could you have contacted him, when I specifically asked you not to do so?"

"He's the child's father." Mattie lifted her chin in defiance. "He deserved to know of her existence."

Another bout of shame took hold. She'd been willing to keep a man's own daughter from him, never mind the reason. "Maria didn't want him to know about Sarah."

"She didn't want you to know about her, either."

True. Annabeth had found out quite by accident. She'd been home from Miss Lindsey's less than a week, humiliated and at a loss about what to do with her life after her expulsion from her position at the school. Mattie had insisted she return to Boston and make her fresh start there, going so far as to threaten to cut off financial support if Annabeth didn't abide by her wishes.

At the time, Annabeth hadn't seen the point. One city was as good as another to start over, and who needed Mattie's money, anyway?

She'd been so naive, so headstrong.

Following that initial argument, there'd been many more heated discussions on the subject. A slip of the tongue on Mattie's part, a bit of investigation on Annabeth's part, and she'd discovered Sarah's existence. One look at the child had been enough to give her a new purpose in life. And so she'd set out to provide a stable home for her niece.

Unfortunately, Mattie had followed through with her threat and had pulled all financial support. Annabeth had been forced to take a job teaching at Charity House. Neither of them had expected Annabeth to fall in love with her new life.

But now, with Hunter's appearance, all her hard work of the past year stood on the precipice of collapsing.

Fear swept through her. "You should not have interfered," she said again, more forceful than before.

"I stand by my decision."

"He might take her away with him."

Mattie dismissed the comment with a sniff. "It would be within his rights."

Yes. It would. Hunter was Sarah's father; Annabeth merely her aunt. Her *half aunt,* as Mattie constantly reminded her.

Giving into despair, Annabeth pressed her back against the shut door, slid to the ground and hugged her knees to her chest.

"I can't lose her." She tangled her fingers in her skirts. "I just can't."

"I understand, far better than you realize. But listen to

me, Annabeth." Mattie tried to smile, but her blue eyes, the same color and shape as Annabeth's, had turned earnest, anxious, a little desperate. "I did not send you to Boston for an education alone. I sent you there to provide you with a better life than the one I could offer you here in Denver. No one knows me there, who I am, *what* I am. It was supposed to be your chance for a clean break."

Sighing, Annabeth lowered her forehead to her knees. "I know all that. But things didn't turn out so well, did they?"

"That doesn't mean you can't still go back and—"

"Mother, please."

In a move completely out of character, Mattie joined her on floor. "You're my daughter, Annabeth." She squeezed her arm. "You know I love you."

Annabeth swiveled her head to look at her bossy, annoying, pigheaded mother and a roll of affection spun in her stomach. Why did their relationship have to be so complicated? "I know you do. I…love you, too."

The words were far easier to say than she'd expected. Regardless of what Mattie did for a living, she was Annabeth's mother. Flawed and the source of much embarrassment, she'd done her best. What more could a daughter ask from a mother?

"I sent for Hunter for your protection. You'll ruin your life over that child if you don't have a care."

Annabeth knew that, too. "I'm twenty-three years old." Long past the first blush of youth. "I'm quite capable of knowing what's best for me. And contrary to what you think, I'm happy."

"You're wasting your education."

"How can you, of all people, say such a thing? I'm helping break the cycle of sin in those children's lives."

"I—"

"No, hear me out. I'm providing a solid, Christian education for boys and girls in desperate need of love and unconditional acceptance. It's really no different than if I'd stayed on at Miss Lindsey's and continued teaching there."

"Don't kid yourself, Annabeth." Mattie spoke in her most patronizing voice, the one she reserved for rebellious employees. "You're at Charity House because of Sarah."

It might have started that way, but Annabeth had changed. Her desires and goals had changed, too. Where once, everything had been about her, she now acted for the benefit of others.

A blessing she couldn't have imagined a year ago.

"If Hunter takes his child away with him," Mattie continued, "you could return to Boston and marry a good man."

"So that's what this is all about? That's why you contacted Hunter? You're counting on him to take Sarah away, thereby giving me no reason to stay on at Charity House?"

"It's the best solution for all parties."

How could her mother look so casual, so unconcerned, when her interference was tearing apart the life Annabeth had made for herself?

"What if I never go back to Boston?"

"Now, Annabeth, let's not be too hasty. You could still—"

"What if, Mother, I don't leave Charity House after Sarah is gone?" Her voice hitched as she spoke, the reality of all she was about to lose settling over her like a millstone tied to her neck. "*What if* I choose to stay and teach at the school indefinitely?"

Mattie's eyes narrowed. "You wouldn't dare."

Oh, but she would. Not to spite her mother, but to fulfill her calling, a calling she hadn't realized existed a year ago. Better still, she'd achieved a level of respectability she'd thought lost to her for good.

"This discussion is over." Annabeth jumped to her feet.

Mattie followed suit, a little slower, but with surprising agility for a woman her age.

"Move aside, *Mother.*" Annabeth looked pointedly at the door behind Mattie's head. "I have an early day tomorrow."

"Now, Annabeth, don't do anything rash. I know Hunter better than you do. Don't make the mistake in thinking he won't fight for what belongs to him. And like it or not—" Mattie leaned forward "—Sarah belongs to him."

"Is that supposed to frighten me?"

"I'm simply warning you to be careful. If the man wants to claim his daughter, there's nothing you can do to stop him."

Perhaps. But he hadn't taken Sarah away yet. There was still time for Annabeth to prepare.

One thing was certain. Hunter Mitchell knew nothing about raising a nine-year-old daughter on his own. All Annabeth had to do was make him realize that before it was too late.

It was all very simple, really. If Hunter wanted to be reasonable, she would be reasonable. But if he wanted a fight, well then, she would give him the fight of his life.

Chapter Four

Hunter jolted awake from a restless sleep. His pulse scrambled through his veins as if he'd been running all night, heading toward a shadowy image in the distance. He reached out even now, unable to stop himself, but came away empty.

Only a dream, he told himself, the same, mind-numbing nightmare he'd had every night since Jane's murder.

Would he ever find peace? Would he ever be free of the guilt? Did he deserve such mercy?

Dragging the back of his hand across his mouth, he lowered his head back to the pillow and shut his eyes.

The sounds in the room slowly separated from one another, each one becoming distinct and specific. The rhythmic tick of a clock. The slap of a shutter banging against a brick wall. A lone coyote howling for its lost mate.

Hunter hauled in another pull of air. The scent of clean linens stood in stark contrast to the usual stench of the state prison. Memories of the past week surged. Once he'd been released he'd traveled north as quickly as possible, stopping only long enough to earn the money necessary to make the journey to Mattie's brothel and beyond.

It was the beyond part that had him sitting up and rubbing at his eyes. The gray dawn light had spread its fingers of gloom into every corner of the room. Long shadows danced sinisterly along the walls, shivering across the white plaster like dark secrets woven inside whispers.

Whispers. Secrets. *Lies.*

The events of the previous evening slammed through his mind. Mattie Silks and her exposure of Maria's duplicity. Annabeth's unexpected arrival. The shocking reality of meeting again the girl he remembered better than he should, all grown up, her exotic beauty and soft nature enough to make a man stop and evaluate every wrong choice he'd ever made.

By all appearances, Annabeth was sweet and innocent, yet full of backbone. Fiercely loyal, too. During their brief encounter, she'd made Hunter's heart ache for something… more. Something he could never have. Stability was the best he could hope for now.

Or so he told himself. Annabeth Silks had surprised him. She'd made him feel things he'd thought long dead, things he had no right feeling.

Leave it alone, Hunter.

Solid advice. But he couldn't seem to shove the mesmerizing Annabeth Silks out of his mind. He wanted to know her more. Wanted to know where she'd been these past eight years. Was she at Charity House solely because of Sarah? Or had something else driven her to the orphanage?

Too many unanswered questions. Too many uncertainties.

The fact that Annabeth was heavily involved in his daughter's life might make matters complicated.

Hunter was used to complicated.

Frowning, he tossed off the covers and made his way to the window overlooking the street below. Hands flat on the glass, he squinted into the colorless morning mist. He could just make out the shapes of vendors setting up their wares for the day. A pair of dogs darted between the carts, probably scanning for fallen scraps of food.

He turned his back on the scene, his mind moving to more important matters. Today marked his first step toward making a new life for himself, because *today* he would meet his daughter.

His daughter.

Pleasure surged from the bottom of his soul, adding just enough force to pound ruthlessly behind his ears. He still had hours before he could make the trek across town to Charity House. He knew exactly how he would fill the time.

Once he'd washed, shaved and was sufficiently fed, Hunter stood directly across the street from his destination. He studied the unassuming brick building with growing unease. Even from this distance he was able to read the words embossed on the plaque nailed to the door. *Sheriff's Office and Jailhouse.*

He'd come full circle. But this time he had nothing to hide, and no sin to atone for. He'd served his time.

Yet he still felt as if he was being watched, hunted by some dark force. He checked his perimeter, rolled his shoulders and glanced to the heavens.

The sun had fully risen in the sky, shining so bright Hunter's eyes watered, and his head throbbed. Even his throat ached as he swallowed the foul stench of Denver's underbelly that wafted on the cool, March breeze.

Nothing had changed on this side of town. A depressing discovery. He jammed his hat on his head, then froze at the sound of familiar footsteps approaching from behind.

Instinct had him reaching for the gun at his hip, the gun he hadn't worn in years. Forcing his fingers to relax, Hunter let out a slow hiss of air and reminded himself he had nothing to hide, nothing to defend. His outlaw days were over.

"Looking for me?"

At the sound of that low, amused drawl, Hunter spun around to face the man he'd come to see. Trey Scott. Smiling that half smile of his. On any other man, the gesture would have softened his face. Not Trey. There was nothing soft about the seasoned lawman. His hair was still black as midnight, his eyes nearly as dark beneath the brim of his hat, his presence as menacing as ever.

Hunter remained motionless, refusing to give an inch of ground, or to show any sign of weakness. Trey did the same.

This was a ritual of theirs, this stare down. Welcoming the familiarity of the routine, Hunter settled in, keeping his mind on his goal—pay off the debt he owed this man. Not in money. But in words.

Money would have been easier, cleaner.

Shifting his weight to the balls of his feet, Hunter flexed his fingers. "Sheriff," he said in a bland tone. "Been a while."

"Too long, by my estimation."

Hunter didn't disagree.

He hadn't seen Trey since the other man had handed him over to the U.S. marshal assigned to escort him to the Colorado State Prison in Canon City. In the weeks leading up to his trial, Trey had shown Hunter what it looked like to live as a man of integrity, what it meant to show mercy where it wasn't deserved. To understand God's forgiveness in all its infinite wonder.

The irony that Trey had made such an impact on his life wasn't lost on Hunter. Logan, Hunter's estranged brother, looked up to this man, as well. They'd served together as U.S. Marshals for years, with Trey teaching Logan everything he knew about law enforcement. On principle alone, Trey should have been Hunter's enemy. Instead, the sheriff had turned into his greatest ally during the trial and his confidant in the endless hours of waiting for a verdict.

Hunter owed the man his life.

He'd never be able to repay him, not in worldly measures. Nevertheless, he was here to try. But first...

"I have something of yours I need to return."

Trey nodded solemnly, showing no surprise at this. "Come with me."

The other man stepped off the sidewalk into the busy street. Hunter kept easy pace with the sheriff as they wove through the morning traffic. At the threshold of the jailhouse, Trey swung open the door, then stepped back, indicating Hunter should proceed ahead of him.

He paused a fraction of a beat, then entered the building first. His gaze darted around the room, taking in the stark interior. Cold, bleak memories took hold. He'd spent a lot of time in this jailhouse, specifically the cell on the far left.

Like always, a fire crackled and spit in the black stove on his right. The air beyond the fire's reach shimmered with cold, all the way into the dank, empty cells.

"Slow week?"

"Blessedly slow." Trey shifted around him.

Rubbing his palms together, Hunter moved deeper in the room, too, then dropped a cursory glance at the desk cluttered with unruly piles of paper. "Still ignoring your reports?"

Trey let out a low laugh. "What can I say? Got an image to uphold."

Brow arched, Hunter cut his friend a speaking glance. They both knew Trey's legendary reputation had nothing to do with filing late reports.

Trey simply studied Hunter in return, with that quiet, reflective air of his. "This your first stop?"

"No." Hunter shook his head. "I went to see Mattie Silks last night."

Trey stared at him, infuriatingly calm as always.

Hunter stared back, reminding himself—*again*—that he had nothing to hide. Even though his past was littered with the wreckage of his mistakes, Hunter was a new man.

A changed man.

Still, he waited for Trey's expression to fill with disappointment, waited for him to say something about the ills of stopping in a brothel his first night in town. But Trey's gaze never changed. There was no lecture forthcoming, no leaping to conclusions. The complete lack of censure proved he had more faith in Hunter than Hunter had in himself.

"That couldn't have been easy," Trey said at last.

"You have no idea." Hunter paused, remembering. No, it hadn't been easy at all, walking into Mattie's last night. There'd been painful moments of self-recriminations, a lot of regret, guilt, raw emotions he hadn't been able to sort through then, or now. "I went to Mattie's because of this."

He dug in his jacket and pulled out the letter the interfering woman had sent him last month—bless her ornery soul.

Trey accepted the paper without looking down.

"Go ahead," Hunter urged. "Read it."

Trey lowered his gaze. A moment later, he drew in a sharp breath, looked up, then back down at the letter.

He continued reading in silence, flipped over the paper and scanned the back. When he was finished, he refolded the letter along the well-worn creases and handed it back to Hunter.

A thousand words passed between them, reminding

Hunter of the last day he'd been in this building, and their final conversation. He'd spilled his guts to this man, admitting his deepest anger at God for forsaking him, at Jane for dying on him. Most of all, he'd raged over the dream that had vanished with the death of his infant son and murder of his wife a few days later.

After too many years on the wrong side of the law, Jane had been Hunter's chance for a new, wholesome life that had lasted barely two years.

Trey was the only person in the world who knew Hunter's desperate wish for a family of his own, why he'd married Jane in the first place, and why he'd sought revenge for her murder. He wanted the stability he'd denied himself for years, but had been snatched from him so ruthlessly. Now, here he was, on the brink of achieving that dream, after all. Answered prayer, if in a different form than he'd ever dreamed.

"I take it you had no idea about the child until Mattie contacted you."

"None."

"You're sure she's yours?"

The question of the hour. "Not completely. But Mattie claims the child resembles me enough to eliminate any doubt."

He went on to explain the circumstances of his brief first marriage, leaving nothing out, including Maria abandoning her vows to return to her former life.

"So the child might not be yours."

Hunter hesitated, fighting off a wave of alarm. What if Sarah wasn't his daughter? What then? "I'll know more when I see her for myself."

His mouth pressed in a thin line, Trey pulled out a chair and indicated Hunter take the seat.

By the time he did as requested, Trey had already disappeared through a door behind his desk. He reappeared with a steaming mug of coffee. "You look like you could use this."

Grateful for the distraction, Hunter took the offered mug and buried his nose in the strong aroma.

Perching on the edge of his desk, Trey dived back into the conversation. "Where's the child now?"

"Charity House."

Other than a slight widening of his eyes, Trey didn't outwardly react to the news. "Then she's in good hands."

"Yes." The relief was still there, a reminder that Maria hadn't been completely duplicitous. Enough, though, and now Hunter had to build a relationship with a nine-year-old child who didn't even know he existed.

Temper reared, dark and ugly, but he shoved the emotion down. What good would it do to become angry with Maria? What was done was done. Hunter had to focus on the future, not the past. "I'm heading over to the orphanage this afternoon to meet my daughter."

The joy was still there, too, riding alongside the relief, reminding Hunter he had a chance to redeem his past, to prove he was more than his mistakes, by becoming a loving, responsible father to his child.

He'd once lost hope of ever achieving such a blessing. He wouldn't muck up this opportunity.

"You're going to claim her as your own." A statement, not a question.

"That's the plan."

As soon as he spoke the words, all the tension in his shoulders disappeared. He'd thought long and hard last night, blinking up at the cracked ceiling of his hotel room. His mind had worked through the multitude of problems—*and* the possibilities—facing him. Hunter still didn't have a concrete plan of attack, not yet. But there was no doubt he was going to step up and become the child's father. In every sense of the word.

Assuming, of course, she was his.

His gut roiled. Surely, the child was his.

"What's your daughter's name?"

"Sarah." Hunter's heart thumped as he said her name, surreal and yet not at all. "She turned nine years old a few weeks ago."

Trey fell silent, his brow furrowed in concentration, as if he were sorting through the faces of every nine-year-old girl in residence at Charity House. The likelihood of Trey knowing Sarah was high. He had several personal connections to the orphanage. Not only was he related to Marc Dupree, Trey's wife, Katherine, was the custodian of Charity House School.

"There's only one child around that age named Sarah. But, if I remember correctly—" his eyebrows slammed together "—she's not alone in this world, nor is she without family."

"I know. She has an aunt. Annabeth…" Hunter paused, wondering how much Trey knew about Annabeth's connection to Mattie. Deciding not to risk exposing either woman's secret, he gave Annabeth's alias instead of her real name. "…Smith. Her aunt is Annabeth Smith."

"You know Annabeth? How?" Icy stillness fell over Trey.

"She was Maria's sister." He didn't elaborate, didn't go into the details of how he'd discovered Annabeth's connection to Mattie Silks. Although he hated lies and had vowed to avoid them at all costs, this particular secret wasn't his to tell.

"Right. Of course." Again, Trey's face crumpled in a look of concentration, and then a spark ignited in his dark eyes. "Annabeth is very devoted to Sarah. Is that going to be a problem?"

Such a loaded question. Such a loaded situation. All of this would be so much easier if Annabeth wasn't so deeply involved in Sarah's life. But she was.

"Honestly? I'm not sure." *No, that was a lie.* "Probably." *Definitely.* "All I know for certain is that I'm going to do right by my daughter."

He was ready for a second chance at a new life. Nobody was going to stand in his way of providing a safe, stable home for his daughter, and himself, not even Sarah's *devoted* aunt.

"Noble, to be sure, but let me give you a piece of advice."

Hunter knew that look in his friend's eyes. Trey was about to say something profound. Hunter silently prepared himself.

"Think long and hard about what you want, both in the long term and the short, before you go charging over to Charity House and make your claim."

"Understood."

"I mean it, Hunter." Trey leaned forward, hands on his knees, his gaze intent. "Make sure you have a solid idea of what the future looks like in your mind before you start formulating plans. Your actions will impact a lot of people at Charity House, some good some bad."

"I get it, Trey."

"Do you?"

"Yeah, I do." Awash with joy, with terror, with expectancy, he continued, "You're telling me I need to be in this for the long haul. And whatever I do, make sure I don't hurt Sarah, or Annabeth, or anyone else at Charity House. That about cover it?"

"I'd say we're on the same page."

"Good. And Trey…" Hunter carefully set the mug in his hand on the desk and let out a slow breath of air. "Thank you."

Trey shrugged. "Happy to help."

"I wasn't referring to my current situation, though I certainly appreciate the advice." *Mostly.* "I meant, thank you for what you did for me two years ago. You helped settle some things in my mind, including the matter of my salvation."

"You came to your own conclusions."

That might be true, but Trey had guided him toward those conclusions. He'd patiently explained the difference between godly justice and worldly justice. He'd explained the notion of giving mercy where it wasn't deserved, as only a man who'd sought vengeance with his own hands could do. In that, they'd shared a common bond. Trey's first wife had been brutally murdered by a man as evil as Cole Kincaid.

Trey had moved past his anger at God. An example Hunter wanted to follow but still wasn't sure how. Not completely.

"I also came here today to return this." He dipped his hand in one of the inner pockets of his coat and retrieved the small Bible Trey had lent him during the trial. The book was frayed at the spine, nearly falling apart in places.

"I see you spent some time in there."

Hunter attempted an easy smile. "A bit."

Giving him a long look, Trey took the Bible, flipped through a few pages at random, then offered it back to Hunter. "Keep it."

Hunter didn't overthink the suggestion. He simply accepted the offered gift with a single nod of his head.

They spoke a while longer, both settling into the conversation as they had years ago. The fact that this man regularly chewed up outlaws and spit them out like a used-up wad of tobacco wasn't something Hunter tended to forget. Not while sitting in the man's jailhouse.

But Trey was more than a tough, dedicated lawman. He was a family man, too, equally devoted to his wife and three children.

"Our daughter is fifteen now." He shuddered. Trey Scott actually shuddered. "She was always a handful, even as a child, often one step away from open rebellion, but now she's downright...*difficult*."

Hunter remembered his own sisters at that age. Both had been...*difficult,* too. "I'm sure it's just a phase."

"A phase?" With a visible effort, Trey unclenched his jaw. "A man can certainly hope so."

Hunter smiled at his friend's obvious discomfort. Talk of Trey's daughter brought his mind back to Sarah. Would she hit *a phase,* too? Would Hunter be ready for that eventuality? Would they navigate Sarah's teenage years with ease, or awkwardness, or a combination of both?

Something remarkable and completely unexpected moved through him as he pondered the questions running through his mind. Anticipation. Followed immediately by dread.

Hunter's heart nearly split open at the thought of parenting a female. What did he know about raising a girl? What did he know about parenting at all? His gut spun into a ball of sickening doom. He checked the clock above the door, noted the time and slowly rose to his feet.

He had some serious thinking to do before he made the trek to Charity House. "I should go."

Trey followed him out of the building. "How long are you in town?"

As long as it takes to win over my daughter. "I haven't decided."

"Make it a point to stop back by. Coffee's always on."

"I'll do my best." He turned to leave.

Trey stopped him. "Hunter. God has given you a well-deserved second chance in life." Trey clapped him on the back and smiled. "Pray for guidance in the coming days and the Lord will direct your path."

Translation: keep his head on straight, his eyes on God and his priorities properly aligned.

With that in mind, he left for Charity House.

Chapter Five

By late afternoon, the wind had picked up, swirling cold air beneath Annabeth's collar as she stood on the front porch. She hardly noticed the discomfort. She was too busy watching Hunter's approach from halfway down the block.

Just looking at him did something strange to her insides. His walk was all his, a smooth, even gait with easy strides that ate up the ground with remarkable speed. He'd taken off his hat and now held it in his hand, swinging it loosely by his side. His hair was disheveled, as if he'd shoved his fingers through it more than once. Eyes dark with banked emotion added to the whole menacing gunslinger look.

Helpless against the pull of him, Annabeth sighed. Apparently, she had a thing for the whole menacing gunslinger look.

He's not here for you. She told herself this, repeated it several times, but her heart still skipped a few unwelcome beats. And her head grew far too light for her peace of mind.

A clock from inside the house marked the hour. Four distinct chimes. She'd known he'd arrive on time. Hence the reason she'd taken up her post on the front porch of the orphanage.

Hunter hadn't noticed her yet. He looked solemn and maybe a little nervous, his gaze darting around as if he was looking for trouble. Did that come from his former life on the run, that constant checking of his surroundings, even on the safest side of town?

For some reason, the thought made her sad. Every muscle in Hunter's back and shoulders seemed tense. He raked a hand through his sand-colored hair and then opened the short wooden gate with a jerk.

He took a few more steps before his gaze caught hers. He stopped. A silent message filled his amber eyes, one she couldn't quite decipher. There was a lot going on in the man's head, and she wasn't entirely sure all of it had to do with Sarah.

What was she supposed to do with that?

She forced a cheerful note in her voice. "Good afternoon, Hunter."

He didn't reply. Just nodded, once, abruptly, then traveled his intense gaze over her face once again. She shifted slightly under the bold perusal. When he still didn't speak, she sought to still the beating of her heart.

There was no reason to be alarmed, she told herself. She'd had all day to prepare for this meeting.

Nevertheless...

She felt an odd pain in her heart, an ache that had nothing to do with the thought of losing Sarah and everything to do with this man.

Oh, Lord. Oh, Lord. Whether she was voicing a plea or a prayer, Annabeth wasn't certain.

She was, however, convinced that standing out on the porch, staring at Hunter Mitchell like a lovesick cow was getting them nowhere.

"Come inside," she said, pleasantness personified. "I have someone I wish for you to meet."

* * *

Annabeth directed Hunter into the house and then down a darkened corridor. Shadows swirled around them as they walked, their footsteps filling the silence between them— hers light and graceful, his clipped and efficient. Despite the nature of this visit, the atmosphere in the quiet house was oddly comforting, as if the orphanage was welcoming Hunter into its world.

Or maybe it was Annabeth's presence that was soothing him, little by little. Whatever the cause, a sense of well-being spread through his hollow soul. He didn't understand how or why, but this woman soothed him. Relaxed his restless heart.

His throat tightened and he swallowed, hard.

Not the direction his thoughts should be taking.

Annabeth led him into a small parlor overlooking the back of the house. Hunter set his hat on the closest chair and moved to the window. He looked out just as a burst of warm, golden light washed over a pack of children at play in the wide, manicured yard. A group of boys was tossing a ball between them, while some girls were holding hands and spinning in a fast circle. Was Sarah among them?

This time it was his heart that tightened. With expectation, hope, jumpiness.

"I thought you and Sarah would have your initial meeting here." Annabeth's voice came from directly behind him. "Will that be acceptable?"

He turned slowly around, taking in the parlor with a practiced eye, locating the exits first then the rest of the room in stages. He ignored the fancy furniture, and focused on the textures and nuances. The attention to detail was impossible to miss, the small area elegant and stylish.

On the surface, this parlor was far too formal a setting to meet a child in for the first time. But if a person looked past the Persian rugs, the expensive furniture, and the crystal vases filled with fresh-cut flowers, there was warmth in the décor.

Another sense of homecoming filled him. He felt at ease. "This room is perfectly acceptable."

Eyes wide, Annabeth's face went through a series of odd little contortions.

He stifled a chuckle at her reaction. "You thought I'd find the room too fancy." He made a point of sitting on the most delicate piece of furniture he could find. "You wanted me to feel uncomfortable."

"I… Yes. I suppose I did." Her cheeks turned a becoming shade of pink as she made the admission.

Well, well. The timid girl had turned into a scrappy fighter. Rather than finding her tactics insulting, Hunter found himself amused at her attempt to gain the upper hand in such a sneaky manner. And maybe he was a bit impressed, too. Not that she needed to know any of this. In fact, best to keep *her* on the defense. "Badly done, Annabeth."

"Yes, it was. I—" she tangled her fingers together at her waist "—apologize."

Feeling gracious, he inclined his head. "Apology accepted."

The tension between them lessened. Not that it mattered. He hadn't come to see her. Or so he told himself. Yet here they were, holding one another's gazes, both breathing slowly, something good and right swirling between them.

He cleared his throat.

At the same moment, Annabeth threw back her shoulders.

"I… I'll just go fetch Sarah now." She sounded practical and brisk, but sorrow pooled in her eyes, a sadness so deep Hunter drew a sharp breath.

He went to her.

Not sure what he meant to do, he took her hand. There were faint shadows beneath her eyes, a sure sign she'd endured a sleepless night.

He tightened his hold on her hand. A moment of shared pain passed between them, so raw, so fresh, neither pulled away. He must have stared too long, seen too much, because she frowned, then yanked her hand free of his. "Wait here."

"Of course."

Alone with his thoughts, he felt a bout of nerves kindle and fire through his blood until he could remain in one place no longer. Letting out a hiss, he paced the room. Back and forth, back and forth. Back. And. Forth.

Hope squeezed in his chest. If he played this right, if he stayed on the narrow path and settled down once and for all, he could have the life he'd always wanted, the one he'd nearly achieved with Jane.

Dare he try again? Did he deserve to have a family of his own, not in the role of a husband to his wife, but as a father to his daughter? Or were there too many mistakes on his ledger to hope for a smooth, uncomplicated existence?

The fine hairs on the back of his neck prickled, sending alarm tripping down his spine. The same sensation had kept him alive in more than one gunfight. Motionless, afraid of what he would see, he didn't turn around to face the parlor's entrance. He closed his eyes and opened his other senses instead.

Holding steady, he sorted through the sounds coming from various points throughout the house. He focused in on the high-pitched prattle of a young female voice mingling with an older, more familiar one. The rapid staccato of the conversation made it impossible for him to decipher the words.

But he knew those footsteps.

Annabeth. Her return was a mere seconds away. That meant the other voice must belong to Sarah.

Sarah.

Hunter's hand started to shake. Flexing his fingers, he opened his eyes and resolved to keep his emotions contained.

No mistakes.

No loss of control.

Calm. Cool. Careful.

The wait was endless, an eternity. The voices grew louder, closer. The individual words were muffled as they mingled with the footsteps, but there was obvious affection in both female voices. Love, too.

Hunter's throat closed shut.

His daughter—*if* she was his daughter—was well loved. By Annabeth. And no doubt others who lived in this house. His shoulders shifted, then went still again. He forced himself to turn toward the doorway, to remain calm as he did so.

With his arms hanging loosely by his sides, he planted his feet a little apart and tried not to hold his breath.

Another moment passed.

And then…

Annabeth entered the room, her jawline tight. The moment their gazes connected her eyes deepened to a dark violet, the color of thunderclouds. The unmistakable warning beneath the turbulent expression was easy enough to read.

A wasted gesture. Hunter had no intention of hurting his own daughter. Or Annabeth. Regardless of what she thought.

A young girl suddenly shifted into view. And smiled directly at him.

He fell back a step.

Oh, Lord. Lord.

Restraint shattered. Calm evaporated. Well-thought-out speeches died on his tongue. The only emotions left were shock, and longing. Painful, heartrending longing for something always just out reach.

He hurt, at the core of his being. The sense of loss was overwhelming, loss over all he'd missed in his daughter's life.

And, yes, this happy child was his daughter. He had absolutely no doubt. Her hair was the exact color of her mother's, her dark coloring the same. But it was *his* eyes staring back at him in that small, thin face.

His daughter had his eyes. And his tall, lean build, mostly lanky at her age. He'd been lanky as a child, too. As had all of his brothers and sisters. It was a Mitchell trait.

This girl was a Mitchell, through and through.

What was he supposed to say now? Nine years ago he'd created this beautiful child with a woman who hadn't wanted him, who'd rejected him. Lied to him, prevented him from knowing his own flesh and blood.

Feeling mildly desperate, torn between anger and distress, he glanced at Annabeth for assistance. She was studying her feet as though all the secrets of the world were in the flowered rug beneath her toes.

No help there.

Sarah solved the problem for him. "Hello." She continued beaming up at him. "I'm Sarah. Who are you?"

There was no nervousness in the child, no fear. Just innocent curiosity. And a welcoming smile that cut straight to the bottom of Hunter's black heart. The child had his smile, too.

"Hello, Sarah." He swallowed, cleared his throat, swallowed again. His voice sounded too raw, too hoarse with emotion. He swallowed one last time and tried again. "I'm your fa—"

He cut off the rest of his words, something preventing him from declaring himself, something that ran deeper than his silent vow not to act on impulse. Perhaps he simply wanted the child's easy manner to continue, didn't want to watch that beautiful smile disappear when he declared who he was, and why he'd come here today.

"My name is Hunter Mitchell. I'm a friend of your aunt's."

Not entirely true, but he had so little to work with here. He'd planned poorly for this moment, he realized that now. Annabeth wasn't helping matters. She was now staring fixedly at some point over his shoulder, not acknowledging Hunter at all, as if afraid to give him an ounce of encouragement.

"Did you say you were Hunter *Mitchell?*" Sarah's dark eyebrows drew together slowly, her mind working fast, her eyes lit with excitement. And the sweetest emotion of all. Acceptance. "I know several people with that same name."

"Yeah?"

"Uh-huh. Let me see." She pressed her fingertip to her lips. "There's Garrett, the twins and little Janie. Miss Megan." She paused, her little eyebrows scrunching together. "Did you know Miss Megan used to live here, at Charity House, just like me?"

Hunter smiled. He might not have kept his family abreast of his life, but he'd managed to keep up with theirs. "Actually, I did know that."

"And did you know that Miss Megan is married to Mr. Logan, and—" She stopped talking midsentence, her eyes wide. "Hey." She moved closer, staring up at him with a fierce, concentrated gaze. "Anyone ever tell you that you look just like Mr. Logan?"

Despite his turbulent history with the man in question, Hunter felt a slight smile tilt up one corner of his mouth. "He's my brother."

"No!"

"It's true."

"Does that mean you grew up on a real ranch? With horses and cows and…and everything?"

"I did. My childhood home is called the Flying M, the largest cattle ranch in Colorado."

"Oh, oh." Sarah clapped her hands together in glee. "How exciting."

"Very exciting," he agreed. And he'd been fool enough to scorn the blessing of his birthright, to run away from it, to seek adventure wherever he could find it, no matter the consequences.

No more running.

He leaned down and set his hands on his knees, capturing Sarah's attention as he did. "Visitors are always welcome at the Flying M."

"You think I could go there one day? For a visit, I mean."

He wasn't going to take her for a visit. He was going to take her to live there, permanently. The future unfolded in his mind, starting with the small ranch house he would build on the land he would lease from his folks, the cattle he would eventually raise, the mended relationships he would enjoy.

But again, he held back from telling Sarah all this. One step at a time. "I think a trip to the Flying M is definitely in your future."

Sarah squealed in delight. Her joy was contagious.

Hunter smiled at Annabeth, wanting—needing—to include her in this moment. She stared back, unsmiling, looking positively morose as she smoothed a hand across Sarah's hair. "We've discussed this, Sarah. It isn't polite to invite yourself to someone else's home."

Striking an exasperated stance, Sarah frowned up at her aunt. "I didn't invite myself. He offered." She gestured at Hunter with a jerk of her chin.

So. His daughter had a stubborn streak. Another trait they had in common. Charmed by the discovery, he had to fight very hard not to laugh.

Annabeth struggled to maintain her composure, while she noted Hunter was trying not to laugh. At her? Or the situation? Either way, he'd been in the room with Sarah for a total of five minutes and was already making promises. What happened to taking this one step at a time?

Worse yet, Sarah and Hunter were getting along rather well. Really well. Annabeth had counted on the opposite. At the very least, she'd expected this first meeting between father and daughter to be awkward.

Nothing could be further from the truth.

Hunter had overcome his initial shock at seeing the child and was now conversing with her as though he spoke to children on a regular basis. Which made an odd sort of sense when she worked the notion through her mind. He was, after all, the eldest in a large family of brothers and sisters.

But that had been a long time ago. Ten years to be exact. Before he'd become an outlaw.

Except...

He didn't look much like an outlaw now. His eyes exuded kindness as he spoke to Sarah, genuine interest, too. In fact, he looked very much like a loving father. And a man of integrity, both trustworthy and constant. He suddenly laughed at something Sarah said, a low, deep rumble of amusement, and Annabeth realized she'd missed a large portion of their conversation.

She forced herself to pay better attention.

"...and my newest, bestest friend is Molly Taylor Scott. She's Sheriff Trey's daughter. She's teaching me how to turn my plain bonnets into pretty masterpieces."

"Masterpieces?" Hunter turned the word into a question he lobbed in Annabeth's direction. His mouth twitched slightly, presenting a momentary dimple in his cheek so fast she nearly missed it. The floor shifted beneath her feet for a brief, disorienting moment.

Focus, Annabeth.

"I had no idea bonnets could become masterpieces," he added when she continued to stare at him, unresponsive and dumbfounded.

Unclamping her lips, she said, "You have no idea."

His smile widened.

Oh, perfect. The man was incredibly charming and appealing when he smiled like that. All big and charming and muscular and handsome. And...and...*charming*.

Annabeth strove to match her detachment of moments before. An impossible feat when she couldn't take a decent breath.

She suddenly felt brittle, on the verge of breaking.

As if sensing the change in her, a shadow crossed over Hunter's face, giving him a concerned expression. The face of a man Annabeth could see putting the people he loved first, protecting them and bearing their burdens at times.

What would that be like, she wondered, to know she was safe, always, never needing to fear the unknown? What would it be like to no longer worry about the future, or her reputation? To have someone stand by her side, no questions asked, a man who knew who—and what—her mother was but didn't care? Who maybe enjoyed Mattie, accepted her, understood her even.

Shifting impatiently between them, Sarah tugged on Hunter's arm. "Want to see one of my bonnets?"

"I would indeed." The smooth amusement was back in his voice and Annabeth let go of some of her hostility toward the man. Sarah was so *happy*.

"I'll be right back."

The child skipped out of the room, leaving Hunter to stare after her. For a brief moment, he didn't bother hiding his expression. Shadows swirled in his gaze, dark and emotional, full of longing, hope and pain. So much pain.

Annabeth felt like an intruder, watching him this closely, and yet pulled toward him, too. The need to comfort stronger than the need to keep up her guard, she took a tiny step toward him, reached out and touched his arm. She didn't expect to feel anything, but the impact was like a physical blow.

She quickly dropped her hand.

Seemingly unaware of her disturbing response to him, Hunter slowly turned his head in her direction. His face was paler than usual, his features taut and intense. "She's really my daughter."

Why deny the truth? "Yes."

"I— She—" He wiped the back of his hand across his mouth and cleared his throat. "It's…astonishing. She has my eyes."

That had been the first thing Annabeth had noticed when she'd met Sarah a year ago.

"And my smile," he said, wonder in his voice.

"She has your build, too."

He nodded absently. "Tall and lanky, like all the Mitchells at her age, even the girls."

He looked fierce and proud as he spoke, and completely

unashamed of the joy spreading through him. But then his expression changed, bursting with other emotions. Determination, conviction. Unrelenting resolve.

Hunter Mitchell was going to claim Sarah as his daughter. Annabeth tried to follow all the threads to their logical conclusion, knowing the gesture was a waste of time. She'd already lost the niece she'd grown to love as her own child.

The Lord giveth and the Lord taketh away.

How would Annabeth ever survive without her niece?

Sarah was so sweet, so eager to please, so willing to accept a stranger in her life without question.

Annabeth sighed. It hurt to love this much.

Breaking her train of thought, Sarah darted back into the room, her hands overflowing with ribbons and pieces of silk, her smile full of excitement.

An identical expression spread across Hunter's features.

Again, Annabeth felt like the intruder.

"Here it is, Mr. Mitchell, my latest creation." Sarah hopped from one foot to the other. "Look, see, right here. And here. And here. I sewed all the ribbons on myself."

"I'm thoroughly impressed." The words were mild enough, but his eyes glistened with emotion, and not just any emotion. Love. The man was already bursting with love for his daughter.

His hand slightly shaking, he took the bonnet and examined the hat from every angle, showing the sort of care one would a fragile piece of china.

Sarah moved in closer, pressing against him as she pointed out various spots of interest.

The moment was full of quiet gravity. Father and daughter, together, united at last, with only one of them understanding the unique blessing they'd been given.

Never having known her own father, Annabeth could hardly look at the scene playing out in front of her. By all practical measures, it was too soon to tell if Hunter would make a good father. But deep in her heart, where pain and loss resided, Annabeth knew the fight was over before it had begun.

Hunter would take very good care of Sarah.

The back of Annabeth's eyes stung and something painful lodged in her throat, sharp as a sliver. She was happy for her niece. So very happy. But she knew she wasn't going to see Sarah grow up. Not on a daily basis.

"Aunt Annabeth?" Sarah's face took on a look of deep concern, identical to the one Hunter shot her way. "Why are you crying?"

Unaware she'd allowed her emotions to get away from her, Annabeth lifted her hand to her cheek. And felt the wetness on her face.

Horrified, she glanced at Hunter, praying he didn't notice. But just as he had last night, in Mattie's private suite of rooms, he looked at her with kindness in his eyes. And understanding and maybe a little pity.

Oh, no. Annabeth would not allow him to feel sorry for her. She would not feel sorry for herself, either. This reunion between father and daughter was a good thing, a dream come true. A blessing from God above.

Exasperated with herself, Annabeth let out a long-suffering sigh, turned her back on Hunter and focused on her niece. "I wasn't crying, dear." She laughed softly to make her point. But there was something broken in the sound so she rushed to fill the moment. "I simply had a piece of dust in my eye."

Chapter Six

Hunter watched wordlessly as Annabeth swiped discreetly at her cheeks. The gesture was a valiant effort to erase all signs of emotion from her face, even if she didn't succeed very well. At least she wasn't trying to insinuate herself in his conversation with Sarah. He should feel triumphant over her lack of interference. Instead, he felt…

Guilty.

His gain was Annabeth's loss. Somehow that didn't seem fair, on any level.

How was it possible Maria's younger sister had grown into a beautiful, compassionate woman—no longer a girl who'd once ignited his curiosity, but a woman—confident and intelligent and devoted to her niece? Hunter was starting to like her, on a personal level.

No good could come from that.

He splayed his fingers and pushed them through his hair, anything to prevent himself from doing something foolish. Such as pulling Annabeth in his arms and soothing away her sadness.

"Well," Sarah said, chewing on her bottom lip, "if you're sure you're not upset…"

"I'm fine. Truly."

Seemingly convinced, Sarah went back to pointing out various details on her bonnet for Hunter. "Notice how the different colored ribbons work together so nicely. My friend Molly says that's because they have the same tone."

Hunter didn't know much about colors or ribbons or similar tones. "Isn't that…interesting."

"I know." She chattered away on the subject, her young voice pitched two octaves higher than his own. She sounded similar to his younger sisters at that same age. He wondered if Sarah loved to sing as much as Fanny and Callie did.

So many details still to discover about his daughter, her likes and dislikes, her favorite color, her food preferences, whether she enjoyed playing indoors or out, or both. Things her aunt probably already knew about the girl.

His gaze sought Annabeth's again. She smiled politely in his direction but didn't quite make eye contact. It was as if she looked right through him.

He understood.

Wasn't that the same expression he'd worn most of his adult life? On Annabeth, the look made her seem wounded and lonely.

They'd all suffered from Maria's lies. Sarah, praise God, seemed to have made it through her young life unscathed. By all outward appearances, she was happy and well-adjusted. Hunter owed that blessing to Marc and Laney Dupree.

And Annabeth, too. He couldn't forget her influence on his daughter. Sarah was a healthy, normal child because of the people in her life.

Hunter made a decision, then and there. The time for sorrow was over. There would be no more pain, no more anger, and definitely no more lies in any of their lives, only down-to-the-bone honesty from this moment forward.

He waited for the child to take a breath. "Sarah, I have something to tell you."

"You do?" She looked up at him with mild curiosity in her eyes. "Is it a secret?"

"It is," he confirmed, laughing at her excited gasp.

"Oh. I like secrets."

"Most women do."

She nodded sagely, her face a study in little girl seriousness. "That's because we're good at keeping them to ourselves."

Not in Hunter's experience. And definitely not the point. "Once I tell you this secret you don't have to keep it to yourself. You can tell anyone you wish."

"Oh." The bonnet slipped from her fingers to the floor. She leaned over and picked it up again, her smile wavering. "I suppose that's good, too."

Sarah's uncertain expression reminded Hunter of Maria. He waited for the anger to come, the frustration over not being able to confront his first wife about her deception. All he felt was regret for what might have been. No matter what Maria had done, or why, Sarah would never know her mother.

From this day forth she would know her father. "Sarah, I'm your fa—"

"Hunter." Annabeth cut him off, pushing past Sarah and settling in a spot directly between him and his daughter. "I'd like a word with you in private."

He gave her a hard look. "Now?"

"Now."

So much for not interfering.

"But, Aunt Annabeth." Sarah scooted around her aunt

and jammed her fists on her hips. "Mr. Mitchell was about to tell me a secret."

"Yes, I know." A slight hesitation. "And he still will." A heavy sigh. "After I speak with him first."

Clearly confused, Sarah looked from her aunt to Hunter and back again. "Can't whatever you have to say to him wait?"

"No, dear, it can't."

"But—"

"No arguments." Annabeth cut her off with a firm shake of her head, then smoothed a hand over the child's hair in a gentle show of affection. "Mrs. Smythe is baking cookies in the kitchen. I'm sure she'd welcome your help."

"Yes, that sounds like fun, but—"

Annabeth cut her off again. "Go help Mrs. Smythe, *now*."

The command was spoken firmly and with unbending authority.

This time, Sarah clamped her mouth shut. With a mutinous twist to her lips, she cast a silent appeal in Hunter's direction.

Knowing better than to get in the middle of a fray between the two females, he raised his hands in the universal show of surrender.

Sarah's face fell.

He could hardly bear all that little-girl despair.

"I'll be right here when you're finished helping with the cookies."

Her eyes narrowed ever-so-slightly. "Promise?"

"Promise."

"All right." Sighing, she headed toward the hallway.

It took every ounce of control not to call her back to him and dispel his daughter's obvious dejection. Hunter had no idea what Annabeth had to say to him—or why she felt the need to do so now—but he wouldn't undermine her authority in front of Sarah.

Once the child was out of earshot? Well, that was another matter entirely.

Annabeth waited for Sarah to slink out of the room, grumbling all the way. Only after the girl was too far away to overhear their conversation did she turn to face Hunter directly.

He didn't look any happier about the interruption than his daughter. Less so, actually. But where Sarah had set out to argue with her, Hunter simply held Annabeth's gaze, still as a stone, quiet, severe, his lips flattened in a grim line.

This was the man who'd faced down some of the most ruthless outlaws in the country, and won.

No matter.

She could not—would not—allow herself to be intimidated by Hunter Mitchell in his big, bad gunslinger stance. There was something far more important going on here, something that went beyond the happy reunion of a father and his daughter after years of unnecessary separation.

Poignant, to be sure, but this was no fairy tale playing out, where everyone got exactly what they wanted and they all lived happily-ever-after. This was real life, where secrets had been kept for nine long years. A child's future was at stake, her well-being, too, *and* her safety. Emotion must not rule the moment.

There was a beat of silence, weighing heavy and thick in the air between them.

And then another.

And one more.

Finally, Hunter spoke. "You better have a good explanation for interrupting me."

Even his tone had changed, becoming hard, more

pointed and direct, the voice of a man used to others bending to his will.

Annabeth refused to flinch.

She did, however, need a moment to gather her thoughts.

Pushing past him, she went to stare out the window. Poised on the razor-thin edge of panic, she hardly noticed the children at play. *Stay calm, Annabeth. You have an important point to make.*

And now she was stalling.

She turned back around. "You were about to reveal who you are to Sarah."

"The timing was right."

Perhaps. Perhaps not. "You don't know that for sure. You've known her for what? All of ten minutes?"

"The truth has been withheld from her for far too long." A pause, an accusatory look, reminding her she'd played a part in the duplicity for an entire year. "I won't begin my relationship with my daughter based on a lie. The deception ends today."

His point hit home. Yet Annabeth couldn't find it in her to agree with him, not openly. Until recently, he'd been serving a two-year prison sentence for killing a man. How could she have known he would return to Denver ready to start anew?

How could she be sure now? "I stand by my decision to withhold your identity from her."

He gave her a long look.

"There was no evidence you would step up and take on the responsibility of raising your daughter."

And Annabeth was getting tired of defending herself. She'd acted on the reasonable assumption that he wouldn't want to be a father to Sarah. "Most of the Charity House children have indifferent parents."

"And, yet, here I am, attempting to do the right thing

by my daughter." He fixed his amber gaze on her face and, with the ease of man comfortable in his own skin, paced toward her. He moved slowly, with efficient, purposeful strides.

Annabeth remained perfectly still. Perfectly. Still.

Another two steps and the distance between them was a mere foot. Up close, she could see the various hues of gold in his eyes. She could also see his frustration.

Well, she was frustrated, too.

So, no, she wasn't going to buckle under all that masculine intensity bearing down on her.

"I mean to be a good father to Sarah." His chest heaved in an unsteady rhythm and his voice sounded raw, emotional, but also determined. "I have changed, Annabeth."

Although he spoke very deliberately, with his jaw tight, it wasn't hostility she saw in his eyes but some sort of murky promise, something that went beyond words, something personal and solely between them.

"Hunter." She sucked in a hard breath. "I don't think—"

"Stop, Annabeth. Stop arguing with me and let me finish." With a move so swift she didn't see it coming, he took hold of her hand.

His touch was so foreign and yet somehow comforting, familiar even.

He rubbed the pad of his thumb across her knuckles. Warmth spread up her arm.

"I'm not going to hurt Sarah." He moved closer, too close, and in a voice pitched to a deep, husky note, added, "Or you."

She snatched her hand free, her fingers curling into a fist. "Words, Hunter. Those are just words."

"Then here are some more words for you to consider. No matter your motivation, I won't let you stand between my daughter and me."

No, he wouldn't. She'd been foolish to think otherwise. She'd known this was how it would end. She'd *known*. Hunter would take Sarah away with him now. And there was nothing Annabeth could do to stop him.

Heart beating madly against her ribs, she stared up at him, teeth ground together, angry and frustrated and... afraid. Not of him, but of what he'd come here to do.

"You're Sarah's aunt." Everything in him softened, as if he actually understood and valued the sacrifices she'd made over the past year. "I don't know what happens next, but we'll figure it out. Together. For Sarah's sake."

So, he was going to be reasonable and fair-minded, putting his daughter's needs above his own. Annabeth would have preferred a fight.

Battling another round of tears, she turned her head away. "I'll get Sarah now." She took a large step to her right, creating some much-needed distance from the man who was breaking her heart in ways she couldn't explain fully. "I know she'll want to hear what you have to tell her."

There was a brief pause, brimming with the same charged emotions as before. Then he nodded. "Thank you."

"You're welcome." Resigned, she turned on her heel.

"Annabeth?"

She stopped, waited for the rest, but didn't turn around.

"I won't let you down."

Another promise, one she could tell he intended to keep. She flattened a hand over her heart and heaved a sigh. "Just don't let *her* down."

She found her niece in the kitchen, rolling dough under Mrs. Smythe's attentive tutelage. The older woman was smiling as she gave her instructions. Short, round and gregarious, the housekeeper had tucked her iron-gray hair in an ordinary bun at the nape of her neck. There was nothing ordinary about her, though. Mrs. Smythe loved life. She was always cheerful, always smiling.

Even now, her bright blue eyes sparkled with good humor as she explained the basic steps for making her *world-famous* cookies.

"Aunt Annabeth." Sarah squealed her name in childish glee. "Look at me. I'm making cookies all by myself."

"I see that." Annabeth's heart kicked fast and hard, her breath catching in her throat. How she loved this child. So very much. "Sarah, your fa—"

She swallowed the rest of her words, blinking hard at the mistake she'd nearly made. "That is…Mr. Mitchell wants to speak with you again."

Sarah beamed up at Mrs. Smythe. "He's the one I told you about. Mr. Logan's brother." She leaned in close. "He's going to tell me a secret."

"Well, then." The housekeeper shared a quick look with Annabeth then took the rolling pin from Sarah and set it on the counter. "You better get on in there."

Sarah hurried around the table, practically tripping over her own two feet in her haste. She sped past Annabeth then stopped cold two steps later. "Aren't you coming?"

Torn between holding on to her niece a while longer, and allowing Hunter a moment alone with his daughter, Annabeth chose the middle ground. "In a minute."

"All right." Sarah charged down the hallway.

As the sound of her footsteps grew ever more distant, doubt reared. What if Sarah didn't react well to the news that Hunter was her father?

Annabeth set out toward the parlor.

"Stop right there."

She froze, took a deep breath then slowly turned back around to face Mrs. Smythe.

The older woman rested her hands on her hips, paying no heed to the flour she was getting on her clothing. "You want to tell me what's going on with that child and Hunter Mitchell?"

"He's Sarah's father."

"Her father?" Mrs. Smythe's mouth fell open. "Well, now, isn't that something." Understanding flashed in the other woman's eyes, a look that said puzzle pieces were fitting together in her mind. "I always did like that boy."

"You know Hunter, personally?"

Mrs. Smythe nodded absently. "I served his meals to him during the trial, as a favor to Sheriff Scott. You get to know a man when you feed him on a regular basis." She shook her head, her mind fixed on some distant memory. "He didn't deserve prison time."

"He killed a man."

"I still say it was self-defense."

Annabeth agreed. Unfortunately, the jury hadn't. They'd based their verdict on the fact that Hunter had sought out Cole Kincaid for the sole purpose of extracting justice for his wife's murder. There hadn't been enough hard evidence to prove that the fight had been a matter of kill or be killed, and so Hunter had gone to prison for manslaughter.

Tragic, really.

He'd been punished for loving his wife too much. Did he still grieve her loss? Of course he did. That depth of feeling never fully faded away.

A moment of defeat spread through her, so unexpected it stole her breath.

Mrs. Smythe touched her arm and Annabeth nearly jumped out of her skin.

"How long have you known that Hunter is Sarah's father?"

"Annabeth has known since the day she moved in with us here at Charity House." The response came from the woman standing in the doorway behind Mrs. Smythe. Laney Dupree, the owner of Charity House, entered the kitchen, her gaze locked with Annabeth's.

Dressed in a faded blue gingham dress with a simple lace collar, Laney managed to look serene and beautiful. Like always, she had an air of sophistication that transcended her casual attire. "So you changed your mind and contacted Hunter, after all."

Shame had Annabeth breaking eye contact with the woman who had become as much a friend to her as an employer. They'd had an ongoing discussion about this very topic, ending the same way every time. Laney urging Annabeth to send word to Hunter that he had a daughter living at Charity House and Annabeth balking, making excuses, procrastinating.

"Actually, Mattie Silks wrote him with the news."

"I…see."

Yes, Annabeth was afraid Laney saw entirely too much. At least Mrs. Smythe wasn't adding her opinion to the discussion. The older woman had slipped into the pantry with the excuse of needing more flour for her cookies.

"When did Mattie contact him?" Laney wanted to know.

"She wrote him about a month ago. He came as soon as he was released from prison. He's in the parlor with Sarah now, probably telling her who he is as we speak."

"He wants to be a father to her, then?"

"Yes." Annabeth was struck by a strange, sweet sensation of…relief. Regardless of her personal stake in this, she was happy for Sarah. The child would never have to go through life wondering why her father didn't want her.

"Oh, Annabeth. Don't look so sad." Laney reached out and pulled her into a fierce hug. "This is an answer to prayer, an answer to *your* prayers for the child."

"I know." She resisted the urge to cling to Laney, accepting how selfish she was being, while at the same time wanting to lash out at the unfairness of the situation. "What if he fails her?" she whispered into her friend's shoulder.

Another tight squeeze and Laney released her. "You think he won't be a good father to Sarah?"

"No. I mean, yes, I mean…" She drew in a tight pull of air. "I believe he'll make a very good father, if he stays on the straight and narrow."

"Word is he's changed," Laney assured her in a careful tone. "Trey has already vouched for him, and Marc has done his own checking on the matter."

"Marc checked on Hunter?" Annabeth blinked at Laney, sensing she was missing a valuable piece of information. "When?"

"A few months ago, when we got word he was being released from prison."

"But I don't understand. Why would Marc want to keep tabs on Hunter?"

"The obvious reason, of course, because he's Sarah's father."

Annabeth gasped in outrage. "I told you that in confidence."

"Yes, you did."

"And you told Marc?"

"Yes, I did." Laney spoke without an ounce of apology in her words. "Annabeth, you know what sort of orphanage we run here. It's our responsibility as guardians to find out as much information as we can on each child's parent."

"Information," she repeated, stunned at Laney's lack of remorse. "Such as, when a father is being released from prison?"

"Among other things." She lifted a shoulder. "We never pressure a man—or woman—to do the right thing for their child, but we don't hinder them from stepping forward, either, not if we feel it's in the child's best interest."

Annabeth absorbed what Laney was saying. She'd known this, in her heart, but hearing her friend explain the reality of what they faced here at Charity House made her all the more ashamed by her own actions. She'd intentionally kept a father from his daughter.

What sort of person did that make her? "Now what do I do?"

"Now you step out on faith. You let go and trust God."

Let go and trust God. Sound advice, under normal circumstances. But when it came to her niece, Annabeth's faith wasn't strong enough to wait and see what the Lord had planned. Too much at stake. Too many unknowns.

Including her father. *Especially* her father.

"I better go check on Sarah." And Hunter.

"If you think you must."

"Oh, I must." As she set out toward the parlor, she could hear Hunter's deep voice wafting on the air. His tone was too low for her to make out the individual words. Except one.

Father.

A loud gasp from Sarah had Annabeth increasing her pace. She rounded the corner just in time to see the child launch herself into Hunter's arms.

Chapter Seven

Hunter clutched his daughter to him and held on tight. His eyes burned, and he had to swallow several times to release the air lodged in his throat. Attempting to sort through his thoughts, he stared up at the ceiling. Somewhere in the deepest, darkest folds of his soul a stronghold of banked emotion struggled to break free.

Nothing had prepared him for this melting of his heart, this wondrous, piercing mix of pain and hope tangling in his gut. He hadn't expected to love this hard, this fast.

Lord, what if I fail this child?

What if he didn't? What if every piece of his life, every mistake, every wrong turn, and every confessed sin had led him to this moment in time?

It was only as the thought took hold that he caught a movement off to his left. Annabeth stood in the doorway, a sheen of tears in her eyes. She released a shaky smile. The gesture sent another sharp ache spearing through his chest because she wasn't looking at him. She was staring at Sarah.

When Annabeth glanced up at him, finally, a slight buzz of something he couldn't identify shot through his veins.

His arms flexed involuntarily around his daughter.

Making a soft squeak, Sarah shifted out of his hold. "If you're my father," she said, her heart in her eyes, "does that mean I'm a Mitchell, too?"

Hunter laughed. It seemed better than giving in to all the other emotions warring inside him. "That's exactly what it means."

He'd discovered from Sarah herself that Maria had given their daughter the last name of Smith, no doubt to keep Hunter from finding out about her.

He experienced a pang of hostility at that.

In an attempt to halt his temper, he allowed himself a long look at Annabeth, an indulgence that only managed to send his pulse skidding faster through his veins. He still had that peculiar feeling inside his chest, the one he'd fought against since he'd noticed the woman standing in the doorway.

"Good. Because I want to be a Mitchell," Sarah declared, shoving out of his embrace, her head high, her chin set at a stubborn angle that reminded him so much of his brother. Logan could be bone-stubborn on occasion. But then, so could Hunter, as could every other person with Mitchell blood running through their veins.

Sarah would fit right in with the family.

"Then we'll call you Sarah Mitchell from this point forward." Hunter's throat constricted as he spoke. He wasn't sure if there was a legal process involved in making the name change official. Nor did he have any idea what sort of agreement Maria had made with Marc and Laney Dupree in terms of Sarah's care.

Was their guardianship backed up by legal paperwork? Had Maria been that wise? Or had she given Sarah away on a verbal agreement alone?

He'd have to find out, the sooner the better. Then he

would hire a lawyer, and gather whatever legal counsel necessary to win permanent custody of his daughter.

From this point forward Hunter would follow the law down to the letter. He would also trust the Lord. He'd tried life the other way, relying solely on himself, only to fall in with bad company that resulted in nothing but pain and hurt and in two instances, death. As his mother always said, *If a man hangs out with the wrong people at the wrong time he's bound to do the wrong thing eventually.*

The story of Hunter's life. Or rather, the story of his past.

Everything changed today.

As if recognizing that he'd come to some sort of conclusion, Annabeth chose that moment to step fully into the parlor.

The movement caught Sarah's attention. She rushed to her aunt's side. "Have you heard the news?"

"What news?" she asked, brushing the child's hair back behind her ear with a fingertip.

"Mr. Mitchell is my daddy."

"Why, that's…wonderful." She spoke with a soft inflection, soothing, sweet, and Hunter sensed a vastness of feelings within her. It was clear she loved her niece.

Hunter couldn't fault her that.

Could he separate the two? Could he be that cruel? No, he couldn't. He'd made mistakes in the past, shocking, painful mistakes that had changed lives, but he'd learned from them, too. He would make better choices now, and in the future.

He had ideas about what came next. However, he needed to sort through them before he began making plans. He would have to include Annabeth in some of the decisions. That much was clear by the simple fact that Sarah was attached to her.

And, besides, he didn't want to see Annabeth hurt. "We need to talk," he said.

She winced. "Yes, I suppose we do."

He recognized her trepidation in the tense angle of her shoulders. No wonder. He'd spoken bluntly, with little care for how his words would impact her. He used to know how to talk to women, how to charm them into doing his bidding. He'd forgotten the use of subtlety during his years in prison.

Perhaps that wasn't all bad. Perhaps living a life of integrity meant coming at matters head-on, rather than glossing over the difficult conversations or using his charisma to get what he wanted.

Let your yes mean yes and your no mean no.

Silence hung between him and Annabeth like a thick, gloomy fog. Sarah didn't seem to notice, though, as she continued to chatter away about her new family. "Cousins, Aunt Annabeth. Can you believe it? I have cousins of my very own."

Annabeth made serious business of leaning down and listening to the child's every word, nodding at the appropriate times.

Midprattle, Sarah swung to face Hunter. "Does this mean I get to live on a ranch with you, like a real Mitchell?"

Strong, unnameable emotions tried to break through the surface of his outward control. He'd like nothing better than to raise Sarah on a ranch near his family's spread, to become a rancher again, as he'd always meant to do one day. He'd had a taste of the dream once before. With Jane.

They'd settled on a piece of land near Pueblo. Everything had seemed fine, almost perfect, but then the baby had died and Cole Kincaid had come back into their lives...

"Is that what you want to do?" he asked, shoving aside the unhappy memories. "Live on a ranch?"

"Oh, yes. Yes, please." His daughter certainly seemed to know what she wanted.

"But, darling." Annabeth draped her arm across Sarah's shoulders and tugged her close. "That would mean you would have to leave Charity House and your friends and…everyone else."

Annabeth gave Hunter a speaking glance, leaving him no doubt what she meant. Sarah would have to leave her aunt. If he took his daughter away with him, Hunter would be ripping her away from the only family she'd ever known.

Unless…

Perhaps there was another solution.

"Well, yes, that's true, Aunt Annabeth. But we could come back for visits, like Mr. Logan and his family do all the time." She looked up at Hunter, a plea in her rounded eyes. "We could, right? We could come back and visit Charity House?"

Hunter rubbed the back of his neck, sighed. He clearly had a lot of thinking to do. Starting a ranch required hard work and dedication. There would be no time for trips back to Denver, at least not in the early years. But if his daughter wanted to visit Charity House occasionally he would figure out a way to make that happen. "I don't see why not."

"See?" Sarah swung back to face her aunt, the trust of youth in her voice. "We'll come back lots and lots."

He hadn't said that, exactly.

"What about your schooling?" Still holding on to Sarah, Annabeth directed the question at Hunter. "Do you have a plan for her education?"

Sarah answered for him. "That's a silly question. You'll teach me, Aunt Annabeth."

"Me?"

"Well, of course. You're coming with us to the ranch." Her sweet little face crumpled with indecision. "Aren't you?"

"Sarah, I have a job here, responsibilities that I can't just up and quit and—"

"But we're family." The child stomped her foot, looking every bit like a Mitchell. "And families stick together. Isn't that what you always say? Didn't you promise you'll never leave me now that the Lord has brought us together?"

"Yes, I said that."

Tears wiggled to the edges of Sarah's thick eyelashes and her shoulders stooped a little. "Didn't you mean it?"

"Of course I did." Annabeth bent to look in the young girl's eyes. "But things have changed." Her voice was very small when she spoke, and full of grief. "You're a Mitchell now. You don't need me anymore."

"I need you." The child's voice broke over the words. "I'll always need you."

Sarah's eyes were red-rimmed, her lashes spiky with moisture. She looked downtrodden, sad and on the verge of crying. Annabeth appeared to be fighting tears herself. Hunter had never been good with female emotion. Feeling helpless, he glanced from one to the other, caught between running and wanting to fix the problem.

He went with the latter, offering up the one solution that would serve them all. "You'll come with us, Annabeth."

He hadn't meant to speak so bluntly, or so forcibly, but he wanted the tears to *stop*. Besides, it was a good idea. Someone had to look after Sarah. Why not her devoted aunt?

As the thought took hold, he felt himself relax. He wouldn't have to say goodbye to Annabeth anytime soon.

The burst of satisfaction that came was unexpected, and a little unsettling.

"I suppose I'm open to discussing it." Despite her words, Annabeth still looked miserable, her face pale and taut.

Sarah, on the other hand, had cheered up considerably. She bounced from one foot to the other, practically vibrating with little-girl excitement. "I have to go pack."

She bounced again, did a little twirl. And one more for good measure.

"Not so fast." Annabeth stilled the child with a hand on her shoulder. "We have a lot of details to work out before you can leave Charity House."

"Your aunt's right," Hunter said when Sarah's face took on a mutinous expression. "These things take time."

The magnitude of all the tasks that lay ahead cramped his brain. He needed to contact his family. He assumed they would welcome him home. They'd said as much during the trial, and in their subsequent letters to him in prison. But as much as he wanted to return to the Flying M, he couldn't just show up with a previously unknown daughter and her aunt in tow.

And there was the other, more pressing problem that needed addressing, too. Hunter still had to convince Sarah's guardians that he was serious about taking on the responsibility of raising his daughter. He had to prove he was a changed man.

No better time than the present.

Ten minutes later, Hunter followed Annabeth through the back of Charity House, silently preparing his speech to Marc Dupree in his head. Annabeth had sent Sarah off to find her friends. No doubt the child was sharing the news that her father had returned to town and was here to claim her.

How would that affect the way the others treated her? Would they be happy for her, or jealous? A combination of both, probably. There would be questions. Where had he been all these years, why had he shown up now? The same questions Marc and Laney Dupree would ask of him.

Hunter's pulse raced in anticipation, and maybe a little dread. Watching the back of Annabeth's head, he had to fight the urge to reach out and spin her around to face him, to determine if she was his ally or his adversary.

Why it mattered what the woman thought of him, he couldn't say. She'd affected him so swiftly—and so deeply—his head was still reeling.

She'd stormed into his life last night, all fiery and determined and beautiful, ready to protect the child she loved—even if that meant keeping Sarah safe from her own father. *From him.* Her loyalty was humbling, as well as frustrating. Whatever it took, Hunter would prove to Annabeth that he was worthy of his daughter, that he could be trusted.

Peace and stability had always been elusive, just out of his reach, often because of the choices he'd made himself. God willing those days were over. He was going to take a leap of faith this time around. And believe in the dream of returning home, of setting things right with his family and settling down to a rancher's life.

One step at a time.

At the end of the hallway, Annabeth stopped outside the last door on their right. Fingers wrapped around the handle, she looked at Hunter over her shoulder. "I assume you will want to speak with Marc alone?"

"I would prefer that, yes." He had things to say he didn't want Annabeth to hear, things about his past that Sarah's guardian needed to know, but Annabeth didn't. Not yet. Maybe not ever.

"I told him you were coming by today." She shifted, her gaze tracking everywhere but in his direction. "And why."

"Annabeth, look at me." He waited until she did as he requested. "I meant what I said in the parlor. I want you to come to the Flying M with Sarah and me."

Her hand dropped to her side and she sighed. "If only it were that simple."

"It can be."

Her jaw muscles tightened. "Making promises again?"

At the sight of her agitation, tenderness welled in his heart, a sensation he hadn't felt in years. "Only ones I intend to keep."

Another sigh seeped out of her. The way she folded her arms around her waist made her look small and vulnerable.

He reached to her.

She shook her head, then turned back to the door and knocked once, twice.

A voice called from within. "Enter."

Squaring her shoulders, she pushed open the door.

As Hunter drew alongside her, Annabeth surprised him by reaching out and touching his arm.

He looked down at her. It was his turn to sigh. She seemed so sad, so…beaten, as if her last hope had been taken away. By him. He'd done this to her.

No, not him. Maria. Maria had done this to her.

To both of them. Sarah, too.

Lies. Secrets. No good came from either.

He fought the urge to drag Annabeth in his arms and make more promises, the kind he had no right to make to any woman, not anymore. "Thank you, Annabeth. Thank you for everything."

She closed her eyes a moment, pulled in a deep breath and then nodded. "You're welcome."

As one, they entered the room together.

Marc Dupree sat behind his desk, wearing a deceptively bland expression on his face. Hunter had never met the man personally, but he remembered him sitting with Trey during his trial on several occasions.

Dark-haired, clean-shaven, Marc was dressed similarly to the last time Hunter had seen him in the courtroom. The red brocade vest and matching tie were made of the finest material available, the kind a banker might choose for his clothing.

With efficient, clipped sentences, Annabeth made the necessary introductions then said, "I'll leave you two alone."

"Thank you, Annabeth," Marc called after her retreating back.

Not bothering to turn around, she waved a hand over her head in response.

The moment she shut the door Marc pointed to one of the two worn leather chairs facing his desk. "Please, Hunter, have a seat."

The man's tone was as formal as his attire and an uneasy feeling clutched Hunter's heart. Everything hinged on Marc releasing his guardianship of Sarah.

Or did it?

Again, Hunter made a mental note to seek legal counsel as soon as possible.

Maria had hidden his daughter from him. That couldn't have been legal, or ethical. Had Marc played a role in the deception? Had the other man known Hunter was the child's father from the beginning, and done nothing to contact him?

Hunter wouldn't leave this room until he had his answers.

Clearing his expression, he lowered himself into the offered chair and looked around the office. He took in the decor with one, quick sweep. The room was a man's sanctuary. The dark furniture and deep, rich colors in the rugs added to the masculine feel. Even the smoky scent coming from the fire in the hearth seemed to proclaim: no females allowed.

Hunter fought back a smile.

Watching him closely, too closely, Marc tented his fingers under his chin and got straight to the point. "I understand you're Sarah's father."

Always appreciative of the direct approach, he nodded. "I found out in a letter penned by Mattie Silks."

This information didn't seem to surprise Marc. "Maria never told you about your daughter?"

"No, never." Hunter forced a casual note in his voice. "Did she tell you?"

Marc shook his head. "No. She didn't."

He was so calm, so matter-of-fact, the quintessential man in charge, holding all the power. Hunter frowned as a twinge of resentment took hold.

"Is that standard?" he asked, his tone going low and just short of deadly. "A mother simply hands over her child, without attempting to contact the father first?"

Marc let out a slow, careful breath, as if trying to decide how much to reveal. "Nothing is ever simple or *standard* when a child ends up at Charity House. Some of the women who bring their children to us don't even know who the father is. Other times, the father is already married. Or, worse, refuses to acknowledge his son or daughter."

"Unfortunate, to be sure, but none of those describe my situation." Hunter held Marc's stare for a beat, then reiterated, "Like I said, Maria never told me about Sarah."

Marc nodded.

"I've come to claim my daughter."

Not a single reaction from Marc to this statement. Not

a shift of an eyebrow, or a twitch of his jaw. Nothing. The man would make a deadly opponent in a gunfight. "How did your first meeting with your daughter go?"

"Better than expected," he admitted.

"I'm not surprised." Marc leaned back in his chair, his shoulders visibly relaxing. He looked pleased. He *sounded* pleased. "Sarah is a sweet child with a big heart."

And Hunter already loved her. One meeting with his beautiful, happy daughter, and he was willing to do anything, give up anything—*everything*—for her.

Feeling as though he'd been gut-punched, he looked down at his hands, found them balled into fists. A fight. He was ready to fight for his child.

"I have always found," Marc began, his voice falling heavy between them, "that speaking plainly is the best route in situations such as these."

Yes. Complete, raw honesty, that's what he'd come here to give this man. "Maria made the right decision," Hunter admitted. "Choosing not to tell me about Sarah."

Marc arched a brow. "Why is that?"

"At the time, I was in no position to care for a child." The truth hurt, but the past was the past, and there was no rewriting history. "I'd already had a pattern of failing everyone I cared about. Sarah would have been no different."

Memories churned, most of them bad, but Hunter continued, anyway. He explained his relationship with Maria, how they'd met, *where* they'd met, and the volatile lifestyle they'd led before she'd returned to her former life in her mother's brothel. He left nothing out, refusing to gloss over the worst of his past and the destructive nature of his choices.

When he finished, Marc remained silent for a long time. "And all that's done now?"

It'd been done years ago. "Yes."

Marc considered him a moment longer. "So what comes next?"

Hunter's heart beat fast, his mouth went dry. "I make the right choice, the *only* choice, to be a father to my daughter. I plan to provide a home for her near my parents' ranch."

For another long, tense moment, Marc simply held his gaze. No judgment in his eyes, no threats, just thoughtfulness. "Legally, I can't stand in your way. Laney and I only had a verbal agreement with Maria."

A range of gut-wrenching emotions spread through him, relief at the top of the list. He could take Sarah away today, now, this very moment.

"But I'm warning you, Hunter." Marc flattened his hands on his desk and leaned forward. "Make sure you have a solid plan mapped out before you take Sarah away from Charity House. Like all children, she deserves stability in her life. I expect you to provide that for her."

Trey had said something similar to him just this morning. Hunter hadn't been discouraged then, and he wasn't now. Nor was he intimidated or cowed or hesitant over the task that lay before him.

He was ready.

Chapter Eight

In the guise of supervising the activity in the backyard, Annabeth stood alone on the porch and watched the orphans at play. Desperate to distract her mind from the conversation occurring in Marc's study, she paid avid attention to each and every child. Two of the older boys had organized a rousing game of baseball. In typical Charity House fashion, there was as much laughter as ball playing.

The sight of so much unfettered happiness should have calmed her nerves. Instead, the idyllic scene reminded Annabeth of all she would leave behind if she agreed to accompany Sarah and Hunter to his family's ranch. She'd found a home here, and had achieved a level of respectability she'd thought lost to her for good.

She had an important decision to make, one that required time and attention to think through all the details.

If only Hunter hadn't returned a new man. If only he wasn't so willing to be Sarah's father.

If only, if only, if only…

Annabeth inhaled the rich, pine-scented air and prayed for the right answer. Unfortunately, her mind was a vast storehouse of doubts, concerns and an odd quickening of some unfamiliar emotion moving through her soul.

This would not do!

She lowered to the steps and clasped her hands around her knees just as a loud cheer erupted from the team up at bat.

Annabeth released a small smile.

Fifteen-year-old Molly Taylor Scott squealed in delight as the ball she'd just whacked sailed toward the back fence. Giggling, the girl pranced around first base, skipped across second, and kept right on going.

She eventually skidded to a stop at third, did a little jig, and then spun around to wave at Annabeth. "Did you see that?"

Annabeth laughed. "I did, indeed."

Not through celebrating, Molly danced around the makeshift base, singing a made-up song about female supremacy in all matters concerning a ball and bat.

Smiling at the girl's antics, Annabeth felt herself relax for the first time since Hunter had arrived at Charity House this afternoon. She'd never met a male or female more secure in her own skin than Miss Molly Taylor Scott.

Annabeth supposed that confidence came from the fact that the girl had a mother and father who adored her, even if they weren't her real parents.

Sarah had two people willing to step up and parent her, too—one her actual father. But unlike the Scotts, Annabeth and Hunter weren't married. Could they find a way to provide Sarah with a happy childhood, anyway? What would their lives look like? What sort of arrangement could possibly work for all parties involved?

Annabeth wanted to be close to Sarah, yes, but that now meant unavoidable interaction with Sarah's big, handsome, rugged father. A man who was proving himself less an outlaw and more the man she'd met ten years ago. Kind and considerate.

Overwhelmed with confusion, she buried her face in her hands and welcomed the blessed darkness that came as a result.

A moment later, a husky voice fell over her. "You gonna hide in there all afternoon or come out and deal with me head-on?"

Hunter. She should have known he would seek her out as soon as he'd finished speaking with Marc.

Not ready to face him yet, she kept her hands firmly in place.

"Annabeth."

She held firm.

He softened his voice. "Annabeth."

She sighed. "Give me a moment."

"Hiding from me?"

No. "Maybe."

That earned her a dry chuckle. "I never would have branded you a coward."

She was no coward. Lowering her hands, she cracked open an eye and found the likable lug watching her from a heavy-lidded, amused gaze.

She shaded her eyes and scowled up at him.

It wasn't fair. It just wasn't fair. The man looked good—really good—with the sun backlighting his hair, almost lovingly brushing the tips with a perfect blend of gilded copper and gold.

And then he did it. He smiled. At her.

Her heart skidded to a stop.

"Hello," he said.

She swallowed. "Hello."

Be calm, she told herself. *No need to panic.* So the man was attractive. And muscular. And…and…dazzling in the sun. She'd met handsome men before. It was a real shame none of them had made her heart trip over itself like Hunter managed to do. Every. Single. Time.

He was one big, bad, dangerous man. And that had nothing to do with his past.

His smile still in place, he settled on the step beside her and watched the activity in the backyard. After a moment of careful searching, not only the immediate area, but the neighboring lawns as well, his eyebrows pulled together. "Where's Sarah?"

"She went upstairs with Camille and Meredith to play dolls."

"She's playing…dolls?"

"It's a typical activity for a girl her age."

"What do you know? Sarah likes to play with dolls." His gaze warmed as he considered the idea a moment longer.

Charmed by his reaction, Annabeth felt herself leaning toward him, her heart softening as she studied his profile. Her fingers itched to touch his jaw. Would the beginnings of the light stubble already shading his face feel prickly to the touch?

She resisted reaching up. Just barely.

Her smile suddenly felt brittle on her face.

Still facing the backyard, Hunter placed his elbows on his knees and leaned forward. His gaze traveled lazily over the ball game, his shoulders less tense. "Marc and I had a good talk."

"You were in there a long time." Nearly an hour.

He inhaled slowly. "We had a lot to discuss."

"Come to any conclusions?"

"A few."

She waited for him to say more. And waited. And waited.

That was it? He wasn't going to expand? He was just going to sit there and watch the ball game?

The passing moments seemed to be marked by the loud beat of her heart. Tilting her head, she shifted so she could see Hunter better. In the unfiltered sunlight his skin had taken on a deep golden hue. He'd probably spent many hours outdoors during his time in prison.

What had his days been like? His well-honed muscles spoke of hard physical labor.

Had there been pain, too? Loneliness?

Another cheer rose up from the game, followed by a collective groan from the outfield. Annabeth glanced over in time to see Molly twirl across home plate.

Hunter watched, as well. A flash of something came and went in his eyes, amusement, maybe, then he shook his head and returned his attention to her. "We aren't going to do this here."

"Do what?"

"Discuss our future."

Our future, as if they were a team, a unit. A couple. No, ridiculous. She was overthinking, something she rarely did. "Where would you suggest we *do this*?"

"Somewhere more…private."

The rough velvet of his voice slid over her and Annabeth couldn't seem to formulate a proper response.

No wonder. Her future lay in this man's hands. She could pretend otherwise, but the truth wasn't overly complicated. If she wanted Sarah in her life, she had to take Hunter, too.

Life is no fairy tale, she reminded herself, intentionally repeating the words in her mind until they stuck. No handsome prince was going to ride in on his white horse and proclaim his love for her. Oh, she might have achieved a certain level of respectability in her position at Charity House School. But she wasn't delusional enough to think she was getting her own happy ending.

At least she would have Sarah.

Raising her niece, watching her grow into a happy, healthy woman, was worth every lost dream Annabeth had ever had.

"Annabeth?" Hunter's voice had gentled. "Did you hear what I said?"

She nodded. "You said we should speak in private."

"No. Well, yes, I did say that." He shook his head, masculine exasperation in the gesture. "But I also asked you to dine with me tomorrow for luncheon, at a restaurant, just the two of us."

Just the two of us. The words echoed in her mind, threatening to spin out of control.

Hunter took her hand. "A restaurant makes the most sense. I don't want to endanger your reputation, but I want us to have relative privacy when we discuss Sarah."

Discuss Sarah. More words. More chaos in her head. One incoherent jumble on top of another.

"We need to come up with a workable plan."

A plan. Right. *Right.* They needed to make a plan. For their future together. With Sarah at the core. Annabeth finally untangled her tongue. "I agree, completely."

"Good." He unfolded his large frame and stood, pulling her up with him. "I'll make the reservations for noon tomorrow."

"Noon, tomorrow." Tomorrow was Saturday. "Yes, that'll be fine."

He continued holding on to her hand. "I'll pick you up a half hour prior to our reservation."

"Yes, that'll be fine," she repeated, feeling oddly lightheaded.

And *still,* he didn't release her hand.

Chewing on her bottom lip, she tugged gently. At last, he let her go.

The sense of loss over the broken connection startled her. She let out a shuddering sigh and did her best to appear completely unmoved. But in the recesses of her mind, Annabeth admitted she was deeply attracted to Hunter Mitchell. She'd been attracted to him from the moment she'd first laid eyes on his handsome face ten years ago.

He'd been larger than life back then, a little scary, a lot dangerous and completely unattainable. Even after Maria had died, he'd been too much *man* for Annabeth.

Now, with time and the wisdom of age, the scary gunslinger was far more human in her mind, a little less menacing, a lot more approachable.

Guard your heart, Annabeth.

The impossibility of a real relationship with him, beyond Sarah, made her want to cry. He'd been married twice. The second time to a woman he'd loved so much he'd set out to avenge her murder.

Guard your heart. Too, too late, her foolish, rebellious soul whispered in return. Too, too late.

The next day, Hunter began making preparations for the trip north to his family's ranch. As much as he wanted to bring Sarah along with him, he should probably make this first venture alone.

He would leave sometime next week, after his appointment with Reese Bennett, of Bennett, Bennett and Brand Law Firm. Although Marc had said there were no legal issues to address, Hunter wanted to be sure. He wouldn't take Sarah away from Denver unless every detail had been reviewed and ultimately conquered.

There was also the matter of his daughter's official name change. She wanted to be a Mitchell? Then she would be a Mitchell. Legally.

No shortcuts. No cheating. Everything by the book.

Pacing across the room, Hunter looked out the window. Out of habit, he checked for danger. Off to his left, he thought he recognized a silhouette in the shadows, but when the man came into the light Hunter didn't know him, after all.

He breathed a sigh of relief.

He knew he was being overly cautious, paranoid even, but he'd been caught off guard once before. And Jane had ended up dead.

Although the remaining members of Kincaid's gang had dispersed long before Hunter had confronted the outlaw in Mattie's brothel, he would continue to watch his back. Complacency had no place in his world. Even when he left Denver and settled on his own parcel of land he would stay alert, ever watchful. No one would catch him off guard again.

Turning away from the window, he allowed his mind to drift back to the Flying M. Back to his family. Back…

Home.

Comforting thought. As reassuring as the worn Bible he kept close at all times. Even now, he could feel the weight of it in his pocket, reminding him he wasn't ever truly alone. *With God all things are possible.*

Facing his parents would be easy enough. They would welcome him without question and would allow him to find his way back into the family fold in his own time. His younger siblings would be easy on him, too, especially Garrett. Despite the twelve-year gap in their ages, they'd always had a special bond.

Logan, on the other hand…

A bleak heaviness settled on Hunter's shoulders. His do-good, virtuous brother had never made a wrong turn in his life. Even in marriage, the younger man had gotten it right from the start. Not like Hunter, whose first marriage had been an impulsive decision at best. And his second? Perhaps he'd put more thought into that one, but he hadn't valued Jane nearly enough. Until it was too late.

In contrast, Logan never took his blessings for granted. He was rock-solid, wise beyond his years, and full of Christian integrity. Hunter had spent a lot of years resenting his younger brother for that. As the older of the two, he should have long since tried to mend their relationship.

He hadn't.

In fact, the last time they'd spoken directly, Hunter had knocked his brother out cold. He'd never expected—or wanted—Logan's support during the trial. He suspected Logan had known that, respected it even, and sent Trey Scott in his stead.

The time had come for Hunter to make amends.

He would follow the biblical model and go straight to the source. But not today. Today his attention belonged to Annabeth.

Smiling, Hunter retrieved his hat from the bed where he'd left it earlier, resting on its crown. He made the trip to Charity House in a rented carriage, for Annabeth's sake, not his own. Although the restaurant was a relatively short walk from Charity House by his standards, it might not be so by hers.

The late-morning air was cool and crisp on his face, the sky clear, the sun a brilliant ball of fiery orange. He'd barely alighted from the carriage and stepped onto the walkway leading to the house when Annabeth appeared on the porch.

Their eyes met across the short distance. Hunter's heart slammed into the back of his throat and stuck. Looking into those blue-blue eyes that seemed to have gone lavender in the sunlight, he felt as if the world had ground to a halt.

With considerable effort, he unclamped the hinges of his jaw and continued forward. "Good morning, Annabeth."

He sounded—and felt—like a schoolboy still in short pants. Which made little sense. Hunter had faced down some of the meanest outlaws in the West, yet couldn't seem to untangle his tongue at the sight of a pretty face.

Not just any pretty face.

Annabeth Silks, a woman who, for all intents and purposes, was completely out of his reach. Innocent and pure, she deserved a decent man in her life.

He was not that man.

"Good morning, Hunter."

Her voice sounded huskier than usual, deeper. *She's as nervous as I am.* The thought helped his shoulders relax, yet he couldn't seem to tear his gaze away from her beautiful face. For a dangerous moment he allowed himself to wonder what this meeting would have been like under different circumstances, if his past had been less volatile, less ugly.

The door behind Annabeth swung open again.

Startled out of his thoughts, Hunter looked over her head and saw Marc Dupree making his way onto the porch. The woman by his side had to be his wife. Petite and fine-boned, Laney Dupree was as beautiful as her home.

She was dressed more casually than her husband in a simple, pale green dress with a white, lace collar. Her mahogany hair was piled atop her head in an elegant twist that showcased her face.

The couple held hands, and moved as a single unit. There was no question they were finely attuned to one another.

A gnawing ache twisted in his stomach. Hunter had never had that sort of connection with a woman, not even with Jane. He'd loved his wife, had wanted to provide for her and protect her, but had always felt slightly out of step with her. She'd been too good, too sweet, too…godly. Hunter had been destined to fail her.

As he'd failed everyone else in his life.

The past, he reminded himself, *all of that was in the past.* His hand automatically patted the Bible in his pocket and his thoughts settled. He was a new creation now, starting life with a clean slate. Perhaps he could still achieve some peace, maybe even happiness.

At the bottom of the stairs, Marc pushed slightly ahead of the woman on his arm and made the introductions. "Hunter Mitchell, this is my wife, Laney Dupree."

"Mrs. Dupree." Hunter removed his hat and nodded in the woman's direction. "It's a pleasure."

"Such formality. Call me Laney." She offered him her hand, her gaze running across his face before her brows pulled into a thoughtful expression. "It's a little startling, you know, how much you favor Logan."

"I assure you." He swallowed back a snort. "Aside from looks, I'm nothing like my brother."

Her eyes widened at his bluntness. Then she smiled at him, a lovely, brilliant slash of straight white teeth. "I think," she said, gazing at him as if she could see directly into his soul, "you're more like him than you realize."

Hunter didn't know what to say to that. She was so completely wrong.

His mouth worked but nothing came out.

"Sarah hasn't stopped talking about you," Laney continued, taking pity on him perhaps. "She'll be sorry she missed you."

Speaking of Sarah…

He looked around. "Where is she?"

"She ran over to Trey and Katherine Scott's home to spend the morning with their daughter, Molly." Laney gave a little flick of her wrist at a house across the street then laughed softly. "You do realize, Hunter, how completely you have won over your daughter."

"I'd say it was the other way around. Sarah is a beautiful child. I couldn't be more proud." A wave of affection and gratitude filled him. "You and your husband have done an exceptional job raising her."

Laney blinked up at him. "What a lovely thing to say."

"It's the simple truth. You willingly took Sarah into your home when she was but an infant." He felt a cold sweat break out on his forehead and the back of his throat felt like sandpaper. "I can never repay you for your kindness."

But he would try. Somehow, he would find a way to compensate this couple for their generosity toward his daughter.

Clearly uncomfortable with the direction of the conversation, Laney shifted from one foot to another. Did no one thank her for the services she and her husband provided here at Charity House?

Marc patted his wife's back then spoke for them both. "Like I said yesterday, Hunter, your gratitude is all the payment we need."

Hunter disagreed. He'd spent too many years skirting duty and responsibility. Although that behavior had ended the day he'd turned himself in, he still had a long way to go to make up for his past.

Some errors couldn't be erased with good intentions or well-meaning prayer. Sometimes consequences stuck.

Annabeth shifted beside him, drawing his attention from his emotionally charged thoughts. He looked down at her.

She looked as if she wanted to say something, but held her tongue. Not finished having his say, Hunter took

Laney's hand in a gesture of friendship. "Thank you for taking care of Sarah all these years." He included Marc with a sweep of his gaze. "I'm forever in your debt."

The couple shared a look. A thousand words passed between them, as if they were having a silent discussion only they understood. Eventually, Laney nodded to her husband.

Marc turned to Hunter. "Sarah is fortunate she has you. We'll work with you to make sure the transition from our home to yours goes smoothly."

Knowing that Marc and Laney were on his side humbled him beyond words. The back of his eyes stung. Not that he let his ragged emotions show on his face. He kept them carefully contained.

The mood turned light, casual even, as if they were four old friends catching up after a short separation. When a comfortable lull settled over the conversation, Hunter turned to Annabeth. "Ready to head to the restaurant?"

She nodded.

He offered her his arm. After a brief hesitation, she wrapped both hands around his biceps then smiled up at him.

His gut squeezed.

And he realized just how much he liked this woman. Liked her a lot. Too much, perhaps.

A new tension coiled through his ribs, settling in his chest. He didn't want to hurt Annabeth. He wanted to keep her safe, to cherish her, to be the man she most deserved. A desperate wish on his part, born of a hope not yet realized.

Bringing Annabeth into his life was probably a bad idea. The very worst. He was going to do it, anyway. For Sarah's sake. As for what *he* wanted?

Hunter dismissed the thought. It didn't matter what he wanted. It couldn't. He had a daughter to consider now.

Chapter Nine

Heart in her throat, her mind battling a thousand thoughts at once, Annabeth watched Hunter walk around to his side of the open-air carriage. She thought she'd learned to be levelheaded since leaving Boston. Hadn't she tried to view the world with cold, hard reason? To set aside her childish fantasies of happily-ever-after?

Yet every thought that tumbled through her head was unrestrained, full of rekindled hopes and forgotten dreams. All because Hunter had thanked Laney and Marc Dupree for taking care of his daughter through the years.

How was Annabeth supposed to remain unaffected?

Not many men received a second chance in life, even fewer recognized the blessing they'd been given. Hunter was a man like none she'd ever met. Any more insights into his character and she might do something foolish, like fall in love him.

No, no, no.

Eyes holding hers a moment too long, he climbed into the carriage and shut the door behind him with a soft click. They were alone. Just the two of them. His leg nearly touching her skirt.

He was so close she could smell his fresh clean scent, a little woodsy, like a summer afternoon in the high country.

She sighed. Looked away.

He chuckled softly.

A flick of the reins and they were off. He had such masculine hands, she noted out of the corner of her eye, strong and capable, tanned from the sun and a little battered from work.

Under normal circumstances, riding alone with a man like Hunter would be considered highly improper for a woman like her. Well, not *highly* improper, but skirting the edges of respectability. Annabeth was in the singular company of a notorious gunslinger, without the benefit of a chaperone. One false move on either of their parts and her reputation might suffer a decided hit.

To his credit, Hunter had thought ahead. He'd chosen an open carriage for their short ride into town. There would be no cause for whispers, nothing to warrant speculation, other than the fact that Annabeth was fortunate enough to be riding alongside the most handsome man in the territory.

One who'd recently served a two-year prison sentence for killing a man. She'd craved respectability for too many years not to pause over that. Except…

There was so much more to Hunter than his recent incarceration. Despite evidence to the contrary, he was no outlaw. He was thoughtful, considerate and whenever Annabeth was in his company she felt cherished and special, as though she mattered. For herself.

Careful, careful, her heart warned.

As if sensing her watching him, a tiny smile danced at the corners of his mouth, playful and more than a little roguish. For a frightening moment Annabeth was sure her heart would stop beating altogether.

His smile widened and she felt a shift in her stomach.

"Hungry?" he asked, his voice full of casual familiarity. He was close enough that she could feel the heat he gave off, and the restless energy he exuded.

Oh, the pull this man had on her. She prayed it didn't show on her face. "Not particularly, no."

He let an arched eyebrow speak for him.

"Well, if you must know…" She folded her hands together in her lap. "I'm too preoccupied to think about food right now."

"Preoccupied?" He dragged out the word in his low, masculine drawl. "With…?"

"*With* trying to figure out what makes you, well—" she lifted a shoulder "—you."

"What makes me, me?" He laughed at that. The sound came out a bit rusty, as if he wasn't used to giving in to his amusement. And, glory, if his eyes didn't crinkle at the edges.

"I'm not overly complicated, Annabeth."

"I beg to differ. You're a complete mystery to me. I find myself quite confounded whenever I'm in your company."

He laughed again and her stomach tumbled to her toes. She couldn't decide what compelled her more, her attraction to him or her desire to see him happy like this all the time.

She was in trouble. Big, bad trouble. And her rebellious heart reveled in the knowledge.

Slowly, his laughter died away. His smile faded next and he returned his attention to the road. Because she was watching him so closely, she saw the exact moment he completely pulled away from her. Not physically, but mentally.

The silence stretching between them was broken only by the creak of the carriage wheels over the dry dirt road.

Annabeth wanted to shout in frustration. Instead, she inhaled slowly and steered the conversation into the one area she'd resisted introducing out of fear Hunter would shut her out. Since he'd already done so…

"Was it terrible?" she asked. "Your time in prison, I mean."

A muscle knotted in his jaw. He looked so solemn, so intense. She immediately regretted asking the question.

"I'm sorry, I didn't mean to pry." She rubbed her hands over one another, again and again and again. "Forget I asked."

He nodded.

She thought that was the end of it, and was glad, but then he cleared his throat and said, "My time in prison was strictly controlled, every minute well-ordered and regimented by someone else. I worked when I was told to work, went to bed when I was told to sleep, and ate my meals when I was told to eat."

His words were so cold, so unemotional, so unhelpful in giving her a clear picture of his life in prison. Except, after a moment of quiet contemplation, Annabeth realized his explanation was all the more telling because of its vague nature. "So it *was* terrible."

He lifted a careless shoulder, his gaze firmly fixed on the road. "It was what it was."

She hated the raw emotion she heard in his voice, aching for him on a whole new level.

"I'm sorry, Hunter." The words seemed so inadequate.

He shook his head. "Don't feel sorry for me, Annabeth. I deserved every moment I spent in prison."

"No." She gripped his arm, held on tight. "I don't believe that. You were given too harsh a sentence."

He laughed again. This time, the sound held no amusement at all. "Don't make me out to be someone I'm not. I've always been a hard man by nature. And I never—"

"No. Hunter, *no*. Don't say that. Don't even think it. I saw you with Sarah yesterday, the care you took with her, the patience. Whoever you were before, whoever you *thought* you were before, you aren't that man. You are kind and good and—"

"Don't romanticize me or what I've been through." He swung his gaze to meet hers, held steady a moment longer than necessary. "I went to prison because I killed a man."

He'd killed in self-defense. Even if the jury hadn't agreed, Annabeth knew the truth in her heart. She needed him to know she believed in him, even if he didn't believe in himself. "You might have entered my mother's brothel with vengeance in mind, but you didn't go through with it."

Everything in him went still, even his breathing stalled in his throat. "What makes you think I didn't go through with it?"

"Because I know you. I know who you are under that hard exterior you've wrapped around you like a piece of armor."

"You know nothing about me."

"I know everything that matters."

His eyes narrowed to two mean, ruthless slits. It was a terrifying look.

And completely wasted on her.

She jerked her chin at him. "I'm not scared of you."

And wasn't that the problem she was having with the man? This former convict should strike fear in her heart. Yet she found herself drawn to him, as a woman was drawn to a man.

"You should be scared of me." He looked down on her from his superior height. "I've done terrible things in my life."

He didn't look mean now, or frightening, or even hard of heart. He looked bereft, sick to his soul. "Oh, Hunter." She paused, commanding his gaze with a quiet intensity of her own. "You are more than your past mistakes."

He blinked at her.

"I'm right, you know."

He blinked again.

She leaned forward, until their breathing joined into one perfect rhythm. "You're a decent man who will make a fine father to my niece."

The muscles in his neck tensed, and he slowly looked away, pulled away. From her. "What if you're wrong about me?"

"I'm not."

His mouth twisted at the corners. The gesture made him look more confused than angry. Clearly he wasn't used to people believing in him. The thought made the backs of her eyes sting.

"You seem overly confident in your assessment of my character." She heard the bewilderment in his voice. "Why?"

"Because you're determined to step up and do right by your daughter. That alone tells me what I need to know about the condition of your heart."

When he said nothing, she continued, feeling bolder. "The Lord has forgiven you, Hunter. It's time you forgave yourself."

He pulled on the reins and they stopped abruptly. Too abruptly. Annabeth had to place her palms on either side of her to avoid careening headfirst to the floorboard.

"Easy now." He reached out to steady her.

She smiled up at him.

He smiled back, carefully, maybe even reluctantly.

"Annabeth." He made her name sound like an apology.

"Oh, Hunter." She placed her hand over his. Warmth spread up her arm.

Slowly, their smiles faded, first his, then hers. There was nothing left but the staring. And a whole lot of emotion.

The gravity of the moment danced a shiver up her spine.

There was something exciting about this man's masculine good looks, a powerful vibrancy that was all his. The tilt of his head, the slash of his cheekbones, the haunting sorrow lurking in the depths of his eyes called to the part of her she kept ruthlessly locked away.

She was not passionate by nature. She wanted a staid, comfortable life with a staid, comfortable man by her side. She wanted safe, easy, not…messy.

She was supposed to be immune to men like Hunter. She wasn't supposed to like him. And she definitely wasn't supposed to be attracted to him. But she was.

Apparently, some things just couldn't be helped.

Hunter kept his hand on Annabeth's arm a shade past polite. Caught in her gaze, stunned by the words that had passed between them, he couldn't seem to move. Did she really believe he was more than his mistakes?

No.

She didn't understand what she was saying. She didn't understand who he was, who he *really* was, at the very core of his being. He'd done bad things and hurt a lot of people. He would never outrun his past.

That didn't mean he hadn't tried and would continue trying.

He'd already spent a lot of time reading the Bible over the past two years. It was only in recent months that Hunter had learned to turn to God first, rather than rely on his own wisdom. Hard, physical labor had taught him restraint and he thought he'd conquered the worst of his selfish desires.

But no.

Case in point, he was still holding on to Annabeth, in a very inappropriate manner, with a host of unsuitable thoughts battling his resolve.

She was so beautiful, with such a giving nature. He wanted to kiss her. She deserved better than to be pawed at by him. Whatever softness might have been in him once had been destroyed in prison.

That didn't mean he didn't like touching her, holding her, feeling her muscles bunch beneath his palm. He also liked her scent, a soft floral mixture of lavender and honey. So calming, this woman beside him. And despite his best efforts to remain unmoved, a sense of homecoming washed over him.

He leaned forward, not sure why. Well, yes, he knew why. He wanted to be close to her. Just…a little…closer.

Her eyes widened with…

Was that fear?

No, something far, far worse. *Encouragement.*

He stopped his pursuit.

Eyes still locked with his, she thanked him for his assistance, her voice rich and throaty, then added, "I believe I have caught my balance now."

"Right." He slowly lifted his hand, palm facing her in the universal show of surrender. It was a highly vulnerable position for a man with his outlaw history.

Looking everywhere but at Annabeth, he alighted from the carriage in a rush of movement. Out of habit, he circled his gaze around the surrounding area, looking for trouble. As was becoming the custom, he found none. Horse-drawn carriages trotted past. Vendors hocked their wares. Men and women hustled about their business, some herding their children beside them. An idyllic scene, to be sure, one that spoke of a modern-day city coming into its own.

He drew in a lungful of pine-scented air and turned back to assist Annabeth's exit from the carriage. He wrapped his hands around her waist. She placed her palms on his shoulders for support.

Time slowed, then…

He swung her into the air.

The moment her feet touched the ground she stepped back. He dropped his hands and balled them into loose fists.

"Thank you, Hunter."

The soft lilt of her voice was soothing against the backdrop of the noisy street. He could almost hear her reading bedtime stories to the children at Charity House, the gentleness of her tone lulling the boys and girls into a relaxing sleep.

This once pretty girl who'd become a beautiful, mesmerizing woman—she made him want to rethink his future, to try to—

And there he went again, having inappropriate thoughts about Annabeth Silks.

"Shall we?"

She nodded.

Placing his hand at the small of her back, he guided her into the restaurant as if they were a couple, them against the world.

Impossible, of course. Too much stood between them, including his resolve never to marry again. Only pain and despair came to the women foolish enough to marry him. The risk was too great. He couldn't—*wouldn't*—subject Annabeth to a potential life of disappointment.

That didn't mean he was ready to let her go. Sarah needed her too much.

Hunter needed her, too, though he'd never say so out loud.

He kept his hand on Annabeth's back, leading her past the threshold of the restaurant and into the main waiting area. He gave the maître d'hôtel his name and they were immediately escorted to a table at the back of the restaurant.

The drone of the other diners' conversations drummed in his ears, but his focus stayed on Annabeth. She walked slightly in front of him, her spine erect, her head high. There was so much strength in her, strength of character, strength of conviction.

He was blessed to have her in his life. *His daughter's life,* he mentally corrected.

This meeting today was not about him, or this beautiful woman. It was about Sarah. Everything he did from this point forward had to be about his daughter.

At last, they arrived at their table.

Once they were alone, with menus placed before them, Hunter took Annabeth's hand. "I haven't thanked you properly for all you've done for my daughter."

Her mouth formed a perfect O. "I…I didn't do it for you."

His conviction increased, conviction to do right by his daughter. And Annabeth. "Nevertheless, thank you."

"No need to thank me. Sarah shares my blood. Not as much as yours, that's true." She pulled her hand free. "But she's my family, too."

She tried to mask her emotions with a smile, but the smile never made it past her lips. He recognized the loneliness in her eyes. The sadness. The grief.

Because he knew exactly how she felt, he gentled his voice. "Come with us to the Flying M."

He saw the hope in her, the eagerness to accept his request. But, again, she tried to mask her emotions with a bland smile. So much pride in the woman, so much bravado.

He should know. Like recognized like.

"Sarah needs you, Annabeth." *I need you, too.* "I'm ill-equipped to raise a young girl on my own."

She was shaking her head before he even finished speaking. "You won't be on your own, Hunter. You'll have your entire family to help you. Brothers. Sisters. Both of your parents."

Such brave words, but her voice hitched over the majority of her little speech. "You're Sarah's aunt, equal in stature as any of my siblings, more so because of the past year."

"Where would we live?" she asked. "With your parents?"

"At first. But not indefinitely. There's a cabin on the north range that will suit our needs until I'm able to build a larger house for the family."

He had her. He heard it in her sharp gasp, saw it in the dreamy look she couldn't quite hide from him.

"Say yes, Annabeth." Taking her hand again, he rubbed his thumb across her knuckles. "Say you'll continue to be a part of my daughter's life." *And mine.*

The waiter chose that moment to return to their table. Annabeth shot the man a scowl full of female frustration. "We aren't ready to order just yet."

Clearly baffled, the man's eyes shifted to Hunter. He dismissed the waiter with a curt nod. "We'll let you know when we've made our decisions."

"Very well, sir."

By the time the young man scurried off, Annabeth had freed her hand again and was sitting back in her chair. She made a grand show of placing her napkin in her lap. "Regardless of how I personally feel on the matter, leaving Charity House presents certain difficulties."

"Such as?"

"I have responsibilities at the school."

"They can find another teacher."

"Perhaps." She picked up a fork and twirled it around in her palm. "Perhaps not. It's not an ordinary school. Marc and Laney can't simply put an advertisement in the *Denver Chronicle* and expect a horde of applicants."

Of course not. But they had other resources, with contacts all over the territory. Annabeth was making excuses. And Hunter knew why. "You're afraid."

The fork in her hand stilled. "That's ridiculous."

"Is it?"

"I…" Her gaze shot around the room, landing everywhere but on him. "Yes. Yes, it is."

Something in him shattered, because he knew what was really holding her back. "Annabeth, look at me."

She slowly did as he requested.

"I'm not asking you to play any role in my home other than tutor and guardian to my daughter."

She simply stared at him. Surely she understood what he was saying. Surely he wouldn't have to spell out the obvious.

Apparently, he did.

"I don't expect you to become my housekeeper, or my—" he paused, held her stare, lowered his voice so the other diners wouldn't hear him "—mistress."

The fork slipped from her fingers and tumbled to the table with a hard clank. "I should think not. On either account."

Her embarrassment was endearing. He nearly stepped away from the conversation, but this topic needed to be addressed, now, before they moved on to the other, less unpleasant particulars of their arrangement.

"I was thinking we would hire a housekeeper, an older woman who would live with us. A working chaperone, of sorts." He reached for her hand again, then decided touching her was a bad idea, considering. "Your reputation will remain above reproach."

"You'd do that for me? You'd hire a housekeeper just to spare my reputation?" He wasn't sure what he heard in her tone. Relief? Gratitude?

"That's one of the details I thought we might work out together. I expect you'd want a say in choosing the person I hire, especially since you'd spend much of the day with her."

Interest fell across her face. She opened her mouth to respond but stopped at the sound of a commotion breaking out at the front of the restaurant. Conversations around them halted momentarily, then picked up again with alarming speed.

Hunter caught sight of the cause for all the whispered speculation and inwardly groaned. Mattie Silks had decided to deign them with her presence, wearing highly inappropriate attire for the afternoon—black lace over red silk, gaudy jewelry and maternal outrage.

The thunderous scowl on her face, focused solely on Hunter, said it all. She'd heard about his offer to her daughter. The inevitable confrontation had arrived. He was ready. But was Annabeth? It was a bit too late, if she wasn't.

Bracing for impact, he pulled a palm down over his mouth. "We have company."

Annabeth glanced over her shoulder. "Oh, dear."

Indeed.

Chapter Ten

Annabeth swallowed a groan. Her stomach flooded with trepidation, with dread, with sheer, raw panic. The sensation climbed to her throat and squeezed. She couldn't breathe, couldn't stop shaking. Mattie was here—in the restaurant—bearing down on their table with unmistakable intent in her eyes.

What was she thinking? One wrong word, one slip of the tongue, and everyone in the restaurant would know they were related. Again...

What was she thinking?

That was just it, Annabeth realized. Mattie wasn't thinking. She was acting. On impulse. And outrage.

The restaurant and all the patrons faded from Annabeth's consciousness, leaving nothing but Mattie.

She knew that look on her mother's face. She was here to cause a scene. The thought snapped Annabeth's spine straight.

"We're in for it, now," Hunter said with an amused twist of his lips.

He thought this was funny?

How could he find this situation amusing? How could

he be so calm when Mattie's very presence had disaster written all over it?

Rounding a crowded expanse of tables, Mattie avoided the maître d'hôtel's attempt to grab hold of her arm—for the third time—and charged onward. She hopped to her left, dodged to her right. She didn't seem to notice the whispers that followed her, or perhaps she didn't care about the speculation.

Which made no sense.

When it came to Annabeth, Mattie always noticed the whispers. And she always, *always* cared about the speculation.

Mattie must be extremely upset to put Annabeth in such a precarious situation, especially when she'd gone to such lengths to keep her safe from the gossips through the years.

As soon as the thought took hold, another, more dreadful one emerged. What if, in an attempt to give Annabeth no other choice than to return to Boston, Mattie revealed their connection today? No decent man would have her then, not one who lived in Denver, anyway.

Surely, her mother would never be that shortsighted, that cruel. *Please, Lord, let me be wrong.*

Mattie skidded to a stop beside Hunter and growled at him. She actually growled!

The maître d' caught hold of her arm and yanked. "Miss Silks." He yanked again, harder. "You cannot be in the main dining room, not without a reservation."

Mattie flicked off the man's grip as though he were a troublesome bug. He sputtered in outrage, then resorted to speaking in a mixture of French and accented English, his tiny little mustache twitching furiously as he spoke.

"Enough," Mattie snapped. "Not another word out of you."

He fell instantly silent under the imperious order, perhaps too shocked to continue.

"As for you, Hunter Mitchell, you have some nerve." Jamming her hands on her hips, Mattie leaned over him until her nose practically touched his. "I expected better of you."

He remained perfectly still, his power humming below the surface of his calm but contained nonetheless. "Now, Mattie—"

"And you." She spun to face Annabeth, her voice lowering to a hiss. "How could you be so careless? Your… mother would be appalled at your behavior, dining with this man in front of all and sundry."

Whispers exploded around them. The other diners speculated behind their hands over how Mattie knew the two at the table, Annabeth in particular.

Annabeth stifled another groan.

Mattie sauntered over to the closest table and glared the entirety of gawkers into silence.

Taking charge, Hunter stood to his feet. The move drew Mattie's attention back in his direction.

"Miss Silks." He bowed at the waist, all politeness and good manners. "Would you do us the honor of joining Annabeth and me for luncheon? We were just about to place our orders."

Mattie opened her mouth. "Now see here—"

Hunter cut her off with an imperceptible shake of his head. The gesture only seemed to antagonize her further. "Don't you shake your head at me, Hunter Mitchell, as if I were a—"

"Think, Mattie." He took her arm and pulled her gently back toward their table. *"Think* about where you are, and why."

"Release me this minute." She jerked out of his grip. "I will not be manhandled by you, or anyone else. I—"

He talked right over her. "Mattie. Have a care. You are on the verge of making a grave error in judgment."

"I—"

He leaned over her and continued speaking in a much softer tone, so soft Annabeth couldn't quite make what he was saying, which meant no one else could, either.

Whatever words he used, Mattie's fury seemed to lessen, ever-so-slightly, enough to make her snap her mouth shut. For a total of three lengthy seconds.

Then…

"Since you asked so nicely, yes, Hunter, I would very much like to join you and your guest for luncheon."

Annabeth fought back a sigh. She had a bad feeling about this. But she knew that short of being bodily removed from the premises, Mattie was here to stay. Hunter must have known this as well, hence his attempt to contain the problem to their table as quickly as possible.

Full of masculine confidence, he smiled broadly, the gesture all but transforming his face, and turned to the maître d'hôtel. "Miss Silks has graciously agreed to dine with us."

"But, sir, I don't think—"

"If you would be so kind as to round up another chair and place-setting we would be grateful." Hunter lowered his voice. "It is for the best."

"Yes, sir, I… At once." With a resigned sigh, the maître d'hôtel nodded at a passing waiter and set about carrying out Hunter's request.

For her part, Annabeth could only watch the two men bustle around their table in speechless wonder. Hunter had just defused an emotionally charged situation with efficient speed.

More than that, he was treating her mother with genuine respect, and a level of kindness she didn't deserve at the moment. Not many people would be so generous to a woman like Mattie Silks, bad mood or not, and that included her own daughter.

Hunter was proving better than them all.

Guard your heart, Annabeth.

Drawing her bottom lip between her teeth, she cast sidelong glances at the other diners in the restaurant. Praise the Lord. They were fast losing interest now that Mattie was calmly allowing their waiter to settle her at the table. In fact, most had already gone back to their own conversations.

With a deep sigh of relief, Annabeth glanced back at her mother. Her embarrassment immediately evaporated, replaced by a wave of concern. Mattie looked especially tired this afternoon. She kept a brutal pace most days, and nights, never taking time off for herself. Her schedule would make any woman look weary.

Unfortunately, Annabeth sensed this recent change in her mother's appearance was due solely to her.

Was Mattie that upset over Annabeth's desire to care for Sarah? Or was there something else bothering her, something that had more to do with Sarah's father?

The waiter set the final piece of silverware on the table and then snapped to attention. "Are you ready to order, sir?"

Hunter focused on Annabeth, a question in his eyes. "Shall I order for the table?"

"Please." She didn't especially care what he ordered, or so she told herself, but when he chose Apricot Chicken a soft gasp escaped from her lips.

He looked back at her. "No?"

"Oh, please." Mattie rolled her eyes. "Apricot Chicken is her favorite dish."

"You don't say." He smiled, looking rather pleased with himself. Annabeth was rather pleased with him, too.

She returned his smile. Something not altogether unpleasant passed between them.

"Oh, no. No, no." With a swoop, Mattie's shoulders slumped forward. "It's worse than I thought."

The moment the waiter took his leave, Annabeth asked, "What's worse than you thought?"

"Must you ask?" Mattie's tone was not unkind. But there was sadness beneath the words. "I had hoped I was wrong. But I see I have acted too late."

Confused, Annabeth glanced to Hunter for help. He lifted a shoulder, clearly as baffled as she.

"Again, Mattie, what are you talking about?"

With pursed lips, her mother reached for her glass of water, took a sip, then set it back down with a shaky hand.

"Mattie." Hunter reached out, stopped just short of touching her. "What's gotten you so upset?"

Her expression turned accusatory, a look full of quiet contempt. "I understand you have asked Annabeth to live with you."

"I suppose that's one way to look at it." He flattened his palm on the table. "The wrong way. I have asked Annabeth to come away with Sarah and me as my daughter's—"

"I don't want to hear this from you." She deliberately turned her back on him then glared at Annabeth. "You couldn't have bothered telling me yourself? I had to find this out on my own?"

Annabeth didn't ask the obvious question: How did Mattie know about Hunter's offer? Her mother had eyes and ears all over town.

Feelings of guilt swamped her. She should have told

Mattie. But she hadn't wanted a fight. More the fool, her. She was getting a battle, anyway, in a very public manner. "I haven't agreed to anything yet."

"But you will. Because of Sarah." Mattie's fingers tapped out an erratic rhythm on the table. "And him. You're going to throw away your future on—" she hitched her chin in Hunter's direction "—him."

"It's not like that between Hunter and me," Annabeth assured her mother, desperate to find the words to make her understand this was about Sarah. *Sarah.* "Tell her, Hunter."

"It's not like that between us," he repeated in a bland voice.

Mattie snorted, refusing to acknowledge him.

"Now, Mattie, don't pretend you can't hear me."

She smoothed out a wrinkle on her shoulder.

"I know you're listening," he said to the back of her head.

She gave another inelegant snort.

"I've always admired your courage," he said sincerely.

"Hmmpf."

"You're a survivor, doing whatever it takes to make a living in a hard world. You have a good heart, Mattie Silks."

"Haven't you heard?" She flicked a curl off her forehead. "I am not good, or soft, or even nice. I run a brothel. My soul is quite black, beyond redeeming."

"No soul is beyond redeeming." He spoke forcibly, as if speaking as much to himself as to her.

Annabeth's heart clutched. He was right, but she didn't attempt to join in the conversation. Who better than Hunter to have this conversation with her mother? Who better to understand the Lord's love for the lost, than this man?

"You're delusional, Hunter Mitchell." At last, Mattie

looked at him. "Ask any of the churchgoing folk in this city, they'll tell you who and what I am."

Annabeth had never seen her mother like this. She looked and sounded so...so...beaten.

Was Mattie ashamed of the profession she'd chosen? She'd never let on, not once. And if she really was ashamed, why not change her ways?

"You might not live a clean life," Hunter agreed. "But the Lord knows who you are, deep down, under all that bluster. He sees all of you and still loves you."

Mattie gazed up at the ceiling, her eyes blinking rapidly. "You can keep your fancy church words and charming smile for some other fool woman. I remain unmoved."

Hunter's lips twitched, but his tone remained serious, low, meant only for the people at their table. "Because of your example, Annabeth has grown into a strong, good-hearted woman of integrity who knows her own mind. She's an excellent role model to the children at Charity House, and to my daughter. I'm grateful to her." He paused. "And to you."

"Me?"

He took her hand, holding steady when she tried to wrestle free. "Thank you, Mattie."

"Oh, honestly, you are such a man." She swiped at her cheek. "Full of balderdash and too much charm for your own good."

Chuckling softly, he pulled her hand to his lips and pressed a light kiss just above her knuckles. "I'm going to take that as a compliment."

"It was meant as one, you big, handsome brute."

Winking at Annabeth, he let go of Mattie's hand. "Are we friends again?"

Clicking her tongue at him, she made a grand show of

adjusting her collar. "You're a pushy, pushy man with no sense to stop while he's ahead."

"I like to think of myself as determined."

"I have another term for what you are." She plucked at his sleeve, then smoothed her hand across the length of his forearm. "But it isn't fit for mixed company."

"Best keep it to yourself, then."

She pursed her lips. "Naturally."

It was Annabeth's turn to blink in astonishment. Hunter had calmed Mattie's temper and had kept her from revealing…well, much of anything.

He really was a sweet, wonderful, dangerous man.

And she needed to turn the conversation back to the important matter at hand. "Mattie, I'm sorry you found out about my arrangement with Hunter from someone other than me."

"As you should be."

"Yes, well, the point is that I didn't tell you because he only asked me to leave with him and Sarah yesterday." And now she was rationalizing. *Badly done, Annabeth.* "I haven't yet decided if I will take him up on his offer. There are certain factors to consider."

She looked at Hunter then. His gaze appeared impassive, but there was something explosive contained in all that stillness.

He needs me.

The truth settled in her heart. And that was how she knew. She *knew* she would go with him. Not only for Sarah's sake. But for his, too.

And maybe, Annabeth realized with a start, even her own.

Caught in Annabeth's gaze, Hunter felt a rush of some strong emotion he couldn't define, didn't dare define.

Attraction? Definitely.

Guilt? *Most* definitely.

He reminded himself she wasn't the woman he should be thinking of, yearning for with every breath, as though he'd been waiting for her to come into his life and she was finally here. The dream of finding a woman to love—as a man loved his wife—was over, dead and buried, murdered by Cole Kincaid.

Jane had been Hunter's last hope of marital bliss, his one chance to get it right. He'd lost everything when he'd lost her.

He'd failed two women already. He would not add a third to the list. Marriage to a good woman, a partner who'd stick by his side as they navigated through life, was no longer possible for him. Stability was the best he could hope for now.

He felt a pang of regret.

He could still love, though, as evidenced by his feelings for his daughter. *Love as Christ first loved you.* That, Hunter could do. But romantic love? A ruined illusion.

So, why this strange new emotion running up against his resolve? Why now? And why Annabeth?

She was beautiful, to be sure, with a lovely oval face, haunting blue eyes, a color so rich and deep it seemed to take on a purple hue. And that silky dark hair, pinned up with tendrils teasing free. Under different circumstances…

No. There were reasons that made anything beyond friendship between them impossible. One in particular came to mind. Sarah.

The other sat at the table with them, watching their every move. *His* every move.

"Stop looking at one another like that." Mattie threw her hands up in exasperation. "It's making me ill."

Just then, the waiter arrived with their meals. After he left, the steaming plates of food sat untouched.

"Tell me your concerns, Mattie," Hunter said. "And I'll do my best to address them."

"Annabeth cannot live with you and your daughter, no matter the reason. You must realize it isn't proper."

The irony of Denver's most notorious madam speaking on the subject of propriety was priceless. Of course, that didn't mean she wasn't absolutely correct. "I plan to hire a housekeeper to live with us, as well."

He glanced at Annabeth, waiting for her to join the discussion. But she'd become overly fascinated with her plate of food, moving a lone apricot around with her fork.

"A housekeeper, indeed." Mattie dismissed this suggestion with a toss of her head. "What decent man will have her after she's lived under the same roof with you?"

"Our living situation will be completely aboveboard." He reiterated his point with force. "It's no different than if she took a job as a governess in any other home in Denver."

"It's completely different." Mattie spoke with equal force. "Because of who you are and the nature of your past, she'll be ruined the moment she steps into your home. Guilt by association."

He wasn't insulted by the statement. Well, only a little.

The comment, coming from Mattie Silks of all people, drove home the reality of his situation. Although some people would give him the benefit of the doubt, most would assume he was still a man of many sins, capable of killing in cold blood.

The dream of starting over was always just ahead of him, always just out of reach. He was lying to himself if he pretended otherwise. He would never be able to atone for his sins. Compelled, he touched the pocket where he kept his Bible, reminding himself that atonement wasn't necessary. In God's eyes he was already forgiven.

But not in the eyes of men.

Mattie was right. Annabeth's reputation would be ruined the moment she left town with him. *Guilt by association.*

He opened his mouth to rescind his offer.

"Now you listen to me, Mattie Silks." Annabeth slapped her palms on the table and leaned forward, her eyes taking on a fiery glint. "Anyone who judges Hunter for his past lacks Christian charity." She waited for her words to settle over the table. "I would never want to be with a man who held Hunter's past against him. And you shouldn't want that for me, either."

Mattie stiffened in her chair. "That is beside the point. You will not agree to his job offer. I forbid it."

Hunter cringed. Mattie had just made a big mistake. Annabeth didn't seem to be a woman who caved to ultimatums.

Proving his point, she swung her gaze to his, mutiny in her eyes. "When do you want my answer?"

"I…" Hunter swallowed, looked between the two women, swallowed again, then did what any wise man would do under the circumstances. He dodged the question. "I have found it's never smart to make a decision out of emotion."

"Very wise advice, Hunter, darling." Mattie patted his hand in commiseration. "Very wise, indeed."

Annabeth persisted. "When?"

"I—"

"When?"

All right, then, since she asked. "I'd like to have your answer as soon as possible. If you decide to refuse me, I will need sufficient time to make other arrangements for Sarah's care."

"Very well." She gave him one, firm nod. "I will let you know my decision tomorrow afternoon."

A day. One day to find out whether Annabeth would be a part of his and Sarah's lives. One. Short. Day.

All he had to do was dig in his heels and hold on for twenty-four measly hours.

Chapter Eleven

The next afternoon, Annabeth arrived home from church ahead of the others. With the children several minutes behind her, the house was quiet, eerily so, the silence broken only by the ticking of the grandfather clock in the main hallway.

Tense and full of indecision, her breathing caught the rhythmic tick, tick, tick.

This moment of peace wouldn't last long, she knew. She had precious little time to sort through her thoughts. Running a hand over the banister of the main stairwell, she tried to picture her future outside this house.

The task proved easier than she'd imagined. She'd always wanted a home of her own, populated with a lot of children, a husband that took care of their family and provided a safe environment for them all.

If she closed her eyes she could almost envision walking along the rolling hills of a valley, the mountains in the distance, the sound of cattle lowing behind her. There was a man by her side, tall, with sandy-blond hair and golden-amber eyes. The haunted look was gone from his expression, no more loneliness, no more sorrow, only peace, and love. Love for her, for their children…

Annabeth quickly snapped open her eyes. Hunter Mitchell was not allowed to be the center of her dreams. She wanted a respectable man, maybe a banker or a lawyer, not a former outlaw.

But perhaps she wasn't being fair. Hunter had proved himself a good man already, kind, considerate, accepting of others, including Mattie. Yet, even if he proved dependable, Annabeth had to remember he was a man who'd been so in love with his wife he'd willingly gone to prison for avenging her murder.

Her mouth tightened around the edges. Despite the sunlight streaming in through the windows, she felt a shadow pass over her soul. Was she jealous? Of Hunter's dead wife?

Yes. Sadly, she was.

The thought of Hunter married to another woman—*any* other woman—made Annabeth sick at heart. For whatever reason, no matter how illogical, after a mere handful of days she was beginning to think of him as hers. It was as though they'd always belonged together but only now was the timing right.

God's timing was always perfect. Annabeth believed that truth. *He makes all things work together for our good.* That, too, she believed with all her heart. So if the Lord's hand was in this situation, if He was guiding Annabeth toward Hunter, and Hunter toward her, then everything would work out in the end. Oh, how she wanted…

What? What did she want?

She let out a small sigh.

Hunter. She wanted Hunter. In her life. Forever.

She was going to accept his offer to accompany him and Sarah to his family's ranch. Moving into the parlor, she glanced at the clock on the mantelpiece. Ten minutes past noon. She would forever think of this moment as the one that changed her life forever.

Now, all she had to do was tell Hunter her decision. Then they would begin making plans.

Mattie wasn't going to like this, not one bit.

Of course, her mother hadn't blessed Annabeth's decision to move to Charity House, either, and look how that had turned out. The thought produced a small smile of satisfaction.

The sound of running feet alerted Annabeth her solitude had come to an end. Seconds later the front door swung opened with a bang. Children of all ages and sizes spilled into the orphanage, shouting, laughing, making their way to various parts of the house.

Since the parlor was considered off-limits for anything other than formal occasions and important visitors, Annabeth enjoyed an additional two minutes of solitude.

Sarah, always attuned to Annabeth and her whereabouts in the house, sauntered into the parlor, her smile wide. "I knew I'd find you here. Why'd you leave church ahead of the rest of us?"

"I simply wanted a moment to catch my breath." Annabeth returned the child's smile with a quivering one of her own. "It's been a busy three days."

Sarah angled her head, her brows knit tightly together. "You mean since my father showed up."

The child was far more perceptive than most nine-year-olds, a trait she shared with the other Charity House children. "That's precisely what I mean."

"Oh, Aunt Annabeth, it's really wonderful, isn't it? I have a father of my very own." The child twirled in a circle, arms outstretched, her entire being filled with unspeakable joy. "I have a father of my very, very, very own."

"Yes, you do."

"God is so good."

Out of the mouths of babes.

He makes all things work together for our good. A wave of peace spread through her confusion.

"Will I see my father soon?" Sarah asked.

"Very soon. Today, actually. He's planning to stop by this afternoon." Annabeth didn't go into further detail, primarily because she didn't know exactly when he would arrive. They hadn't set a specific time yesterday when he'd dropped her off after lunch.

"Oh. Oh! He could be here any minute." Sarah shuffled her feet, turning in small, tight circles. "I had better hurry and change my dress."

"You look more than presentable at the moment."

Her words rolled off Sarah's retreating back. The girl was so excited, so happy, even if Annabeth had wanted to prevent Hunter from claiming his daughter, she wouldn't have the heart.

Sarah already loved her father.

That makes two of us.

No. No. Annabeth stumbled back a step. Her knees gave out and she fell into a chair. No. *No.* She couldn't be in love with Hunter Mitchell. Not this soon. This was only an echo of her schoolgirl infatuation with the man.

Yes. That explained this strange sensation. She was merely overwhelmed from the stream of shocks she'd endured over the past three days. Hunter had been nice to her, and to her mother, treating them both no different than anyone else he met.

How could Annabeth not be dazzled by his charm, his large presence, the way he looked her straight in the eye?

This will pass, she assured herself.

So why did the room suddenly become a confusion of

sights and sounds? Why did her breath knock around in her lungs in a series of hard puffs?

And why was the floor moving beneath her feet?

"Miss Annabeth?" A feminine voice broke through the haze in her mind. "You don't look so well. Have you taken ill?"

She swatted at the buzz in her ear. She needed time. Time to analyze what was happening inside her. Time to sort through the emotions that were bursting inside her very soul.

"Miss Annabeth."

She looked up.

Molly Scott frowned down at her.

"Oh, Molly," she breathed the girl's name on an exhale. Tension continued to coil in her shoulders. *Focus, Annabeth, focus.* "I didn't hear you come in the parlor."

Molly's lips quirked at a perceptive angle, amusement dancing in her eyes. Even at fifteen she was a startling beauty with her coal-black hair, clear blue eyes and creamy porcelain skin. Boys were already falling at her feet, much to her parents' chagrin.

The girl was also a handful, always one step away from crossing a line, and one of the most likable people Annabeth knew. Although Molly wasn't officially one of the orphans anymore, and hadn't been for years—not since her half sister had married Sheriff Scott and they'd adopted her—truth be told the girl was one of Annabeth's favorite students. And her most challenging.

"I've been told I'm light on my feet. By, well—" Molly grinned "—you, actually."

"I'm aware." On several occasions Molly had managed to sneak out of class, always on a sunny day when the outdoors called to her rebellious nature. "Did you need something from me?"

"Actually, I was looking for Sarah." She held up a satchel Annabeth hadn't noticed before now. "I was going to help her redesign another one of her bonnets this afternoon."

An activity that would keep the child busy until her father arrived. "What a lovely idea. She went upstairs to change her dress."

This seemed to confound Molly. "Whatever for?"

"She's expecting a visitor later this afternoon."

"Oh. You mean her father." Molly frowned. "Should I come back another time?"

"No, no. Now is good." Better than good. Annabeth could use a distraction herself. "Why don't you go fetch Sarah and bring her back downstairs?"

"You want me to bring her here? In the parlor?" Molly looked intrigued, and more than happy to dive in for the sheer sake of breaking the rules.

Oh, yes, the girl was definitely a handful.

"Not here, no." Annabeth tried to sound stern but she gave in to a quick spurt of laughter. Molly had such a crestfallen expression on her face. "We'll work in the dining room this afternoon so we can spread out the ribbons, scraps of material and pins on the table."

Molly still looked displeased at this explanation, as if Annabeth had ruined a rather fun, if somewhat innocuous, rebellion on her part.

"I'll join you in a few minutes," Annabeth offered.

"That'll be fine." Molly lifted a shoulder and gave in good-naturedly. "I'll get Sarah now."

Twenty minutes later, the two of them—plus six other girls—worked at the dining room table. Ribbons of varying widths, lengths and textures were scattered across every available spot.

Laughter abounded, while suggestions for possible designs flew between various groupings of girls. But as the afternoon passed, instead of enjoying what was usually her favorite activity, Sarah grew more and more agitated. She kept shooting glances toward the doorway, her heart in her eyes.

She was waiting for her father, clearly, and as each moment ticked by, with no sign of Hunter, something akin to fear replaced her excitement.

Annabeth realized too late she'd made a serious error in judgment. She shouldn't have told Sarah about Hunter's visit, not until she'd been certain what time he would show.

How she knew what poor Sarah was feeling. How many times had she herself waited for her own father to show up at Mattie's brothel? One short visit, that's all Annabeth had ever wanted. A visit that never came.

Understanding her niece's disappointment, more than she cared to admit, Annabeth inched next to her. "He said he was going to come," she whispered. "He'll come."

Sarah's mouth twisted into a stubborn line. "I don't care if he does or not."

Of course she cared.

"Relax, darling. He'll be here soon."

"It doesn't matter." Despite her bold words, Sarah drew in a shuddering breath and looked toward the entrance once again. A sigh leaked out of her.

Resisting the urge to follow her niece's gaze, Annabeth thought through her options and decided distraction was her best course of action. She picked up a thin white ribbon with light blue polka dots and ran it along the rim of a bonnet. "This might work here. The hues definitely match and they fit so well here, where they—"

"It's ugly." Sarah shoved Annabeth's hand away. "The whole bonnet is ugly. And I hate blue."

Annabeth prayed for patience. "But, Sarah, blue is your favorite color."

"Not anymore."

The tension in the girl was evident, and so very understandable, but that didn't mean she could get away with ruining the afternoon for everyone else with her foul mood. "If you don't like blue, then try another color. How about this pink one?"

Sarah's bottom lip wobbled. "I *hate* pink."

"Now you're just being ornery."

"Am not!"

Unused to such behavior from her niece, Annabeth drew in a calming breath of air. Either that or give in to her own irritation. "Keep this up, Sarah, and I'll have no other option than to send you upstairs."

"Fine." She crossed her arms over her chest. "I don't want to be here, anyway."

A collective gasp rose up from the table. Annabeth didn't have time for the shout of frustration that clogged in her throat, because at that moment, Hunter stepped into the doorway of the dining room.

Rotten timing, that's what Hunter had, the very worst of all.

Never one for unnecessary drama, he took a step back, realizing a moment too late that he'd arrived just in time for a female snit of classic proportions. The fact that his daughter was at the center of the maelstrom, made him all the more leery.

Sarah's very aggravated aunt tossed him a desperate look that said, "Do something."

Right, sure thing, as if he knew what do with a nine-year-old female temper tantrum. Maybe he should have bought his daughter a doll.

Or…maybe not.

Sarah's chin jutted out at an obstinate angle so reminiscent of Maria in one of her "moods" that he doubted anything could soothe the child.

Fighting off his own desperation, Hunter looked around the room and realized eight pairs of eyes—all female—were focused directly on him. Every person sitting at the table seemed to be aware of his presence. Every person, that was, except his own daughter.

She was too busy glaring at her aunt.

Hunter was way out of his league here. Had he really thought he could raise a young girl on his own? He blinked. Swallowed hard. Blinked again. Sighed. Speared his fingers through his hair.

Cleared his throat.

Sarah finally looked in his direction. And, hallelujah, her face instantly lit with happiness.

Head reeling from the swift change in her, his mouth spread into a flimsy attempt of a smile.

Tantrum forgotten, Sarah shoved back her chair and leaped forward, straight into his arms.

"You came. You really came." A sob slipped out of her throat, far more telling than her words. "I was getting so very worried."

Ah. So that was the source of her *snit*. Sarah had been afraid he wasn't coming back, today, or maybe ever. "Not to worry, sweetheart." He held her tightly against him. "I'm not going anywhere without you."

The tears started then. Why was she crying? What had he done wrong?

"I love you," she whispered.

He had to swallow the hard ache that rose to his throat. His daughter was crying happy tears, because of him. "I love you, too."

"I'm so very, very glad." She pressed her wet cheek into his shirt, and clung, a move that further melted his already battered heart.

Hand shaking, he smoothed his palm over his daughter's silky hair. The magnitude of what he was getting himself into sank in with a vengeance. The weight of responsibility had never felt heavier. This young girl's happiness was connected with his, and his with hers. Every decision he made would directly influence her life, and every hurt she suffered would cut him to the core.

The last time he'd taken on another person's care had been his wife. Though he'd failed Jane, long before Cole had found her in that alley, and in many ways, he'd failed Maria, too.

He would not fail Sarah. By the grace of God, with prayer, hard work and the help of her aunt, Hunter would do right by his daughter. He wasn't leaving today until Annabeth agreed to come with him and Sarah to the Flying M.

Seeking out the woman in question, he captured her gaze and made the silent promise to her, as well. A moment of complete understanding spread between them, as if she understood they were in this together.

He tightened his arms around his daughter. She continued to cling to him—and didn't that say it all? Aware they had a very attentive audience with various levels of speculation being shot their way, Hunter tried to pry Sarah's arms from around his waist.

She was having none of it.

Thankfully, Annabeth moved to stand beside them. Bless her beautiful, kindhearted soul she'd decided to rescue him.

"All right, girls, let's everybody settle down." When the chattering turned to a low hum, Annabeth carefully pulled Sarah free of Hunter's embrace. "Sarah, why don't you introduce your friends to Mr. Mitchell?"

"All right." She darted to the girl at the head of the table. "This is my best friend, Molly Taylor Scott."

Hunter nodded to the girl. "You're Trey's daughter."

Holding her head high, her posture oh-so-proper, Molly allowed a tiny half smile to play across her lips. "I am, indeed."

"I'm pleased to meet you."

"And I, you."

He remembered what Trey had said about his wayward daughter. *She was always a handful, one step away from open rebellion, but now she's downright...difficult.*

Hunter shrugged. The description didn't match the charming girl smiling at him now. Had Trey exaggerated? Didn't seem likely.

Sarah stepped to the next chair. "And this is Constance."

"Constance." Hunter nodded at the blonde girl. "A pleasure."

Smiling broadly, Sarah continued around the table, repeating the process with each girl, naming them one by one. He tried to keep up. Natalie, Jocelyn, Mary, Prudence and, finally, Rachel, or maybe that last one was Rebecca. He'd lost track. Now his head was spinning a little. *A lot.*

He didn't have a prayer of remembering all the names. Nevertheless, he smiled at each girl as Sarah made her way through the introductions.

One of the girls, the youngest if her size was anything to go by, stared up at him with wide, curious eyes. "You know who *we* are. But who are *you?*"

"Isn't it obvious?" The girl next to her jabbed her in the ribs with her elbow. "He's the one Sarah's been telling us about."

"Oh." The first girl still looked confused.

Hunter smiled at his daughter as she drew alongside him again. Understanding the magnitude of the moment, he slung his arm over her shoulders and said, "I'm Sarah's father."

The room erupted with squeals and voices tumbling over one another. Girls jumped out of their chairs in random succession, and rushed forward. Even Molly lost a portion of her earlier dignity.

Completely ignoring Hunter, they shoved and pushed and surrounded Sarah. A symphony of high-pitched voices threw questions at her in rapid-fire intensity. He'd seen bullets fly slower in a five-man gunfight.

"You certainly know how to make an entrance," Annabeth said, speaking over the commotion.

Still watching his daughter, loving how happy she looked, he replied absently, "I learned from the master."

"Some actress, I suppose." Something in Annabeth's tone drew his attention back to her. If he wasn't mistaken, she looked as if it bothered her that he might have once been friends with an actress.

He laughed at that, really laughed. "I was referring to the one and only Mattie Silks."

"Oh, of course." Annabeth laughed with him then, the sound low and musical.

At the sound, something deep inside Hunter simply... let...go.

For the first time since leaving prison, he felt truly at peace, all because of the woman sharing this moment with him. The same woman who'd declared he was more than his past, who'd defended him in front of her own mother.

Annabeth Silks was a marvel.

He'd be a fool to let her get away.

Hunter was many things. A fool he was not.

Chapter Twelve

After all the questions were asked—and answered—Sarah left with Molly in search of more material so she could make bonnets for her new cousins as gifts. At least, that's what Annabeth thought she heard the girl say. Sarah had spoken so quickly Annabeth couldn't be sure.

Her head was still spinning from the constant chatter of the past half hour.

Looking bemused, Hunter glanced around the now empty room, his gaze bouncing off various points of interest.

Alone at last, Annabeth wanted to tell him her decision. Not here, though, not in the dining room where anyone could walk in on them.

She took his hand. "Come with me."

He smiled. "All right."

She led him to Marc's office but stopped on the threshold. "Oh, Marc. Laney. I forgot."

Sunday afternoon was when they reviewed the list of supplies needed for the coming week.

Annabeth backpedaled. "Hunter and I can find somewhere else to talk."

"No need to leave on our account." From behind his

desk, Marc ushered them into the room with a sweep of his hand. "We were just finishing up."

Smiling, Laney looked at them over her shoulder, her gaze zeroing in on Hunter. "Well, now, the man of the hour. I understand you told several of the children that you're Sarah's father today."

"I did."

Laney's smile gentled, her eyes full of affection. "It's a rare occurrence, you know, to have a father show up and accept responsibility for his child."

Hunter's shoulders stiffened, as if prepared for a fight. "It's not a hardship, claiming Sarah as my daughter."

Something swelled in Annabeth's throat at the raw emotion she heard in his voice. He really was a good man. The very best.

"Nevertheless—" Laney nodded at him in approval "—well done, Hunter."

Looking oddly uncomfortable for a man who was usually so sure of himself, he shoved his hands into his pockets and rocked back on his heels. "I never want Sarah to question whether or not I want her in my life."

"I'm glad." Laney walked over to him and patted him on the cheek as she would one of the children who'd done something rather exceptional. "It's an important step for you both."

"Yes."

Shifting at an angle so she could take in Annabeth and Hunter at the same time, Laney looked from one to the other, holding Annabeth's gaze a bit longer than Hunter's. "It's clear you two still have some things to work out between you. Come along, Marc. Let's give them a moment of privacy."

Her husband was already rounding the corner of his desk. "Perfect timing, I could use a break from all those numbers." He clapped Hunter on the back. "Good to see you."

"You, too."

Annabeth waited until Marc escorted Laney out of the room, and then got straight to the point. "I've made my decision."

"I'm listening." So cool, so calm, the man hid his emotions well. But Annabeth sensed the vulnerability in him, the nervousness.

She wanted to say yes.

"I will continue to be a part of Sarah's everyday life." *And yours.*

"So you're coming with us to the Flying M."

Now. This was the moment when she put her future into this man's hands, for better or worse. "Yes. I'll take on whatever role you need of me."

A small smile curled the corners of his mouth. "Interesting choice of words."

Tricky, bad, dangerous, bad, bad man. A terrible influence on her. She nearly laughed. The surge of happiness bubbling up from her soul caught her off guard. She tried to beat it down, but she couldn't.

For once in her life, Annabeth wanted to toss aside care and step out on faith. A frightening prospect, to be sure, but she'd learned long ago that faith with no effort was no faith at all. Sarah was worth taking this risk, she told herself.

So was Hunter, her heart whispered.

He was as fierce as a tiger, had the courage of lion, and was totally, irresistibly charming when he chose to be.

Like now…

There he stood, his gaze traveling across her face with an unspoken promise in his eyes.

"Your mother isn't going to like your decision," he pointed out.

"I'm my own woman."

He reached to her, his hand landing on her arm. "She'll do whatever necessary to stop you from leaving town with me."

"She won't succeed."

He moved his hand to her face.

Annabeth leaned into his touch.

"You deserve a better life than the one I can give you."

His softly uttered words, spoken in that raw tone, staggered her. This beautiful, brave man needed a woman to care for him, to accept him, to love him. She wanted to be that woman.

"I'm doing this for Sarah," she insisted.

"It's a good reason. The right one."

His hand shook ever-so-slightly, then moved to the back of her neck. Slowly, tenderly, he lowered his head toward hers. And she knew. He was going to kiss her.

The inevitability of this moment had her lifting on her toes. She wanted this, wanted it very much.

She longed to be the one to close the distance between them, to prove to him she was as much in the moment as he appeared to be.

"Be sure, Annabeth." His mouth stopped just short of connecting with hers. "Be very sure this is what you want to do."

Was he referring to her decision to leave Charity House? Or this…kiss?

Caught in a whirlwind of emotion, tired of fighting her longing for this man, Annabeth closed her eyes, let go of the logical part of her brain and gave herself over to this new, wondrous feeling of abandon. A sensation that felt strong and lasting, like the first step toward forever.

She whispered his name.

A moment later, his mouth closed over hers. He knotted his other hand in a loose fist around her hair. She'd never thought a kiss could feel like this, exciting, a little frightening, as if Hunter was offering himself to her, asking her to heal him.

Annabeth slid her arms around his neck, trying to get closer.

And then…

He abruptly pulled away from her.

Grim determination flattened his lips. "I'll speak with Mattie as soon as possible." Sad, and maybe a little lost, he gave her a halfhearted smile. "We need to make it right with her before we leave town."

It took a moment for his words to register. "You don't have to do that. Mattie is my problem, not yours."

"She's *our* problem."

"She's my mother," she said. "Not my keeper."

"I won't be the cause of a rift between you two."

How…utterly…sweet.

Annabeth touched his face. He was so earnest, so sincere. Tears threatened, wiggling to the edges of her eyelashes. Did this man know how good he was, deep down, where it counted?

"You're in for a battle." She dragged her fingertips across his cheek, his jaw, back up to his temple. "Mattie can be bone-stubborn when she has an idea stuck in her head, especially when it comes to me."

"Don't I know it." Covering her roaming hand with his, his voice dropped an entire octave, growing silky with amusement and something else. Something that drew her closer to him.

"Mattie's unquestioning devotion to you is what I like most about her."

Something tightened in Annabeth's throat. Hunter liked Mattie. He genuinely liked her, despite the hard exterior she presented to the world, despite what she did for a living. "Don't ever tell her you think that. You'll only encourage her outrageous behavior."

He gave a mock shudder.

They dropped their hands simultaneously, laughing, smiling, sharing the joke. But when their eyes met, the laughter died away.

"Annabeth." He pulled her against him again.

"Hunter."

"This is a bad idea," he muttered.

"The very worst," she agreed. And yet, she lifted on her toes and, this time, she pressed her lips to his.

In that moment, Annabeth accepted the truth about the situation, *about herself.* Hunter wasn't a bad influence on her. She was a bad influence on him.

Hunter needed to step away. He needed to release Annabeth, this very instant.

He also needed...had to have...longed for...

Her.

She wrought emotions in him he'd thought buried, such soul-deep longing he could hardly take a breath. How had Annabeth become so important to him? When had she become such a part of him that he couldn't imagine a day without her in it?

She was a good woman, the kind that could save a man from himself, which was why he should ask her to stay with him and Sarah, permanently, *before* she found someone else who appreciated her. Dangerous thinking on his part.

With considerable effort, he set Annabeth away from him. "I have to go."

"You're leaving? Now?" The narrowing of her eyes emphasized their pale color and the thickness of her black silky lashes. "When we just…you know…just…" She looked at him helplessly, as if she couldn't find the proper word for what had happened between them.

"Kissed?" he supplied helpfully.

She flinched. "Do you have to be so blunt?"

Had he been blunt?

"Annabeth." He ran his thumb along her jawline, wondering how he could have ever thought he would be able to remain neutral toward this woman. Dangerous, dangerous territory.

"I believe it's important to be honest with one another, always, wouldn't you agree?"

"I…" Her brows snapped down over her stunning eyes. "Well, yes, I agree completely."

"Then I need to tell you something before we go any further."

Eyes wary, she pressed her fingertips to her lips and waited for him to continue.

"No matter how much I have come to like and admire you, I could never give you what you need, or what you deserve."

"Oh." She dropped her hand to her side. "Because of your wife?"

Partly.

"I let her down, in the worst possible way." He reached for her, needing to touch her, just this one last time, but pulled back before making contact. "I'm a risky prospect. I never want to hurt a woman like that again, especially if that woman is you."

"Oh, Hunter."

He didn't want her pity. *Lord, anything but that.* "Do you understand what I'm trying to say?"

"Yes. No more kissing." She actually sounded…disappointed. "But, I thought, we kind of, got it…you know, right."

Yes, they had.

More than right, pretty close to perfect.

He ignored the swell of regret that spread through him.

"You're a beautiful, intelligent woman." He didn't mention specifics, not her light blue, heavily lashed eyes, or her full mouth, strong chin, high cheekbones, her…

He cleared his throat.

"Any man would be blessed to have you as his wife. But that man won't be me."

Looking as if he'd slapped her, she went very still before affecting a bored expression. "One kiss, and you think I'm dreaming of marriage. My, my, don't you have an ego."

He deserved her sarcasm. But her words cut deeper than he would have expected. "If memory serves, it was actually two kisses."

Her cheeks turned a becoming pink. "True. But I only initiated one of them."

He could see the embarrassment she tried so hard to hide.

He could see the moment the emotion turned toward something darker, something more like shame.

His annoyance melted away and he allowed a touch of tenderness to soften his voice. "It was nicely done, by the way. Your kiss, I mean."

She smiled, and a new tension shifted between them. *Dangerous, dangerous territory.*

"It was a kiss, Annabeth. Remarkable as it was, you don't have to be afraid I'll expect more from you in the future."

He didn't move any closer to her, nor did he try to touch

her, but with their gazes locked so firmly together, it felt as if they'd made a physical connection, anyway.

"You don't have to expect the worst from me," he promised in a low tone. "I will never hurt you."

It was a promise he intended to keep, a promise that seemed to take her by surprise.

Her eyes turned glassy and her teeth clenched tightly together, so tightly he feared she might grind the back ones into powder. "No need to worry about me," she said at last. "I can take care of myself. I've been doing so for years."

Yes, she probably had, especially with a mother like Mattie. Even though she'd gone to school in Boston, she'd come home during the holidays and had lived in the brothel for short stays.

Annabeth's mixed heritage made her a rare beauty. She could wear a potato sack and men would want her. There had to have been occasions when one of Mattie's customers had seen her and tried to take what they saw.

For her daughter's sake, why had Mattie never tried to earn money in a more respectable manner? Anger, strong and visceral, burned through Hunter. Annabeth deserved to be cherished, adored, revered by a good man without a sordid past.

"I want you to come live with me and Sarah. But I'll say this again, and again, until you believe I'm sincere." He held her gaze. "I only ask that you be Sarah's aunt, nothing more."

"I understand, Hunter. I do. No more kissing."

"No more kissing," he repeated, for his own benefit this time, not hers.

It was really too bad, all things considered. Annabeth had felt good in his arms, better than any woman he'd ever held. And that made him a disloyal fiend of the worst kind. Every day he was finding it harder to remember his dear wife's face. Even in his dreams her image was becoming hard to discern, fading with each passing day, more a watery memory than substance.

The disturbing thought stole his breath, but not his resolve. He needed her to understand where he stood. "I promise to behave above reproach at all times while you are in my home."

"You're making a lot of promises this afternoon."

Yes, he was. "I can't raise Sarah on my own. I need your help."

He heard her sharp intake of air, felt her shock and something else. Hope.

"I don't say that to force your hand. I will let you go if you change your mind, now or in the future. And if a decent man offers you marriage, I won't stand in your way."

"How very noble of you," she muttered. At least, that's what he thought she said.

Hard to tell with the blood rushing in his ears.

What would he do if another man sought her favor?

Nothing. He would do nothing.

They might have shared a moment of intimacy in this room, one he would never forget, but she'd made it clear, on several occasions, what she wanted in life. Permanence, respectability, a decent man to cherish her into old age.

He could give her none of those things, not without the risk of hurting her in the future.

He hated to see her stiff posture, hated knowing he'd been the cause of her discomfort. He wanted to see her smile again, to watch her eyes crinkle in amusement at something he said.

He wanted her to know he cared.

Perhaps that explained why he took her hand and placed it against his heart. "The Lord brought us together for a reason, no matter how temporary. It's up to us to figure out what comes next. I'm willing to do the work. Are you?"

She answered without hesitation. "Yes."

They stood staring at one another. The moment should have been charged with tension. Oddly enough, it wasn't.

And he knew why.

With Annabeth, everything felt exactly right, even when everything should be all wrong.

Dangerous, dangerous territory.

Chapter Thirteen

Eyes checking the perimeter of the property, Hunter arrived at Mattie's brothel just as the sun disappeared behind the mountains. The startling array of pinks and oranges was an awe-inspiring end of the day, one usually set aside for rest.

He wasn't surprised the Sabbath had no meaning on this side of town. The vulgar revelry seeping out of every establishment told its own tale. He considered leaving and returning in the morning, but his conversation with Mattie couldn't wait another day.

Hunter had made a drastic mistake this afternoon. He'd let himself have too much free rein in Annabeth's company. Kissing her had been a bad idea. He'd known that from the start. Still, when he'd held her in his arms and stared into her beautiful eyes, he'd forgotten all about honor and duty and the man he was trying to become.

Now, he had nothing but regret.

He suddenly wanted to punch a wall, to howl in frustration, to do something drastic.

No, that was the man he used to be. The new Hunter surrendered his destructive impulses to the Lord.

Praying for control, he set his jaw at a determined angle and entered Mattie's brothel.

One of the girls approached him, hips swaying, intent in her heavy-lidded gaze. He stopped her pursuit with a firm shake of his head.

Frowning, she switched directions. The moment she was out of sight, Jack appeared on the other side of the parlor. He met Hunter halfway across the room. "Not another step."

Hunter blew out a hiss. "I don't want any trouble. Just tell Mattie I need to see her immediately."

"Sorry, Hunter, not tonight."

Here we go again. Praying for patience, he swept his gaze around the room then set out once again.

Jack stopped him with a palm to his chest.

Stone-cold still, Hunter dropped a pointed glare at the other man's hand. "Out of my way." He lowered his voice to a deadly whisper. "Now."

To his credit, Jack didn't flinch. He did, however, drop his hand and step back. "She's entertaining a personal friend."

Possible.

All right, probable.

Hunter paused.

Barging into the middle of one of Mattie's private sessions would only antagonize her. Not the best course of action considering the delicate nature of his own business. "I'll wait until she's free."

"Wait? You?" Jack raised his eyebrows. "Did I hear that correctly?"

Hunter shrugged. "I'm in no hurry."

"Suit yourself." Jack cut a glance over Hunter's head. "But you can't stay in here. This room is for paying customers."

"Fine. I'll wait—" he considered his options "—in the kitchen."

Jack nodded and stepped aside to let Hunter pass.

Entering the kitchen, he looked around for the most advantageous seat. He chose a straight-back chair near the stove, angling it in a position that would ensure he caught Mattie the moment she left her rooms.

After a half hour of cooling his heels, Hunter considered leaving and coming back later. But there was a good chance if Mattie finished up before he returned she would find another "personal friend" to entertain in his absence.

No, Hunter wasn't budging from this spot until he had his audience with the queen, er...discussion with the infamous madam.

Unfortunately, the half hour turned into an hour, which turned into three, which turned into an endless night. He must have fallen asleep at some point, because he jolted awake as the first threads of gray morning light fell across his face.

Stretching his legs out in front of him, he rolled his shoulders and winced. Kinks had taken up residence in every part of his neck and back.

So. Mattie had left him to wait in the chair all night.

Hunter hadn't expected her to pull something this mean-spirited, though he should have. This was Mattie Silks he was dealing with, not some green ingenue. Underhanded tactics were a part of the woman's everyday repertoire. And yet, the fact that she'd kept him waiting—*all night*—actually made him...

Chuckle. A moment later, he gave fully into his laughter.

Ornery, sneaky, devious, devious woman.

Though she may have won this round, he would take the next.

Still smiling, he stood, stretched his legs again, then pulled his watch from a vest pocket. He flipped open the lid and read the time. If he didn't leave now, he'd be late for his appointment with the lawyer across town.

A rumble of thunder had him glancing to the sky just as he exited the brothel. Dark, ominous-looking clouds rolled in off the mountains.

Hunter increased his pace. He thought he saw a shadow dart in the alley behind him. Glancing quickly over his shoulder, he saw nothing out of the ordinary. Just a trick of the light filtering through a seam in the clouds.

Several blocks into the finer part of town, a pair of ladies in pristine walking dresses, hats in the latest fashion and matching pale pink parasols approached him from the opposite direction. They gave him a wide berth, as if they knew who he was and where he'd been.

He gave a mental shrug. This wasn't the first time the "good people" of Denver had avoided him. He doubted it would be the last. Some would always consider him nothing more than an outlaw with loose morals and no conscience.

His thoughts shifted to Sarah and his steps faltered.

As his daughter, would she suffer guilt by association?

It was a question that had plagued him since he'd received Mattie's letter all those weeks ago. The Bible taught that the sins of the father would carry into three generations. But, as the prison minister had also pointed out to Hunter, the Lord's blessings carried into a thousand generations for those who turned from their sins.

Hunter clung to that hope, determined to be a blessing rather than a curse to his daughter.

Resolve quickened his steps once again.

Three seconds later, the rain let loose in driving sheets. People darted for cover.

Not wanting to be late for his appointment, Hunter shoved his hat over his eyes and shouldered through the downpour. He didn't ease up on the pace until he was outside a majestic, two-story brick building. Glancing at the gold-embossed placard, he read the name aloud. "Bennett, Bennett and Brand Law Firm."

He'd been here once before, last week when he'd made today's appointment with Reese Bennett's law clerk. He stepped inside the building. Waiting for his eyes to adjust in the darkened entryway, he removed his hat and shook off the rain as best he could.

Moving forward, he realized the desk where the clerk had been prior was empty. He was alone in the large reception area. Was he too early?

He took a deep breath and looked around, relaxed his shoulders. The place reeked of money and success. Even the smell of furniture polish, leather and wood paneling denoted wealth. Knowing the law offices were down the hall beyond the reception area, Hunter rounded the empty desk and set out in that direction.

Portraits of mature, stodgy-looking men hung on both walls along the corridor. The last portrait stood out from the rest, primarily because the likeness of a much younger man stared back at him. With his black hair, dark, serious eyes and stern expression, the man looked overly determined, as if he wouldn't rest until the job was done to his satisfaction.

Hunter read the nameplate on the bottom of the frame. *Reese Bennett, Jr.* Excellent. The lawyer he'd come to see.

He continued his trek and stopped at the door with Bennett's name on the front. He knocked twice.

No response.

After a moment, he raised his fist to knock again but a voice stopped him midreach.

"You're five minutes early, Mr. Mitchell."

Swinging around to face the newcomer, Hunter connected his gaze with Reese Bennett, Jr. The lawyer was Hunter's same height, and had his same build. But where Hunter had on his usual unassuming attire of black pants, black vest and black coat, Bennett wore a perfectly tailored gray suit with a brocade vest and red silk necktie.

"I'm punctual by nature," he said at last.

"Indeed."

Bennett dropped his gaze and surveyed the puddle forming at Hunter's feet. "Well, now that you're here—" the lawyer lifted his head "—we might as well get down to business."

"Excellent suggestion."

"This is my father's office, Reese Bennett, Sr. I'm at the end of the hallway." Without further explanation, he set off at a clipped pace.

Hunter followed, matching the man's steps with purposeful strides of his own.

Once inside his office, Bennett pointed to one of two chairs facing his desk. The man certainly didn't waste words.

Hunter liked his style already.

Settling in the appointed seat, he placed his hat on the leather chair beside him and took a moment to look around. He was immediately struck by the serviceability of the decor. Understated, masculine, nothing overdone, the kind of office dedicated to work first, last, with no nonsense in between.

Another point in the man's favor.

After moving aside a stack of books from a chair on the opposite side of the desk, the lawyer sat. He checked a ledger, turned the page with a whispery flutter and then he set the book aside.

"So, Mr. Mitchell." Bennett folded his hands on the desk and leaned forward. "What can I do for you this morning?"

"I should think it obvious." He ran a hand through his hair, the only part of him that had avoided a complete drenching. "I've come to acquire legal advice."

"Ah, then I'm afraid I can't help you."

Hunter recoiled at the blunt dismissal. "I haven't even told you what I need yet."

"No. But my primary focus is family law and estate management." He gave Hunter an apologetic grimace. "I do not handle criminal cases."

"You know who I am, then."

"I know who you are, where you've been and how long you've been out."

"You discovered all that in three short days?"

Bennett unfolded his hands, sat back and gave Hunter a placid look. "I make it my business to know my potential clients."

Hunter held the man's stare. He had nothing to hide, not from Reese Bennett, nor anyone else. His past was just that. The past. But some people had no forgiveness in them, and no ability to look beyond a man's mistakes.

Was this well-dressed, serious-minded attorney one of them?

Hunter didn't think so. There'd been no judgment in the other man's tone.

Or had he missed it? "If what you say is accurate, then you know I have paid my debt to society."

"True. Unless you've been up to something in the past few days I don't know about."

A valid point.

Hunter used to be up to a lot of *things* in his former life, bad things. He'd been ruled by impulse, gratifying every desire, every impulse, whenever and however he wished. He touched the Bible in his coat pocket, a physical reminder his sinful behavior was over once and for all.

"Just so we're clear, Mr. Bennett, I have done nothing to warrant needing a criminal attorney at this time."

"Then why are you here?"

"I have recently discovered I have a nine-year-old daughter living at Charity House."

The man's only response was an arched eyebrow.

"It's a type of orphanage, of sorts, for prostitute's children who have nowhere else to go and—"

"I'm acquainted with Charity House." Bennett's mouth tipped in the semblance of a smile. "Marc Dupree is a friend."

Good to know, but not particularly relevant at the moment. "I need an attorney to help me gain custody of my daughter."

Just saying the words reminded Hunter how much he was looking forward to becoming Sarah's father, permanently. He desperately wanted to take her to the Flying M to meet his family, to settle down for good.

I'm homesick, he realized. Had been for years. He could admit that now, if only in the dark recesses of his mind.

Bennett shifted in his chair, the sound breaking through Hunter's thoughts. "Can I assume, then, that the child's mother has had a change of heart since leaving the child at Charity House and is planning to fight you for custody?"

"Maria is dead."

"Ah." Bennett shifted in his chair again. "Was the child conceived out of wedlock?"

"No. I was married to Sarah's mother at the time of her birth." Hunter proceeded to tell the lawyer the story of his estranged relationship with Maria.

When he came to the portion of the tale where Maria had intentionally hidden Sarah's existence from him,

Hunter felt nothing but sadness. Not anger, not even frustration. But sorrow.

Sarah would never know her mother.

But she had an aunt who loved her. The thought of Annabeth made his heart pound in his chest. She was always there in his mind, lurking on the edges, already an integral part of his life. Kissing her had merely sealed the deal.

A portion of him softened at the memory of her wrapped in his arms, filling him with something more than need, more than longing. Joy. Peace.

Was she the one to bring warmth into his heart, and in his home? Would laughter follow?

Maybe even love?

He stopped there, knowing the danger of allowing his mind to go any further down that particular path. Hunter wasn't deserving of Annabeth's love. Someday she'd find that out on her own. And when she did—

"If the child's mother is dead, and you were married to the woman at the time of her birth, why do you need to fight for custody?" Bennett paused, considered Hunter a moment, then began again. "Did your wife have a legally binding agreement with Marc Dupree?"

"No." Hunter shook his head firmly. "Maria only had a verbal understanding with Marc and his wife. They have vowed to make Sarah's transition from their home to mine as easy as possible."

His gratitude increased tenfold with the retelling of their kindness.

"Then there doesn't appear to be anything keeping you from claiming your daughter."

"That's precisely why I've come to you, Mr. Bennett." It was Hunter's turn to lean forward and command the other man's gaze. "I plan to take Sarah away from Charity House and raise her on a ranch outside the city. I want you to ensure nothing stands in my way. No hidden loopholes in the law. Can you do that?"

"I can." There was no hesitation in the man, only confident self-assurance.

"We do this right," Hunter continued, "on the front end. I want no surprises down the road. Not in a week, or a year, or ten."

"You've come to the right man, Mr. Mitchell. I'm always thorough," Bennett assured him. "However, my services aren't cheap."

"How much are we talking?"

The lawyer quoted the cost of his services, an amount Hunter was comfortable paying. "That'll be fine."

"All right, then. Let's get down to business." Bennett pulled out a sheet of paper from a side drawer. After making several notations, he looked up at Hunter. "I will need a copy of your marriage license to the child's mother, as well as the girl's birth certificate."

"I don't have either." Hunter's heart squeezed with unease. "Is that going to be a problem?"

"Probably not." The lawyer made several more notes on the page. Without looking up, he said almost absently, "The originals should be on file at the county clerk's office."

"Good. *Good.*" A relieved breath slipped from Hunter's lungs. "There are two additional matters I will need you to address, as well."

Bennett lowered his pen and waited expectantly.

"No matter what my daughter's birth certificate says, I want her legal name to be Sarah Annabeth Mitchell."

Hunter probably should have consulted Annabeth on the matter first. But after taking time to think this through, he had no qualms making this particular decision on his own.

"Consider it done." Picking up his pen, the lawyer made the necessary notation on the paper. "What else?"

"I want you to draw up my Last Will and Testament." Hunter pulled out the piece of paper he'd tucked behind the Bible in his jacket and handed it to the lawyer. "I want you to include these specifics."

The lawyer took the paper, read quickly, then looked up again. "Are you certain of this?"

"Yes." Hunter rose.

Bennett followed suit.

"How long will it take for you to complete my requests?"

"I'd like to meet again in a week."

"A week? That soon?"

"None of what you want is overly complicated, Mr. Mitchell. Assuming, of course, that I can locate your marriage license and the child's birth certificate."

Hunter left the law offices with a light heart and a lighter step. The rain was still coming down hard. Uncaring, he stepped onto the sidewalk and turned in the direction of Charity House.

He needed to see Annabeth, needed to tell her all that he'd accomplished here today. She would be pleased for Sarah's sake. Hunter liked that about the woman, liked how she put her niece's happiness above her own.

In truth, he liked a lot of things about Annabeth Silks, especially the fact that she would be leaving town with him and Sarah soon. By the grace of God, they'd make their unusual arrangement work.

Unless a certain foul-tempered madam had her way.

Hunter still had to convince Mattie he could be trusted with her beloved daughter. Determined to do this right, every step of the way, he changed directions.

When he arrived at the brothel again, he discovered that the cantankerous woman was still unavailable to him.

Enough of her games.

"When *will* she see me?" he asked Jack through clenched teeth, determined to remain until he had his answer.

"Miss Silks would be more than happy to receive you at five o'clock this afternoon."

Hunter gave a crisp nod.

"That's five o'clock, sharp. If you're a minute late—"

"Don't worry," Hunter interrupted. "I know how the woman works."

Back on the street, the rain was still coming down in a steady rhythm. Unlike the last time he was on this street he felt no danger lurking in the shadows. He felt only peace, as if the rain was washing away his transgressions as surely as the dirt off the planked sidewalk.

Another few steps and he rethought his plan to head directly to Charity House. School was probably in session by now, anyway. He might as well shave and put on a clean set of clothes before venturing out again.

A block from his hotel, he caught sight of his reflection in a passing window and stopped cold. His watery image was smiling like a fool. Except, Hunter didn't look like a fool. He looked...

Happy.

He *felt* happy.

The Lord's blessings kept raining down on him as surely as the water poured out of the sky.

Chapter Fourteen

As soon as the last student left the schoolroom for the day, Annabeth let out a slow, grateful whoosh of air. The whole lot of them had a bad case of spring fever. She'd seen it before, had experienced the sensation herself when she was their age. But until she'd been put in charge of ten boys and girls between the ages of nine and sixteen, she hadn't realized how challenging children could be when they joined forces.

Not that she'd been in any better shape herself. Her mind had spent far too much time on Hunter Mitchell, making her just as restless as her students.

Why couldn't she get their kisses out of her head? Kisses that, according to the man himself, wouldn't be repeated.

Sighing, Annabeth smoothed her skirt then began tidying up her classroom. She worked her way along the aisles one at a time, picking up discarded papers, books, two hair ribbons and—oh, joy—a dried up lizard tail.

She'd worry about that last item later. *Much later.*

By the time she made a pass down the last aisle, her arms were full.

Suddenly, a shadow fell across her feet, stopping her

progress cold. She knew who'd arrived without having to turn around. Still, there was a brief moment of shock when she connected her gaze with the broad-shouldered man in her doorway.

Propped against the doorjamb, with a small satchel sitting at his feet, Hunter looked casually self-assured in his usual black from head to toe. As he stood there, watching her, he looked softer somehow, less tense.

She soaked up the sight of him.

He gave her a long once-over in return.

Mesmerized, she tried to remain cool and unaffected under his bold scrutiny. Nearly impossible when the lump in her throat was as big as a baseball, and her heart pounded out a rapid staccato against her ribs.

Why did the man affect her so?

She knew why. *Of course* she knew why.

It was in the way he carried himself: calm, steady, full of confidence mixed with a hint of stoicism. The loneliness in him called to her, too.

"So." A low, wry chuckle tumbled out of him. "We're back to the staring."

Despite her nerves, she laughed with him. "Apparently, it's what we do in each other's company."

"So it would seem."

Smiling—and, oh, what a smile—he pushed away from the door and paced toward her.

Every bit of moisture dried up in her throat. She couldn't seem to move. Why couldn't she move?

He took the bundle of collected contraband in her arms and set the booty on the desk beside her.

She *still* couldn't move. Not one, single inch.

Crowding her now, he turned his head so that they were face-to-face, their lips inches apart. For a long, tense moment, he said nothing.

Neither did she.

Was he going to kiss her? This tough, beautiful, wounded man who needed her more than he would ever let on.

A little flutter took flight in her stomach. She brushed the sensation aside and waited with anticipation.

Frowning, Hunter took a very deliberate step back.

She tried not to sigh.

"The color of that dress brings out the blue in your eyes," he said, his smile returning. "I approve."

He took another step back, his eyes dancing with amusement, and something more. Something long-lasting, permanent.

Why did she have to care for this man? Especially when he'd made it perfectly clear he didn't plan to marry again?

Best to keep that fact in mind, at all times. "To what do I owe the pleasure of your company this fine afternoon?"

She spoke in a nice, calm, rational voice. Oh, look at her. So cool, so in control, a woman who knew her own mind. It was quite the act. Mattie would be proud of her performance.

"Would you believe I came to see you?" he asked.

To be so fortunate. Knowing better, she raised an ironic brow. "You came to see me, only me?"

"And Sarah." He gave her a sheepish dip of his head. "I came to see my daughter, too."

Now *that* Annabeth believed.

"You just missed her," she said. "She headed back to the main house with Molly and the other children a few minutes ago."

"Ah."

He looked so disappointed she couldn't help but take pity on him. "Give me a moment to tidy up here and I'll walk over there with you."

"If you let me help we'll get done in half the time."

"All right."

Together, they made quick work of setting the room back to rights. Oddly attuned to one another, they moved in flawless harmony, as if they could read each other's next move.

Annabeth told herself it didn't matter that they worked so well together. But it did matter. Their effortless camaraderie made her think of God's perfect timing. And happily-ever-after.

Glory.

There was no use denying the truth any longer. Annabeth wanted the fairy tale, and she wanted it with Hunter.

Once they were outside and heading over to the main house, Hunter stepped around Annabeth and pulled her to a stop.

The jolt of awareness that shot through his arm had him pressing his lips into a grim line and forgetting why he'd halted her progress in the first place. He shook his head impatiently, trying to organize his thoughts.

No easy feat.

Annabeth was right here, staring up at him, waiting expectantly for him to say something.

He shut his eyes a moment. But the image of her remained. Her lovely, oval face, the gentle, bowed lips, and blue-blue eyes. And that silky dark hair, pinned oh-so-primly on the top of her head.

He opened his eyes, and tried to stay in the moment, not think of the future, of forever. He was waging a losing battle with himself, especially after their interaction in the schoolroom a moment before. They'd been so easy with one another, perfectly synchronized, even with the tension they both pretended wasn't there between them.

They were also staring again.

He swallowed.

She did the same.

She looked so proper in her schoolmarm garb he wanted to ruffle her, just a bit, if only to see how far he could push her.

Did they have an audience?

He glanced over his shoulder and realized that they were standing in a small alcove between the two houses. Had he stopped her here on purpose, unconsciously wanting a private moment alone with her?

Seemed he still had a bit of the outlaw in him. He probably always would. Sobering thought.

"Why aren't the children running around outside?" he asked, realizing the utter quiet didn't fit the image he had of Charity House in his head.

"Afternoon chores first, then play."

He let the information settle, calculating the minutes that had already passed since he'd arrived at the schoolhouse. "How long do afternoon chores take?"

"About an hour."

Plenty of time for a kiss. And that was exactly where his thoughts should *not* be heading.

"Hunter." Annabeth whispered his name in that throaty way of hers, encouraging him to tap into the outlaw he'd once been. She sighed against him. And then...

They were kissing again.

The sound of birds chirping in a nearby tree brought him to his senses.

This was wrong. All wrong. If they were caught by one of the children, Annabeth's reputation would be ruined beyond repair. Her good name was the one thing she could control. He wouldn't take that from her for his own selfish gain.

Abruptly, he let her go.

A shaken breath escaped her. Or was that him?

He felt a mixture of emotion, guilt at the top of the list, followed closely by a need to clarify his intentions.

"Annabeth…" He was talking to her back.

"Annabeth, wait."

She stopped several strides later, but didn't turn around. Standing in the open now, she tilted her head toward the sky.

He gentled his voice to a whisper. "Annabeth."

Slowly, she pivoted around to face him.

"I'm sorry—"

"Don't." She held up her palm. "Please, don't apologize."

"But I shouldn't have—"

"Not another word." She gave him a vicious shake of her head. "I mean it. Not a single word of apology out of you."

He fought back a wave of frustration, wondering if she knew how appealing she was when she got that stern schoolmarm look on her face.

Doing his best to keep from doing something stupid, like unraveling that ridiculous bun of hers, or kissing her again, or indulging in any number of other inappropriate acts, he joined her in the sunlight.

"I want to give you something before we head inside."

He should have done so back at the schoolroom, but he'd been a little dazzled under the power of her very-female presence. No, he'd been a lot dazzled. It was like a sickness in him, a slow, pleasant, sweet way to die.

Later, when he was alone, he'd analyze why she was different. Why *he* was different when he was around her.

Giving himself a mental shake, he reached into his bag and pulled out the gift he'd wrapped himself.

Her eyes widened. "You…" She pulled her bottom lip between her teeth. "You bought me a present?"

He shrugged, trying to keep his expression bland, but her pleased reaction took him by the heart and squeezed.

"It's nothing special." He thrust the package toward her. "I saw it in the store and thought of you."

"You thought of me?" Her hand went to her throat. "Truly?"

Apparently, she didn't receive a lot of presents. A happy discovery, Hunter decided. He wanted to be the only man to buy Annabeth gifts, now and in the future.

Again, he was thinking of her in all the wrong terms. She wasn't for him. She was his daughter's aunt. Not. For. Him. This gift was a simple gesture of friendship, nothing more.

Hands shaking, she accepted the package and ran a finger over the lopsided red bow. "It's very pretty."

He chuckled. "The gift is actually *inside* the box."

She laughed. "I know. I just…" She trailed off and glanced at the bag in his hand.

He lifted it in the air. "I also bought a doll for Sarah."

Her gaze swept up to his. That look she gave him. It did something to him, something good and lasting and full of hope.

"You bought Sarah a doll?" She sounded puzzled.

And, now, so was he. "You said she likes dolls," he reminded her. He suddenly felt tongue-tied. "That's what you said, right?"

"I… Well, yes. Of course she likes dolls. She loves them, actually, almost as much as bonnets. I just hadn't thought you would go out and buy her one."

"And yet, I did."

"And yet—" her fingers tangled in the ribbon of her own gift "—you did."

Uncomfortable under the wonder in her voice, he pointed to the package. "Are you going to open that anytime soon?"

"Oh. Yes." She attempted a smile. "I... Of course."

Hunter could see she was trying to appear light, casual. But as she tackled the task of untying the ribbon her blue eyes were full of confusion and seriousness and tempered joy.

Warmth coiled in his stomach. And then came the dread. What if she didn't understand the gesture?

What if she didn't...remember?

After removing the ribbon, she took her time studying the package, perhaps deciding how best to unwrap the plain white paper. Wanting to get this agony over with, *now,* he resisted the urge to hurry her along.

How could one tiny woman affect him so? Feeling oddly self-conscious, he looked to his right, and then to his left, straight up.

Her gasp had him lowering his head.

"Oh, Hunter." Her voice tripped across his name.

The ribbon slipped out of her fingers and fluttered to the ground. The white paper followed. Then the box. All that was left in her hand was the silver-handled hairbrush, the design intricate and delicate, so feminine he'd been afraid to touch it when he'd first seen it in the store.

Annabeth didn't have such qualms. Eyes glistening, she pressed the brush tightly to her heart. "You remembered."

"I..." How could he respond in a way that wouldn't reveal his very soul? He hadn't even realized he'd thought of her all these years until now. "Yes. I remembered."

The day he'd met her came back to him in a blast. He and Maria had taken Annabeth with them on a walk through town. Maria had wanted something new, something shiny and expensive. Flush with cash from a win at the poker tables, Hunter had told both women to pick out anything they wanted.

When they'd entered the store, Maria had gone to the jewelry case to make her choice. Annabeth had been more tentative, her shyness touching Hunter in a way he hadn't expected. She'd walked over to a display case of silver-handled hairbrushes, her gaze full of girlish admiration.

He'd followed her, wondering what had caught her eye. The hairbrushes had been pretty, and certainly an appropriate choice, but Maria had scoffed at her little sister. She'd told Annabeth to think bigger.

Shoulders slumped, Annabeth had immediately stepped away from the display case. But Hunter had seen the wistfulness in her eyes. He'd told her he would buy the brush for her, anyway.

She'd shook her head. "It's too expensive."

No, it had been reasonably priced. Maria had embarrassed her. That was why she'd refused his gift back then.

Now, Annabeth had a completely different expression on her face. A look full of wonder. "Thank you, Hunter."

"You're welcome."

She clutched the hairbrush tighter. "I'll treasure it always."

The sight of her happiness left him speechless. He stood watching her, stricken with some combination of joy and sorrow, wonder and caution.

And now he knew. He knew he would never be immune to this woman. He wasn't sure what that meant for their future, but he couldn't think about that now. Now, he needed to step back, away from this beautiful, heart-rending woman.

He needed to remember his duty was to take care of her, to protect her, even if that meant protecting her from himself.

Under the circumstances, he did what any self-respecting, yellow-bellied coward would do in a similar situation. He changed the subject. "I met with a lawyer today."

The change of subject was so swift, so unexpected, Annabeth felt her mouth drop open. She quickly shut it, trying unsuccessfully to focus on Hunter's words and not the man himself.

She wanted to jump into his arms, to kiss him square on the lips and thank him over and over and over again. He'd remembered the day they'd met. More than that, he'd remembered her girlish desire for a silly hairbrush.

She'd been so young, so frivolous back then. She'd like to think her priorities had changed, but no. She still adored silver-handled hairbrushes.

And now, she adored the man who'd bought one for her.

He made her feel good about her preference for something most women considered utilitarian. He made her feel like a woman, not a silly girl.

Even if he was pretending he'd done nothing remarkable, she knew the truth. Hunter Mitchell was the most special man she knew. And she wanted him for herself.

He wasn't in the moment with her, though, that much was obvious from his strange redirecting of the conversation. It crossed her mind that this was why she preferred dealing with children over handsome rogues with golden eyes. Children didn't confuse her like this.

"You went to see a lawyer?" She felt her eyebrows pull together. "I don't understand."

He stepped closer, so close she had to crane her neck to look into his eyes. Eyes that were shielded now. It was as if they'd never had A Moment. Except, they'd definitely had A Moment. They'd crossed an invisible line toward something good and long-lasting.

"I've set in motion the paperwork to ensure Sarah is mine, legally, on paper."

"Oh." Well, that made sense. With his past, Hunter would want to tie up all the loose ends concerning Sarah's custody before heading out of town. "Whom did you see?"

"Reese Bennett, Jr."

"He's a good lawyer." And a good man. Respectable, well-liked, a pillar of the community, Reese was always above reproach. In fact, he was the kind of man Annabeth had once thought she wanted in her life.

She'd been so terribly wrong.

The man she wanted was standing right in front of her, looking as though he just might kiss her again.

What a lovely, terrifying thought. Hunter wanted to kiss her. But he didn't want to marry her.

Oh, Lord, why does that hurt so much?

"How well do you know Reese Bennett?" he asked, his expression grim.

Hunter looked and sounded…jealous?

Annabeth's heart soared.

"Not well," she assured him. "We've only met a few times in passing."

"I see." He visibly relaxed.

And, then, so did Annabeth.

It was a beautiful day, one of those warm, blue-sky wonders of creation after a hard rain. A soft breeze played in Hunter's hair. With that slight smile on his face it was difficult not to think him the most handsome man in the world. And he'd bought her a hairbrush.

He only did so because he's a nice man.

Annabeth needed to remember that. Before she jumped into his arms and showed him just how grateful she was for his thoughtful gesture. Maybe a kiss on the cheek wouldn't be too forward.

She lifted on her toes, but then Sarah and several of her friends spilled out of the house. Laughing and talking over one another, they scattered onto the porch. As if she sensed his presence, Sarah zeroed in on her father.

A smile spilt across her face. After saying something to her friends, she rushed down the steps.

"Mr. Mitchell. Mr. Mitchell. Mr. Mit—" Her voice ground to a halt at the same moment her feet stopped churning up the yard. A scowl replaced her smile.

"Sarah?" Hunter asked in a gentle voice. "Something wrong?"

Looking uncertain, she glanced at Annabeth then back to her father. Another hesitation and then she heaved a sigh.

"Sarah, whatever's on your mind, I'll listen without judgment."

She nodded. "If you're my father, and, well, you want me and all, then shouldn't I call you something else? Something like—" she scuffed her foot over the grass "—I don't know, something besides Mr. Mitchell?"

Hunter blinked at the child, a soft, hopeful expression on his face. "What would you like to call me?"

"I don't know. Maybe…" She lifted her narrow shoulders, looking everywhere but at Hunter. "Father?"

"You want to call me—" he swallowed several times "—Father?"

The poor man looked gut-punched.

Sarah's shoulders moved with the force of a heavy sigh. "Or Pa. I could call you Pa."

"My sweet, sweet child." He spoke in halting tones, even as he drew her into his arms. "I'd like nothing better than for you to call me Pa."

Hugging him back, Sarah murmured something incomprehensible into his shirt.

Witnessing this touching moment between father and daughter quite simply tore Annabeth's heart in two. She swiped at her eyes.

She loved Sarah, completely and without reservation. And now, she loved Sarah's father, too. Wait a minute…

Oh, Lord help her, it was true. Annabeth loved Hunter.

He would never return her feelings, he'd said as much already. She needed to keep her distance, needed to guard her heart. That was the rational thing to do.

Or…

She could take a leap of faith. She could trust that the Lord was already at work in their lives and their hearts. Hers had simply fallen faster than Hunter's.

It was possible he would grow to love her one day. After all, he had a great capacity for the emotion. The evidence was right in front of them, wrapped tightly in his arms.

But that was fatherly love.

Could he come to care for Annabeth as a man cared for a woman, as he'd once cared for his wife?

Her head told her not to take the risk.

Her heart told her he was worth the leap of faith.

Hunter looked up at her then, and smiled, his teeth white against his tan skin.

Her stomach fluttered wildly in response.

In that moment, Annabeth knew what she had to do. She had to risk heartache, humiliation, *everything,* for the love of this fine, decent man.

Hunter had no idea what he was in for.

In Annabeth's estimation, that made the coming days all the more exciting.

Chapter Fifteen

Sarah wiggled out of Hunter's arms and cast her gaze up to his. Instead of smiling in happiness, her expression was full of heartbreaking vulnerability. She clearly had something on her mind, something he feared he wasn't going to like.

He felt the first stirrings of uneasiness, like a hard blow to his chest, and nothing remotely similar to the sensation he'd just experienced staring into Annabeth's eyes.

"Sarah?" He could scarcely speak her name. "What's wrong, baby?"

She shifted her feet nervously, then stilled and narrowed in her eyes. "How come you're only just coming around now?" Her voice was thick with accusation and little-girl hurt. "Where have you been all this time?"

Hunter's shoulders dropped. This hostility, where was it coming from? Why now, why hadn't she asked this of him sooner? Had she been talking to the other children?

What did it matter where his daughter's doubts had come from? She thought he hadn't wanted her before now, that he'd abandoned her for no good reason.

He couldn't remember ever feeling this brand of fear before. What he said next had the potential to soothe the child's worries, or add to them. If he chose the wrong words he might even create a rift between them.

Lord, what do I do? What do I say?

The answer came at once. The truth. Hunter had to tell his daughter the truth.

"I didn't come around sooner," he began, "because I didn't know I had a beautiful daughter waiting for me here at Charity House."

Chewing on her bottom lip, Sarah considered his explanation in quiet contemplation. "You didn't know about me? Truly?"

"Truly."

The scowl remained in place, as did the hurt in her eyes.

Hunter desperately wanted to fill the silence with words. Instead, he gave his daughter all the time she needed to sort through what he'd just said.

All this time, he'd thought she hadn't been affected by Maria's lies.

He'd been wrong.

"But, Pa—" Sarah cocked her head at a confused angle "—how could you not *know* about me? You were married to my mother, weren't you?"

"Yes, I was married to her. But we'd decided to go our separate ways for a time."

"You didn't want to be with my mother?"

The truth, Hunter, stick with the truth, no matter how humbling. "It was the other way around, baby. She didn't want to be with me."

"But…" This didn't seem to make any sense to the nine-year-old. "Why not?"

Because I was too determined to save her from a profession she didn't want to leave.

"Your mother and I, we didn't—" he swallowed back a pang of remorse "—want the same things out of life."

When Sarah's brows still remained scrunched in a frown, Hunter looked to Annabeth for help. He did that a lot, he realized, turned to her as if she was already an integral part of their family.

Squeezing his hand, she gave him a brief smile, and then moved into her niece's line of vision.

"Sarah, darling, sometimes adults have complicated relationships. Your mother might not have wanted to be with your father, but never doubt that she loved you. That's why she brought you here when she became sick."

"But, Aunt Annabeth, why would my mom bring me here instead of telling my pa about me?"

"I doubt we'll ever know why she made that decision. The important thing is that your father is here now." She motioned him to move closer. "He loves you, Sarah, as much as I do."

"So we're going to be a family? The three of us? You, me and Pa?"

Hunter answered the question before Annabeth could open her mouth. "Yes, my sweet, sweet, girl. Now that the Lord has brought the three of us together we're going to be a family."

She turned to look at Hunter with a painful lack of assurance in her eyes. "And you're not going to leave, ever?"

"Never," he promised.

Smiling at last, Sarah threw her skinny arms around his neck and planted a loud, little-girl kiss on his cheek.

Eyes burning, he wrapped his arms around his daughter. He breathed in her clean, fresh scent. She didn't seem upset anymore—praise God—but he knew he'd only been given a reprieve. They would have many more conversations on this particular topic. As Sarah grew older her questions would become more pointed and would require more detailed responses.

For now, his daughter was satisfied with his explanation and that was a blessing in itself.

"I love you, Pa."

The carefree devotion of a child, *his child,* was so strong, so simple. Why couldn't he be that free with his feelings? "I love you, too, Sarah."

Next time, he would say the words first.

"Hey, Sarah," one of the girls called from the walkway. "Are you coming to Molly's with us, or staying here with your dad?"

Hunter turned his head in the direction of the voice. At the same time, Sarah pulled out of his arms. A handful of little girls stood staring at them from the porch, impatience in their shifting feet.

"I'm coming now," Sarah called out. "I mean, that is—" she swung her gaze up to his "—if it's okay with you."

Hunter told himself he was only mildly hurt that his daughter would rather spend time with five little girls than with him. But then he remembered he would be taking her away soon, and she wouldn't have the opportunity to play with girls her own age anymore. Not on a regular basis.

"Go on," he said. "Have fun with your friends."

"Thank you, Pa." She gave him a quick hug and then sped off. Only after Sarah raced away did he remember the doll he'd bought for her. He would give it to her another time, he supposed, maybe tomorrow. He hoped she liked the one he'd chosen, he—

A soft voice cut through his musings. "Hunter?"

Annabeth. He'd nearly forgotten she was standing beside him. He swiveled around to face her. Her eyes were so serious, so full of emotion.

He knew the feeling. "I meant what I said to Sarah," he said with conviction. "The three of us, we're going to be a family."

"No, Hunter, we aren't *going* to be a family." She gave him the sweetest smile he'd ever seen. "We already are a family."

Yeah, they were. Somewhere in the past few days they'd created a bond that wouldn't be broken easily.

There was one person who would try to tear them apart, though, with every underhanded trick she could think to use.

"I have to go." He touched Annabeth's cheek before setting out.

"Go?" She called after him, "Go where?"

"To Mattie's," he said over his shoulder.

"Oh, no, you don't. Not without me." Scowling fiercely, she moved into his direct path and parked her fists on her hips. "Just try to stop me from joining you."

He felt a chuckle rumble in his chest. "Are you issuing me a challenge, Miss Silks?"

"You better believe I am."

Hunter liked challenges, almost as much as he liked this woman.

After a surprisingly short argument, with Hunter smiling through most it, Annabeth convinced him of the wisdom of having her along when he confronted her mother. Sensing he was still shaken by his bittersweet interaction with Sarah, she expected their journey into town in the hired carriage to be filled with uncomfortable silence.

Not even close.

The easy camaraderie she and Hunter had experienced in her classroom was back. In fact, he seemed to have visibly relaxed around her as if he was finally finished looking over his shoulder, expecting bad things to happen.

She might as well follow suit and let go of her own anxiety. Either that, or succumb to the nerves gnawing in the pit of her stomach. She'd decided to make him fall in love with her, but was only now realizing the massive task ahead of her. Yes, he considered her part of his family, but only as Sarah's aunt.

Annabeth wanted more. She wanted to be Hunter's wife, and all that that implied.

His next words shot holes in her burgeoning dream. "I know there hasn't been much time since we've discussed our arrangement, but have you thought of any woman we could hire for our housekeeper yet?"

Our housekeeper. The equivalent of a chaperone for Annabeth. Another swift blow to her dream. "Not yet, no."

"I was thinking about asking Marc if he knew of anyone suitable."

"I'll ask Laney, and Mrs. Smythe, too."

"Good idea."

Annabeth tried not to sigh at his even tone. She should be pleased. After all, Hunter was following through with his promise. He was actually going to do what he said he would do and provide her with a respectable life in his home.

That's what you've always wanted, a simple, uncomplicated existence with a man you can trust.

A simple, uncomplicated existence, indeed. How could she have been so shortsighted? What an empty dream she'd had all these years. Safe, yes. Secure, absolutely. But empty, oh-so-empty.

She twisted her hands together in her lap and shot a quick glance in Hunter's direction. He appeared to be lost in his own thoughts, his gaze focused on the road up ahead. She shouldn't want more from him than what he was prepared to give her, shouldn't wish he'd care for her like she cared for him, shouldn't…

Ache for him.

"Tell me about the Flying M," she said, desperate for a distraction. "What can Sarah and I expect when we arrive at your family's ranch?"

A pause. A quick tightening of his grip on the reins. Then he turned his head and looked at her. "You want the long answer or the short one?"

She thought she heard tension in his voice, but his eyes were still warm as he looked at her.

Into her.

Shaken all over again, she quickly glanced away and studied the scenery. They were making slow but steady progress through town. "How about something in between? Maybe start with the ranch."

His laugh rumbled in her ear.

Smiling despite herself, she shifted on the carriage seat and waited for him to continue.

"I can't tell you about the ranch without telling you about my family, too." A shadow fell across his face as a cloud passed overhead. "Home and family, for the Mitchell brood they're one and the same."

Home and family.

What did Annabeth know about either? What did she know about the dynamics that made up the "Mitchell brood"? Mattie had done her best as a parent, but she'd never provided Annabeth with a home, or a family.

Mattie's "girls" were employees. Women her mother cared about in her own way, but Mattie had been adamant that Annabeth keep herself separate from them. No friendships allowed in the brothel. No relationship with her half sister.

She'd been so lonely growing up.

Annabeth had carried that sense of isolation with her to school. She'd kept herself apart from the other girls in the dormitory out of habit, never allowing herself to get too close to any of them. She'd maintained her distance even after becoming a teacher at the school.

The self-imposed separation had kept her secret safe, for a time. But her connection to a notorious Denver madam had come out, anyway. That was the problem with secrets and lies. Truth inevitably found a way to shine through the deception.

Would Annabeth fit in with Hunter's family?

Did she want to fit in with them?

Just thinking about the Mitchells—the utter definition of home and family—brought the same warm, puzzling pull she felt every time she was in Hunter's company.

"Annabeth? Are you listening?"

She hadn't been, no, not completely. "You were telling me about the ranch, the largest in the state of Colorado by thousands of acres, and how your family and the Flying M are uniquely linked."

"That's right."

"Do you miss the Flying M?"

"I miss my family more. I should have gone home years ago. No—" he shook his head fiercely "—I should never have left."

"Why did you leave?"

"I don't remember now. I wanted freedom, I suppose. I wanted to make my own rules. I was headstrong, self-centered, a rule-breaker. The quintessential prodigal son who failed to recognize the many blessings right in front of me."

"But you're not that man anymore." She placed her hand on his arm. "You recognize your blessings. And just like the prodigal son, you're returning home with a humble heart."

"It took me too long to return," he whispered. "The pain I've left in my wake..."

His voice trailed off, but not before Annabeth heard the regret in his voice, and the soul-deep guilt.

Needing to soothe his pain, she moved her hand down his arm and squeezed his hand. "You know—" she squeezed again "—as a schoolteacher I've been given a unique insight into what makes people do the things they do."

He didn't look at her directly, but he did rotate his palm to meet hers. "I bet you have."

Holding his hand gave her the courage to continue. "Not that I have any of this completely figured out, but one thing I've gleaned from the classroom is that some people can be told something once and that's all it takes for them to retain the information. Other people have to learn their lessons the hard way."

"People like me?"

"Am I wrong?"

"No. You're absolutely right. Like I said, I'm a hard-headed man."

"I know."

He threw back his head and laughed. "Good to know I can always count on you to speak the truth."

He seemed so approachable in the muted light of the afternoon, smiling at her, revealing a part of his heart she didn't think anyone else knew. She wanted to reach out, to touch his face, to ease away that haunted, guilt-ridden look he tried so hard to hide from the world, and her. "You're a good man, Hunter Mitchell. I'm honored you want me to help you raise your daughter."

"Thank you, Annabeth." He raised her hand to his lips. "Thank you for agreeing to come with us."

"You're welcome."

He released her hand and focused once more on the road. Sighing, she watched the scenery pass by with unseeing eyes. If only Hunter would let her fully into his heart, not just a small portion of it. If only he would give her—give them—a chance.

A hopeless set of wishes, she knew. His wife Jane had been his one true love. Annabeth could only hope to be second best in his heart. She had too much of her mother in her to consider that an acceptable outcome. But she was no quitter, either.

She would win Hunter's heart. She just didn't know how. Yet.

Life is no fairy tale. Her own words flashed through her mind.

Well, why not? Why couldn't she have the fairy tale with Hunter?

"We're here." He pulled their carriage to a stop.

Annabeth looked around and smiled despite her inner turmoil. He'd parked the carriage near a side entrance of Mattie's brothel, where no one would witness their coming or going. In the darkened alley the pink three-story house lost what little charm the front facade presented to the world. The building was decidedly run-down. She'd never really noticed that before.

And if Annabeth wasn't mistaken, the ground was moving. Rats. They loved this part of town, as much as she hated it. She really disliked the nasty little creatures. But she was too proud to let Hunter see her fear.

Setting the brake with easy movements, he unfolded his large body and hopped to the ground. Coming around to her side of the carriage, he placed his hands on her waist and swung her down next to him.

A quiver went through her entire body. Her reaction had nothing to do with the sound of tiny toenails scurrying around in the dark and everything to do with Hunter's sure touch. He had powerful hands, strong yet capable of such tenderness.

Again, she wondered what sort of jobs he'd held in prison. Blacksmithing, perhaps? Quarry work?

"Ready to face your mother?" he asked.

No. "Yes."

They turned toward the house at precisely the same moment, as if there'd been a silent agreement between them.

Hunter's hand slid around her elbow as he directed her toward the side entrance. Even in this, in their arrival at a house no decent woman would enter during the day, Hunter had considered Annabeth's need for anonymity.

She fell a little more in love with him. And for a dangerous moment, she struggled with two irreconcilable facts. She couldn't have him. She *had* to have him.

"Stop staring at me," she whispered.

"How do you know I'm staring at you?"

"I can feel your eyes on me." It was true. She could actually feel the heat of his gaze falling over her.

He released a rich, throaty laugh. The sound rolled over her like a touch or maybe, a kiss. "You can *feel* my gaze? That must be a valuable skill for a schoolteacher."

"You have no idea." She wanted to spin around and smile at him. Yet she couldn't bring herself to do it, not when she knew what would happen when their gazes connected. Her heart would leap into her throat. Her breathing would turn shallow.

His lips would tilt upward at an attractive angle. Amusement would dance in his eyes.

Distance, she told herself. *Keep your distance. Mattie cannot know how you feel about this man.*

Priorities set, Annabeth entered the brothel with as much stealth as possible. She instinctively moved closer to Hunter in the poorly lit hallway.

So much for keeping her distance.

"Is Mattie expecting you?" she asked, grateful the shadowy corridor made looking at him unnecessary.

"She knows I'm coming." His voice hardened slightly.

They must have been speaking louder than Annabeth realized because Mattie threw open her door before Hunter could knock. She looked briefly at Annabeth then turned to glare at him.

Completely unconcerned he was on the receiving end of one of her mother's…moods, Hunter smiled pleasantly. "Good afternoon, Mattie."

Annabeth repressed a sigh at his goading tone. As expected, Mattie's eyes narrowed to two, thin, angry slits.

Hunter widened his smile in such a way that made him appear a bit wolfish. "I say," he continued. "It's a fine day for a serious conversation, don't you think? Far better than, oh, say, last night or even early this morning?"

An irritated sniff was Mattie's only response.

Annabeth looked from Hunter to her mother and back again. "Is there something I'm missing?"

They ignored her question. And her, as if she wasn't standing right there, listening to every word they said.

Oh, yes, something was definitely going on between the two, something she didn't fully understand. Hunter was antagonizing Mattie on a whole new level. And yet, it seemed her mother respected him all the more for his daring.

Maybe this meeting wasn't going to be as awful as Annabeth feared. Then again, it was never a smart idea to presuppose anything when Mattie Silks was involved.

Chapter Sixteen

Hunter was fast losing patience with Mattie Silks. He'd allowed her the upper hand in the last day and a half, but she'd pushed him far enough. It was time she discovered exactly where he stood—and with whom.

Before making his move, he glanced briefly at Annabeth who stood with her arms clasped around her tiny waist. He felt the loneliness coming off her, a self-imposed "pulling away" he understood all too well. Except, she was no longer alone.

She had him.

Perhaps she needed to know that as much as her mother did.

He made the short trek to stand beside her. Shoulder to shoulder now, the two of them became a single unit, solidarity in their common purpose for the future.

But Hunter wasn't through making his point.

Smiling tenderly into Annabeth's eyes, he took her hand and brought it to his lips. For his own pleasure, he lingered several seconds longer than necessary.

Mattie's sharp intake of air confirmed his silent message had been received.

Quirking a brow at the surly woman, he let a smirk play

across his lips. He knew his behavior was in poor taste. But he wasn't feeling especially generous at the moment. Mattie had left him to cool his heels for nearly twelve hours. And for most of today, as well.

No denying Mattie Silks liked her control, too much to go down without a fight. Hunter readied himself for the outburst to come.

She surprised him, though, by remaining perfectly calm as she held his gaze. "You should not have brought Annabeth with you."

No. He shouldn't have. He should have tried harder to convince her to stay behind. A mistake easily remedied.

But before he could ask Annabeth to give him a moment alone with her mother, she made her own move.

"I insisted on joining him." She lifted her chin at an obstinate angle. "Now that I'm here, I'm not leaving."

All right, then. Everyone knew where everyone else stood. He squeezed Annabeth's hand.

She squeezed back.

Mattie gave a long-suffering sigh that expressed her displeasure better than words ever could. For a beat, her tough exterior slipped—just a bit—then returned with a sharp hardening of her eyes. "Annabeth, you are being uncommonly stubborn. I must speak with Hunter alone. I demand you leave us this instant."

"No, *Mother*." The muscles in her back and shoulders went taut as she spoke. "We both know your argument is with me, not Hunter."

Untrue.

Mattie's fight was with them both. Annabeth had to know that. *Of course* she knew that.

Which meant she was trying to protect him, in her own sweet way.

Something inside him softened, turned to mush. He felt

her very essence pulling him to her. She was extraordinary, special, and he couldn't help but stare into her forthright, earnest face.

Captivated inside those big, gorgeous eyes, his own need to protect kicked up a notch. He wanted to hustle her out of this room—out of this town—to a place where no one could hurt her. Not even her own mother.

Especially her own mother.

Unable to stop himself, he cupped her face and smiled. He knew touching Annabeth was a bad idea—it would only further antagonize Mattie—but he did so, anyway. He suspected the gesture revealed a portion of his heart, a portion he didn't quite understand himself.

He really needed to stop this madness.

Unfortunately, Annabeth wasn't helping matters. She was actually leaning into his palm.

Mattie snorted. "That's quite enough of that."

True. And yet…

And yet…

He couldn't seem to pull his hand away from Annabeth's lovely face.

"Let her go, Hunter." It was the panic he heard in Mattie's voice that made him drop his hand.

Annabeth was not a pawn to be used in some twisted game against her mother. She was a beautiful, warm, loving woman who deserved to be treated with respect.

Swallowing, he took a large step away from her.

In the next moment, Mattie proceeded to push and shove until she'd physically moved him halfway across the room.

Seemingly satisfied she'd created enough distance between him and Annabeth, she said, "Don't touch her again." She thumped him on the chest. "I mean it, Hunter."

At the absolute desperation in her eyes, he realized this was no game for Mattie.

He needed to tread softly.

"I have no plans to hurt Annabeth. Quite the contrary. I plan to do whatever it takes to care for her and keep her safe."

"You can't make that guarantee."

Oh, but he could. Lifting Mattie's chin with a curled finger, he looked her straight in the eye. "I give you my word."

"Ridiculous man. You think I'd fall for that false sincerity in your voice?" Lips trembling, Mattie jerked away from him. "Mark my words, Hunter Mitchell, when boys start sniffing around your daughter, you'll understand."

If any boy came near Sarah...

The idea was so horrible to contemplate, he visibly shuddered. "I understand now."

"If you two are quite done pretending I'm not in the room," Annabeth said, "I'd like to speak for myself."

Simultaneously, he and Mattie swung around and silenced her with a look.

"Fine, fight it out among yourselves." She scowled at them both, then sank in a nearby chair.

Satisfied Annabeth was momentarily out of the conversation, Hunter turned his attention back to Mattie. He caught her staring at her daughter with unmistakable pain in her eyes, as if she loved her child more than life itself and was rendered helpless under the weight of the emotion.

Hunter knew that feeling. From the moment Sarah had leaped into his arms last week, he'd been torn between a complicated mix of fear and desperation, hope and love. Such love. Only since meeting his daughter was Hunter beginning to understand the Lord's command to love as He loved.

Annabeth had inspired him, too, in ways he couldn't yet define. Every day she slipped beneath his well-laid defenses, creating an emotional bond he'd never experienced with a woman before. He had no idea what to do with his feelings for her, or how to address his growing attachment. All he knew was that he had to make matters right with her mother.

"Look, Mattie, no more games, no more wordplay. I came here today to assure you that I—"

"No, no. Don't you dare use that low, reasonable tone with me." Mattie's face went cold, her voice turned sharp. "Nothing has changed since the last time we had this conversation."

Actually, a lot had changed.

"If Annabeth leaves town with you, she's as good as ruined."

Not if he kept his hands to himself and didn't kiss her any more. "She will remain as innocent and untouched as she is now," he vowed, a promise to himself as well as to Mattie.

Not that he was immune to Annabeth's considerable charms, or that he didn't want her in the way a man wanted a woman. But there was more to his feelings for her. She brought out a new, deeper emotion in him, one that went beyond the physical, a sacrificial willingness to give up his dreams in order to indulge hers.

He wanted to make her life easier. He wanted to see her happy.

And he had a good idea where to start.

"Come with us, Mattie. Come live on the ranch with Annabeth, Sarah and me. Come be a part of our family."

A sharp intake of air made him cut a quick glance at Annabeth. He recognized the restrained hope on her face, and he knew he'd been right to make the request.

Mattie laughed in response, a twisted, bitter sound that made her daughter cringe and practically fold inside herself.

"Hunter, my dear boy, you can't be serious."

Annabeth's face crumpled.

Feeling her pain as though it were his own, Hunter wanted to go to Annabeth, but not yet. Not until he finished with Mattie. "I'm deadly serious."

"I can't just leave town and go live on a ranch." She shuddered. "The very idea."

"Why not?" The question came from Annabeth, who seemed to have rallied once again. "Why not quit this life and start over?"

"You know why, Annabeth."

"Do I?"

Sighing, Mattie pressed her fingertips to her temples. "Must you play dumb?" She slashed the air with her hand, the gesture full of pent-up frustration. "Too many people count on me for their livelihood to simply walk away."

"Let someone else take on that responsibility." Annabeth's voice turned pleading.

Mother and daughter stared at one another for an unfathomably long beat.

"Sell the brothel," Annabeth beseeched.

"Sell the brothel?" Mattie's eyes widened. "You ask the impossible."

"Then have one of your girls run it in your stead, or put Jack in charge."

Shaking her head, Mattie momentarily turned her back on her daughter. Tension radiated from her, almost palpable as she worked her way over to the bookshelf and ran her fingertips along the wooden shelving.

The sadness in Annabeth made Hunter ache to spirit her away this instant. But he sensed this was a conversation that had been a long time coming. Annabeth deserved her answers.

That didn't mean she had to hear them without the support of someone who cared about her.

He returned to her side and took her hand. The air practically crackled between them. There was something profound in the way she looked at him now, so trusting. He accepted the truth at last. He would do anything for this woman. *Anything.* She had the power to bring him to his knees.

Or perhaps save him from—

"I can't leave the brothel in someone else's care." Mattie sounded sincerely remorseful. Even sad. "My girls rely on me to provide them with a home and a steady income. Someone else might not be so generous, not even Jack."

Hunter's jaw slackened at Mattie's twisted reasoning.

She was no benevolent mother figure to a bunch of wayward girls. She ran a brothel, and she ran it with an iron fist. Men came here daily and paid considerable sums of money to enjoy the services Mattie herself brokered in this house of sin.

Hunter started to remind her of that cold, hard truth, but Annabeth let go of his hand and approached her mother first.

"You provide a home for your girls? A home? This is no home. And your girls aren't family. They're prostitutes." Her voice was quietly calm as she spoke, alarmingly so, as if she was speaking from a considerable distance. "You barter their flesh and you make a considerable profit doing so."

Mattie stumbled back a step as though Annabeth had struck her. "It's not about the money."

"Isn't it?" Annabeth looked pointedly around the room, her gaze landing on a crystal vase, the silk curtains, the bookshelf filled with first editions.

"All right, yes, I like nice things. But try to understand, my dear. Most of my girls have no skills to speak of, not the kind that would result in a proper situation. If I walk away, they'll simply end up doing for someone else what they do for me."

"Then let them." Annabeth's eyes filled with tears. "As for you, stop perpetuating the cycle of sin in their lives."

Sighing, Mattie sank into a chair. She lowered her head momentarily, perhaps to hide her own eyes. Eyes that Hunter noted were fast filling with tears, as well. "What you suggest is the equivalent of abandonment. The world beyond these walls is a cruel one, especially for women like them. You know all this, Annabeth."

"How would I know?" Annabeth choked on a sob. "You've never explained any of this to me before."

"I just did. And I won't continue to defend my lifestyle choices to you." Mattie rose and swept her gaze over her daughter. "We won't speak on the matter again."

Annabeth blinked. "But, Mother, I truly want you to come with us to the ranch."

"With us? As if you're a couple?" Her voice rose with emotion. "Has he made a respectable offer? Of course he hasn't."

Not waiting for her daughter's response, Mattie skirted around Annabeth and approached Hunter. There was something rigid about her expression now, something a little ruthless, even cruel.

Hunter felt his throat thicken with dread. This was the Mattie Silks the rest of the world saw. "You will take Annabeth out of my sight at once, and never bring her here again."

"Don't do this, Mattie. Don't do this to your daughter," he said softly, pained. "Or to yourself."

She ignored his plea. "Annabeth is no longer welcome in this house, nor are you."

"Mattie." Hunter appealed to the goodness he knew was in her. "There are other solutions."

"Oh, please." Annabeth gave an impressive eye roll. "Don't be fooled by this ridiculous display, Hunter. She's bluffing."

"This is no bluff," Mattie warned without an ounce of flexibility in her voice.

Eyes locked with Mattie's, Annabeth stepped forward until they stood nose to nose. "You don't get to control this situation. Not this time."

Mattie flicked a desperate look at Hunter, then threw her shoulders back and hardened her resolve. "Get out."

"Or what?" Annabeth asked. "You'll have Jack escort me out? Go ahead, Mother, call him."

The two women stared at each other. Or rather, glared at each other. Both were bluffing, but each was too proud to be the first to relent.

Hunter considered interjecting himself into the fray, but his instincts told him he would only make matters worse. He held back a moment longer.

"Stop this, Annabeth. Stop this right now. I will not tolerate open rebellion in my own house."

"I'm not one of your girls. Nor am I under your control, financially or otherwise. You made sure of that a year ago when you cut me off. Funny how you didn't have a problem abandoning me."

Mattie's shoulders dropped. "Everything I have ever done has been to protect you."

"Is that right? Well, I don't need your kind of protection." Annabeth drew in a long, slow breath. "You've made your stand. Now it's time I made mine."

She shot Hunter a quicksilver grin. He had a bad feeling about this.

He quickly moved between the two women, fearing he'd waited too late to intercede.

Annabeth skirted around him, said something low to

her mother and then spun around to face him directly. The look in her eyes was full of single-minded resolve.

He swallowed. "Now, Annabeth." He swallowed again. "Don't do anything you'll regret later."

Eyes glittering, she placed both palms on his shoulders. "Who says I'll have regrets later?"

"I do." He grabbed for her hands, but she was too quick, lightning fast.

Next thing he knew, her fingers were linked together behind his neck.

"What are you doing?" he whispered.

Mattie, for her part, sputtered and threatened and warned her rebellious, headstrong daughter to think her actions through to the end.

Ignoring the sound maternal advice, Annabeth's smile widened.

He couldn't help it. He smiled right back, with a big toothy grin of his own.

"Congratulate us, Mother."

Hunter froze. "Congratulate us on...what?"

"We're getting married."

Married? Had Annabeth just told him they were getting *married?* He attempted to pry her hands away from his neck, he couldn't think with her so close. But then she lifted on her toes and went in for the kill. She pressed her lips firmly to his and held on tight.

Time stopped.

His breathing stalled in his chest.

His stomach performed a fast, painful roll.

Coherent thought failed him.

No matter how good the woman felt in his arms, this was wrong. *Wrong.*

He tried to do the right thing. He really tried.

Hadn't he only seconds before promised Mattie he

wouldn't hurt Annabeth? If this really exceptional kiss continued much longer, something was going to end up broken.

Like his head.

Or her heart.

Unacceptable.

He had to remember that Mattie was still in the room, clawing at his arms and yelling at him to let go of her daughter. She spoke so loudly and with such rage that surely someone—everyone—in the brothel could hear her.

That returned him to his senses at last.

He jerked his head back, took a deep breath and gently set Annabeth away from him.

She looked up at him with a self-satisfied grin. How had he allowed matters to get so out of hand?

"What do you say, Hunter? Want to get married?"

Yes. No. *"No."*

Chapter Seventeen

Annabeth tried unsuccessfully to ignore the rapid beating of her heart. Frustrated with herself, she couldn't quite believe what she'd just done. She'd proposed to Hunter Mitchell. Proposed! In a brothel, of all places.

With her mother present.

And he'd said...*no*.

Not "Yes, please, it would be a dream come true to marry you, Annabeth." Not "What a splendid idea. You read my mind." But an emphatic, unequivocal, resounding *no*.

Her pulse picked up speed and she burned hot with the force of her shame.

She knew she only had herself to blame for this moment of complete humiliation. Hunter had warned her. He'd made it perfectly clear he would never marry again.

Had Annabeth listened? No.

Oh, no. She'd allowed her frustration with her mother to lay siege on her good sense. She'd let her pride rule her actions, calling Mattie's bluff with one of her own.

Scripture taught against such behavior. *Pride goeth before destruction, and an haughty spirit before a fall*.

Holding back a sob, Annabeth pressed her lips tightly

together. For a few more thrashing heartbeats, she remained silent, trying her best to discern Hunter's mood. But no matter how long she looked, she couldn't read any emotion on his face. His unmoving stance gave nothing away, either. Even that benign lift of his lips couldn't quite pass for a smile.

"You have made your point, Annabeth." Mattie looked thoroughly disappointed in her. Well, she was disappointed in herself. But at least her mother wasn't attempting to shove her out of her brothel—*or her life*—anymore.

A victory, to be sure, but a hollow one at best. Annabeth sighed. Truly, could there be anything more painful than unrequited love? Anything more mortifying than a man simply staring at her in stunned silence?

She sighed again.

"Step away from her, Hunter." Mattie made a shooing motion with her hands. "Let's everyone sit down and discuss the future like calm, rational adults."

A damaged, almost jagged sound rumbled from Hunter's throat. "Look around, Mattie. Do you see any calm, rational adults in this room?"

"At the moment, no. I do not. But that doesn't mean one of us can't try a little harder. And when I say one of us, I mean you." She wagged her finger at Annabeth. "No daughter of mine—"

She abruptly stopped talking. "Did you hear that?"

"Hear what?" Annabeth and Hunter asked in tandem.

"Footsteps."

A shadow moved at the foot of the door leading into the hallway. Someone was outside, evidently listening to their conversation.

A sense of foreboding filled her. "Mother—"

Mattie shook her head, pressed a finger to her lips then, with a hard yank, threw open the door.

"Oh." One of Mattie's "girls" tumbled forward, landing with a thud in a heap of skirts and incoherent sputtering.

Annabeth stifled a shiver. Though she'd never met the woman, she recognized her. Her name was Camille. She had a ten-year-old daughter living at Charity House, a girl Sarah considered one of her dear friends.

Twisting around, Camille managed to sit up after several attempts. She brushed limp red curls off her face, craned her neck and then stared straight at Annabeth. Her dark eyes were filled with something that looked like cunning.

Annabeth might have turned away from that calculating gaze but that would have branded her a coward, or worse, a woman with something to hide. She forced a smile on her face. "Hello."

Mattie was not so welcoming. "What are you doing listening at my door, Camille?"

Guilt flashed in the woman's eyes. Another wave of foreboding sliced through Annabeth.

"I wasn't listening," Camille stammered. "I was…just about to knock. But you…you…opened the door before I could."

She was lying. Annabeth knew all the signs. The darting gaze, the rapidly blinking eyes, the quick swallows.

Precisely how long had Camille been in the hallway listening to their conversation?

"Get up off the floor this instant," Mattie ordered.

Camille hurried to her feet, her gaze sweeping around the room. As she smoothed her skirt in place her eyes came to rest on Hunter. A brief smile and then she looked meaningfully from him to Annabeth to Mattie and back to Hunter again.

"What do you want, Camille?" Mattie let out a hiss that

spelled doom for the woman. "And I'd advise you to think hard before you answer the question."

"I was…going to request an advance on my…" She eyed Annabeth again, this time looking as if puzzle pieces were fitting together in her mind. "I know you."

"No, we have never met." That was certainly true.

"I *do* know you. You're…yes, you're that teacher at Charity House."

"That's right." Annabeth sucked in a calming breath. "Your daughter is in my class."

Camille nodded, then flicked her gaze down to her toes and back up again. "What did you say your name was?"

"I didn't say."

"Smith," Hunter said for her, stepping forward and commanding Camille's full attention with his large presence. "Her name is Miss Annabeth Smith."

He did not introduce himself, or engage Camille in further conversation. But he did reposition himself so that he was slightly in front of Annabeth now, all but shielding her with his broad shoulders and muscular chest.

"Annabeth…Smith." A pause. "Right. Of course."

She knew, Annabeth thought again. Camille knew she was Mattie's daughter. And from the woman's devious smile, their secret would be all over town by nightfall.

The whispers would follow, subtle at first, then growing bolder, turning vicious, until Annabeth was shunned from every good home in town. Before she could dwell on the terrible possibility, Mattie took charge.

She ushered Camille toward the exit with a considerable lack of finesse. "Yes, well. As you can see, Camille, I am in a private meeting with two old friends." She lowered her voice to an angry murmur. "I will deal with you later."

It was no empty threat.

Still, Camille dug in her heels and opened her mouth

to argue. Mattie pushed her over the threshold and shut the door in her face.

For several seconds the entire room went silent.

Dead silent.

Annabeth's vision blurred. Her head hurt. Her stomach roiled. All this time, she'd fooled herself into thinking her connection to Mattie would remain a secret forever. The illusion was over. The little white lies had been for naught.

The truth shall set you free.

She didn't feel free. She felt trapped, exposed and hot with shame. So very hot. A panic-stricken breath whooshed out of her. This awful feeling, this despair, *this* was what came from telling lies.

She could do nothing now, nothing but inhale slowly, and then exhale. Inhale, exhale. Finally, she found her voice. "She knows I'm your daughter."

It had to be said, had to be addressed head-on.

At least Mattie didn't try to soften the blow with more lies. "Yes, dear, I'm afraid she does."

"That's not to say all is lost," Hunter said as he moved to Annabeth's side.

Smiling tenderly into her eyes, he rubbed his hands down her arms in a show of comfort. His gentleness splintered her thoughts, turning her a bit stupid but also a little less desperate.

He was a conundrum, this man. One moment he was rejecting her marriage proposal, the next, he was making her panic dissolve into something far less ugly and much more manageable.

"I have changed my mind," he said with soft steel, his voice determined but not unkind.

"I'm sorry. I…" Annabeth shook her head. "You've changed your mind about what?"

He held her gaze. Calm, unwavering, so sure of himself.

But Annabeth saw the lines around his mouth, the ones that told her he wasn't as relaxed as he was putting on.

"Yes, Annabeth." Taking both her hands in his, he pulled her forward and pressed a soft kiss on her forehead. "I will marry you."

"You'll—" she felt her heart squeeze *"—what?"*

"I will marry you," he repeated.

"You will?" This was what she'd wanted. But something was wrong. Where were the love words? He wasn't saying them because he didn't love her.

Her stomach did a slow, agonizing roll. Hunter wasn't supposed to be this calm, this steady, this everything when her dreams were shattering at her feet. "Why do you want to marry me?"

"He's being noble, that's why. Misguided fool." Mattie nudged him back a step with her hip.

"I am sincere." He spoke the words to Annabeth.

Mattie scoffed. "Come now, Hunter." She nudged him again. "We both know what this is and what this isn't."

What was that supposed to mean? Was her mother speaking in some sort of code? Annabeth cocked her head in confusion. "I'm afraid you've lost me."

"It's not that complicated, Annabeth." Mattie pursed her lips. "Hunter thinks that by giving you the Mitchell name he will be able to soften the disgrace you must suffer because of your connection with me."

Oh. *Oh.*

"Is that true?" She looked at him for confirmation.

He didn't deny Mattie's accusation. Instead, he took her hands again. "Marry me, Annabeth." He punctuated the proposal with a smile. "Allow me to give you the protection of my name."

No. This couldn't be happening. She wanted to cover her ears. She wanted to run. But her mother was right.

Hunter—the misguided, noble, decent man—wanted to marry her in order to shield her from scandal.

Surely that meant he cared for her, if only a little.

Was it enough? Could she marry him knowing he didn't love her in the same way she loved him?

No.

Yes.

Yes, she could. Because she wasn't ready to give up on him, or them, not yet. What better way to win his heart than by living with him, day in and day out, as his wife?

She opened her mouth to tell him yes, she would marry him, but Mattie wasn't finished mounting her protest. "You should understand, Hunter." She physically pulled him away from Annabeth. "That by marrying my daughter you will also be gaining me as your mother-in-law."

He laughed. "I'm well aware."

"Are you, now?" She jammed her hands on her hips. "Then you should also be aware that I shall have no compunction in hurting the man who hurts my Annabeth."

Annabeth gasped.

Hunter simply walked over to Mattie and took her hands in the same tender hold he'd used with Annabeth. "Message received, my friend. And for the record, I would be honored to have you as my mother-in-law."

He looked sincere.

He sounded sincere.

He *was* sincere.

Annabeth just had to…stare. He was such a good man. She didn't want him to marry her out of obligation. She wanted him to marry her because he loved her.

"You do realize," Mattie began, her whole demeanor softening, "that my objection to you marrying Annabeth isn't personal."

Annabeth suppressed a groan at her audacious mother.

No one could ever accuse Mattie Silks of refusing to speak her mind.

"Of course it's personal," Hunter said, laughing again, this time in genuine amusement. "Can't say I blame you, all things considered."

"Now don't misunderstand." Mattie patted him on the cheek. "I firmly believe you will make some woman a fine husband one day."

"Just not your daughter."

"Well, yes." Remorse flashed across Mattie's face. "Just not Annabeth."

"You do realize my family's reputation is one of the best in the state."

"Yes," Mattie agreed. "But what of *your* reputation?"

"Stop fretting, my friend." Hunter yanked Mattie into a hug, sufficiently cutting off further protest. "If Annabeth agrees to marry me, she will be allowed to change her mind at any point and return to Denver, or wherever she wishes to go."

"That's not an acceptable solution." Mattie shoved away from him. "Divorce is no less scandalous than having a mother like me."

"I was referring to an annulment. Our marriage will be in name only."

What? *What?* "Now wait just a minute." Annabeth stepped into Hunter's line of vision and put on her best scowl. "I never said anything about a marriage in name only."

He set her out of his way. "Not now, Annabeth."

"Yes, now." She scrambled back around him. "This is a most important detail that cannot be glossed over just to appease my mother."

"Please, just…hold on a minute." His unspoken message was clear. *I can only deal with one riled-up female at a time.*

Ignoring her completely now, he guided Mattie into a chair and smiled down at her. There was such warmth in his gaze that Annabeth relented.

Hunter cared about Mattie. He really did.

Crouching in front of her, he began a quiet, heartfelt conversation just between the two of them. He spoke of honor and duty first, then turned to the importance of family. When he reintroduced the idea of Mattie joining them on the ranch, she didn't balk this time. She simply listened.

Hunter had her full attention, all because he looked past her sin and straight to the person underneath. Annabeth was humbled by his approach. Even when he talked about second chances and the freedom in Christ he didn't sound like a preacher. He sounded reasonable, heartfelt and believable.

Annabeth had to look away. She did not look at Hunter again. She couldn't. Because if she did, she would have to accept that her feelings for him weren't reciprocated, and might never be.

If she married Hunter, she would be doing so for all the right reasons, while he would be marrying her for all the wrong ones.

She shook her head, trying desperately to focus on anything but the despair growing in her heart. But then she thought of Sarah. If Annabeth married Hunter, Sarah would have both a mother and a father in her home. That mattered, far more than her own impractical dream of happily-ever-after.

"…and that's the end of it, Mattie."

"Oh, Hunter, my dear, dear boy." Mattie slapped him playfully on the arm. "That remains to be seen."

What remained to be seen? What had Annabeth missed?

Hunter squeezed Mattie's hand, then stood. "I realize you have much to discuss with your daughter." He hooked a thumb in Annabeth's direction. "I'll leave you two alone now."

With efficient, short strides, he headed toward the exit.

Annabeth rushed after him, only catching him after he swung open the door.

"Perhaps I'll go with you," she suggested, having no desire to face her mother alone right now. "You know, discuss the details of our upcoming nuptials and—"

He pressed his fingertip to her lips. "Stay, Annabeth. Talk this over with your mother."

That's all he was going to say to her? Couldn't he give her a few tender words before he left?

Our marriage will be in name only. Not if Annabeth had anything to say about it.

"We'll have our own discussion soon. But first, you need to sort out a few details with your mother."

"You can't just leave me here." She searched her mind for a reason why. "How will I get back to Charity House?" All right, she was reaching now. She'd made the trek back to Charity House a dozen times in the past few months. She didn't need him, or any man, to escort her home.

"Mattie has assured me she'll see you home safe and sound." He pressed his palm to her cheek, a look of affection in his eyes. "We'll talk again tomorrow."

With those parting words, he left the room. Annabeth watched him go, but he didn't look back at her, not once.

Sighing, she shut the door and then pressed her forehead to the wood.

She heard the rustle of silk a second before Mattie placed a hand on her back. "So, you are determined to marry him."

"What does it matter?" Squeezing her eyes shut, she

flattened a palm against the door. "You heard what he said."

"I also heard what he didn't say."

Not sure what that meant, Annabeth lifted her head, thought to turn around and face her mother head-on, but decided she needed another moment. She pressed her forehead again to the door and curled her fingers into the material of her dress.

Hunter's words swam in her mind. *Our marriage will be in name only.* Another sigh leaked out of her mouth. "He doesn't want me."

"Oh, he wants you."

"Not like a man is supposed to want the woman he's about to marry."

"Yes, Annabeth, he does. In this particular area, I'm an expert."

Perhaps that was true. Most of the time. But in this situation, the most notorious madam in Denver was wrong. So very wrong.

"He's just being noble, you said so yourself. I'll be nothing more than a glorified nanny for his daughter."

"Then be his daughter's nanny and nothing more." Mattie's hands closed over her shoulders and then gently turned her around. "I beseech you, Annabeth, don't marry Hunter Mitchell."

"But I *want* to marry him. I want to be his wife."

"Don't make my same mistakes," Mattie warned, her hands still clutching Annabeth's shoulders. "You can't change a man, any man."

"You don't know that."

"I know what it's like to try." Mattie dropped her hands. "You're only setting yourself up for heartbreak."

Was she? Did it matter? "He needs me."

"Oh, Annabeth." Mattie shook her head sadly. "Let some other woman save his soul."

Her mother didn't understand. Annabeth wasn't trying to save Hunter's soul. Only God could do that. All she wanted was to be a soft force in his life, a gentle touch when the world threw him punches.

She wanted to be the woman to soothe away the pain of his past, to watch that haunted look in his eyes disappear over time. She wanted to provide joy and peace and love in their home. Not only for Hunter, but for Sarah as well, and maybe even for herself.

All three of them deserved a chance at happiness and a place to call their own. Why not build that place together?

"There's something else you should consider," Mattie said. "Hunter is *a man*."

"Well, that certainly needed clearing up."

Mattie ignored her sarcasm. "He may say he wants a marriage in name only. He may have vowed that you will leave his home untouched if you change your mind. He may even believe that, but—"

"*I* believe him."

"You shouldn't. He's a strong, healthy, vigorous young man." Mattie sighed. "Eventually, he will want more from you."

Oh, Annabeth hoped so. She really, truly hoped so. Although she wasn't quite sure what marital intimacy involved, how she felt when Hunter kissed her told her it would likely be pleasant. Her cheeks warmed. "If matters change between us in that way, well, that will be our concern, not yours."

"He spent the past two years in prison," Mattie said, trying a different tactic. "There is no tenderness in him."

Annabeth disagreed. He was capable of great tenderness. After the way he'd treated her this very afternoon,

Mattie had to know this. She had to realize her arguments didn't hold up under close scrutiny. "I am willing to take that risk."

"There will be no finesse in his kisses."

Seeing as she had proof otherwise, Annabeth *thoroughly* disagreed. "I am willing to take that risk," she repeated.

"He will break your heart," Mattie reiterated.

Yes, very likely, he would.

But what if he didn't? What if he turned out to be the man of her dreams?

Her heart filled with unspeakable hope. And she repeated her new mantra a third time. "I am willing to take that risk."

"Annabeth, you aren't thinking clearly."

"On the contrary, Mother. I am thinking clearer than I ever have before."

Chapter Eighteen

Hunter twisted right then left, blinking furiously to clear his vision. He was back in the dark alley. His wife a few steps ahead of him. She'd turned the wrong way again, when he'd unwisely let his guard down.

He reached for her in the same way he did every night. This time, he caught her arm. But his grip slipped and she continued on without him. She seemed to disappear a little more with each step she took, her image becoming a watery blur.

"Jane, stop!" Hunter shouted after her, his voice hollow in his own ears.

The shadowy figure of Cole Kincaid materialized just out of Hunter's reach.

"Jane, behind you. He's right behind you."

As if sensing the fear in his voice, she turned to look at him. "Not to worry, my love. I'm in a safe place now."

But she wasn't safe.

Cole was pulling a knife from his pocket. The blade morphed into a gun. Grinning sinisterly, Cole pointed the barrel at Jane's head, and...

Bang!

Jane crumpled to the ground.

Bang, bang, bang.

Hunter staggered forward, reaching for his wife, but he missed and hit the ground hard. The impact knocked the breath out of him. He dragged in choking gulps of air. "Jane. I failed you again."

She came into view again and touched his face. "It's finished, Hunter. You can let me go now."

Another round of gunfire exploded through the air.

This time when Hunter reached for his wife his hands wrapped around Kincaid's beefy neck.

The scenery suddenly changed and they were in Mattie's sitting room.

Cole collapsed to the ground, Hunter's hands still on the outlaw's throat. The man's eyes bulged, his face a dingy, lifeless gray now.

"Hunter, open up."

His brother's voice came at him from a distance, like an unwanted echo inside his head. He shook free of the insistent call to come home. The past beckoned, pulling him deeper into its sinister danger.

The pounding resumed, fist against wood. "Hunter. I know you're in there."

He knew that voice, even if he hadn't heard it in years. Hunter's mind cleared. He sat up slowly and rubbed at his gritty eyes.

"Only a dream," he murmured. The same gut-twisting nightmare that had plagued him every night since Jane's death.

Jane. No matter how hard he tried to hold on to her, her face was growing more obscure in his mind, her individual features harder to remember. It was as if he was losing her all over again.

Losing her? Or letting her go?

Bang, bang, bang.

"Hunter. I mean it. Enough stalling." The doorknob rattled. "You have thirty seconds to open up or I'm breaking down this door."

Logan's low-pitched baritone teemed with frustration.

"All right, all right." Hunter threw off the covers and padded across the room. "I'm coming."

"Ten seconds down," came the harsh warning, "twenty to go."

Strangely, Hunter found himself smiling. Same old impatient Logan.

"Fifteen seconds."

Eyes still gritty, throat raw, he yanked open the door, and confronted his brother's scowl.

It was like looking in a mirror, and no less surprising than in years past. Only eleven months younger, Logan had Hunter's same build, hair color and nearly identical features. The only difference was their eye color.

Arms crossed over his chest, Logan stared at him. He made no move to push into the room. The calm demeanor was a facade. The man hummed with controlled energy, waiting, measuring, gauging.

Outwardly, Hunter remained equally calm, equally controlled, one hand resting on the door, the other on the opposite doorjamb. A sense of inevitability slammed through him. This meeting had been coming for a long time.

When the silence stretched long and uncomfortable, Logan ran his gaze over Hunter and grimaced. "You look awful."

"Good to see you, too, little brother." Hunter touched his brow in a mock salute.

Logan's lips twisted at a wry angle.

Here it comes, Hunter thought. The reproach, the detailed list of his past transgressions, the reminder he'd made a complete mess of his life.

Confronting more silence, Hunter eyed his brother with suspicion, his guard up.

Logan simply smiled. "You going to invite me in?"

Caught in a mild state of surprise, a slow rush of air hissed out of his lungs. Ever since leaving prison Hunter had felt "eyes" on him, as if someone was tracking him. When really his imagination had been working overtime, preparing him for this unavoidable confrontation with his estranged brother. The churning in his gut eased and he moved aside to let Logan pass.

Two steps forward and the man's gaze fell on the rumpled bedcovers. "I woke you."

"I had a late night."

One arched brow was his brother's only response.

"I was at Mattie's brothel."

As soon as he spoke the words, Hunter's mind immediately jumped to Annabeth and her unprecedented marriage proposal. He knew he should stop the insanity as quickly as possible. Marriage to a man like him was a losing proposition for a woman like her. But after considerable thought, Hunter had come to the conclusion that their union made sense.

Sarah needed both a mother and a father, and Annabeth needed the Mitchell name.

"You went to…Mattie's?" Logan's brow traveled higher.

A slew of questions lit in the other man's gaze, but he didn't voice any of them. The restraint was new. By this point in the conversation Logan was usually spouting off the same tired sermon about it not being too late to change his life.

They both knew it was never too late. God's mercy was fathomless and available to all His children. Hunter had needed to come to that realization in his own time, and in his own way.

Again, he wondered why Logan wasn't preaching to him.

"What?" His voice came out raw, gravelly. "No urging me to mend my wicked ways?"

Logan lifted a shoulder. "If you were at Mattie's last night, you had a reason. And I guarantee it wasn't why most men frequent her establishment."

Hunter found himself staring at his brother, unable to reconcile this man with the lawman he'd once been.

As if reading his mind, Logan let out a long-suffering sigh. "Look, Hunter, I know what you're thinking. But I'm not here to lecture you, or judge. Despite the mistakes you've made in the past, I know what kind of man you are."

It was Hunter's turn to arch a brow. Again, he thought, this was not the brother he remembered.

"I sat in the courtroom during your trial," Logan continued. "I listened to all the testimony and…" He trailed off, shrugged.

"And?" he prompted.

"The judge shouldn't have sentenced you to two years in the state prison." Breaking eye contact, Logan moved to the window and looked out, his shoulders tense. "If it were up to me you wouldn't have served any time."

Stunned, Hunter rocked back on his heels. His brother, the former U.S. marshal, the man who always followed the rules, was giving him a pass for killing another man?

There was too much bad blood between them for Hunter to remain silent on the matter. "If I remember correctly, you were the one who told me I should turn myself in to the authorities and face the consequences of what I'd done."

Still looking out the window, Logan ran a hand over his face, drew in a long pull of air. "I thought you would get a fair trial. Then, once you were set free, you'd be able to start fresh, without having to look over your shoulder anymore."

A nice sentiment. But there were some mistakes a man could never outrun, mistakes others would never let him forget. The Lord forgave sin, Hunter knew that, believed it, but He didn't always take away the consequence of the sin.

Clearing his throat, Logan swung around and faced him head-on, his eyes full of regret. "I never thought you'd have to go to prison, Hunter, certainly not for two years."

All this time, he'd thought his brother had wanted him to suffer for his actions. Had he been wrong?

"I owe you, more than I can ever repay in this lifetime." Logan pulled in another harsh breath. "You saved Megan's life that night."

"Let's not rewrite history. I had one motive when I entered Mattie's suite of rooms, and that was to confront the man who'd killed my wife in cold blood. I had no idea Kincaid had tried to attack Megan only moments before. When I arrived, I found him on the floor, near the hearth. Your wife had knocked him out cold." He smiled at the memory. "She'd moved behind one of the false walls, so I didn't see her at first and I certainly didn't go in there to help her."

"The result was the same. Megan is alive because you took out Kincaid." Gratitude filled Logan's gaze. "Let's jump to the end, shall we? You had no choice but to kill the man."

"You don't know that for sure."

"I've faced men like him, men with pure evil in their hearts." Logan clenched his hands into angry fists, as if picturing Kincaid attacking Megan. "He wasn't going down without a fight."

True. Hunter had known it was kill or be killed as soon as he'd looked into the outlaw's soulless eyes. He'd given Kincaid a chance to collect himself and face him like a man.

They'd fought hard. The battle as ugly as Hunter had ever endured. He'd ultimately prevailed, by God's grace alone.

"I still killed a man," he said, a reminder for them both.

"In self-defense," Logan corrected. "I never doubted that, and despite what the jury decided, you shouldn't, either."

His brother's unwavering confidence in him made Hunter rethink the events of that evening, this time from Logan's perspective. If Kincaid had been sadistic enough to engage in a fight to the death with a man his own size, the outlaw wouldn't have hesitated hurting a petite woman like Megan.

Hunter had taken away that opportunity, the one good thing that had come out of that night.

"Now that we've covered the past," Logan said, moving away from the window. "Let's focus on the present. Since you won't offer up the information freely, I see I'm going to have to ask straight-out. Why did you go to Mattie's last night?"

"It's a long story."

"I've got time." Proving his point, Logan pulled out the straight-backed chair tucked under a small writing desk. He turned it around, straddled the seat and then folded his arms over the top.

Unable to remain immobile under his brother's watchful gaze, Hunter paced the room. The movement helped him put his thoughts in order.

He swallowed. He'd kept so much from his family, too much, mostly out of pride. That ended today, now. He started by disclosing the nature of his rocky marriage to Maria.

Logan interrupted him almost immediately. "You got married that soon after leaving home?"

"I was young and determined to have my own way. I was lonely, too." He could admit that now, could accept what he'd refused to see at the time. "That kind of bone-deep sense of isolation can make a man do stupid things, especially a young man just off the ranch with too much kid left in him."

But he hadn't just been young. He'd been selfish, prideful and determined to deny his Christian upbringing, all because he'd craved freedom. Or what he'd thought was freedom. He'd set out to live life on his own terms. No rules. Whatever felt good *was* good.

He hadn't found freedom, but rather his own form of slavery, a self-made prison of unholy desire.

"Go on, Hunter." Logan's voice was patient as he wound his wrist in the air. "Continue with your story."

Hunter did, pacing as he spoke, his steps slowing when he came to the part about Maria hiding his own child from him, his precious, beautiful Sarah.

"Maria didn't tell you she'd borne you a child?" Logan sounded outraged. He also sounded like a…brother.

Had that always been there, the loyal, unwavering support?

Hunter made another pass through the room. "I can't say I blame her. By then I'd fallen in with a pretty rough crowd."

"I remember."

Yes, Logan would remember. They'd met once during that time, the night of Maria's funeral. He'd been half crazed with guilt, wondering if he'd tried harder to make Maria happy maybe she would have stayed with him.

Maybe she would still be alive today.

And Sarah would have both a mother and a father.

She can still have that, with you and Annabeth.

The thought brought a wave of peace, and a sense of

rightness settled over him. He needed Annabeth in his life, as much as he needed Sarah.

He loved them both, for very different reasons. He loved Sarah as a father to his daughter. And he loved Annabeth as—

"What happened to the child?"

Hunter swallowed the complicated emotions warring inside his head. He needed to focus on this conversation, but he couldn't quite make the leap back now that his thoughts had turned to Annabeth. Had he just told himself he loved her?

Of course he loved her. She was Sarah's aunt.

Sarah. Right, he was telling Logan about his daughter.

"Sarah is living at Charity House." His lips lifted and Hunter allowed the smile to spread across his face. "At least Maria got that right."

Rising from the chair, Logan made a sound deep in his throat. "Did you say your daughter's name is Sarah?"

"That's right." Hunter could see Logan's mind working, perhaps sorting through the Charity House children, trying to figure out which one was Hunter's. "She just turned nine years old a few weeks ago. She has Maria's dark hair, her same coloring and my—"

"Eyes. She has your eyes. Hunter, I know Sarah. I *know* your daughter. I've met her on several occasions when we've visited Charity House."

"How often do you go to Charity House?"

"Not as much as Megan. She still has a strong connection with Laney and Marc. For all intents and purposes, they were her parents. She teaches art classes a few times a year. Sarah is one of her favorite pupils." Wonder lit Logan's gaze as he closed the distance between them and clapped him on the back. "She's a sweet girl, smart, inherently kind. The sort of person any man would be proud to call his daughter."

Didn't he know it? "Thanks to Laney and Marc Dupree."

"They certainly had a big part in it." Logan stepped back and angled his head. "This explains why Sarah always seemed familiar to me."

"She's my child, Logan." Hunter let the joy he felt sound in his voice. "I have a *daughter*."

"And I have a new niece." Logan slapped him on the back again, a gesture reminiscent of their father at his most supportive. "The folks are going to be beside themselves with happiness over another grandchild."

For one, brief moment the past fell away and they felt like brothers again. Just as quickly, the moment vanished and the awkwardness returned.

Time. They would need time to find renewed peace between them, to grow comfortable around one another. But Hunter had genuine hope they would eventually forge a strong relationship.

"What are your plans now?"

"I'm coming home."

"Praise the Lord." Logan threw his hands in the air. "You realize this is answer to all our prayers."

"Mine, too."

They grinned at each other, and another layer of hostility fell away.

"Speaking of home." Logan dug in his pocket, pulled out an official-looking document. "The folks told me to give you this when I found you."

Wary again, Hunter took the paper, lowered his head and read. Halfway down the page, his eyes started to burn. "It's a land deed. In my name."

"That's right. Two thousand acres just off the east range. There's a small, furnished cabin already on the property."

"I'm familiar with the place." He'd holed up there a few years back, right after he'd killed Kincaid. He'd still been grieving Jane's death, not sure what to do next. His past had caught up to him, in a single, horrific night, and he hadn't known where to turn.

Home had seemed the place to go, but even then he'd made mistakes. He'd known Logan was looking for Kincaid's murderer, so Hunter had decided to give him what he wanted. On his terms. He'd used Logan's wife as bait, drawing out his brother for a final showdown, thinking that would relieve the haunting pain in his heart, as if Logan was the cause.

He'd been dreadfully wrong. And now he waited for his brother to remind him of that meeting, waited for the words of censure.

Logan said nothing.

Which was for the best. Hunter needed to be the one to cross this particular chasm first. "Logan, about the last time we met. I want to apologize for knocking you out cold. I—"

"It's in the past."

No, it was still between them and always would be if they didn't clear the air. "Let me have my say."

"All right." Logan lowered to the chair again, looking slightly uncomfortable.

"I should have listened to you that day." Hunter paused, then pressed on. "I wasn't in the right frame of mind at the time, but that's no excuse. I could have saved everyone a lot of heartache if I'd turned myself in back then. I have much to atone for."

"You finished?"

"No. Logan, I'm sorry. I'm sorry for the years of animosity between us, for considering you my enemy, for… everything."

"Hunter, you're my brother." Logan rose but didn't move away from the chair. "I forgave you a long time ago."

"You shouldn't be this easy on me." Hunter swallowed, feeling more and more like the prodigal son than ever before, and just as undeserving of grace. "You should demand I make amends."

Logan shook his head. "I'm not that much of a hypocrite. I have my share of sins to answer for, too. Sins against you."

Hunter felt his eyes widen. "What did you ever do to me?"

"I didn't ask you to come home. I judged you unfairly and withheld mercy when you needed it most. Can you forgive me?"

"I…" Hunter blinked in amazement, then answered from his heart. "Yes."

Logan smiled. "To prove there's no hard feelings, Megan and I have a gift for you."

"Your forgiveness is all I need."

"Nevertheless, we want to give you two hundred head of cattle from our herd."

The land from his parents, cattle from his brother, it was enough to start his own ranch. Hunter didn't deserve these gifts. His family was showing him what grace really looked like, offering mercy without question, or demand of payment.

He was humbled beyond measure, ready to go home and rebuild all the relationships he'd lost.

The fact that Logan was the one to bestow his family's gifts mattered most of all.

For years, Hunter had thought his brother would be a

stumbling block to his return home. Instead, he'd become a staunch ally.

Hunter thought of his other ally, Annabeth. "Sarah and I won't be the only ones coming home. Her aunt will be joining us."

Logan didn't pretend to misunderstand who Hunter meant. "You're bringing Annabeth to the Flying M?"

"She's sacrificed everything to become a part of Sarah's life. I won't tear them apart."

And with their marriage Annabeth would forever be in Sarah's life, no matter what happened to Hunter. Although he didn't like the idea of her sacrificing her own future in the bargain, he couldn't let her go, either.

And not just for Sarah's sake, but for his own. The truth hit him at last, staggering in its impact. Hunter wanted Annabeth in his life, now and forever. He loved her, as a man loved a woman.

As you once loved Jane?

No. His feelings for Annabeth were different, because she was different, yet equally powerful. Perhaps he'd been too hasty in suggesting a marriage in name only.

Perhaps he could still convince her they had something special, something lasting, something worth fighting for.

"Have you thought this all the way to the end?" Logan asked. "There won't be any problem bringing Annabeth home with you and Sarah, as long as the three of you live in the main house with the rest of the family. But what happens if you move into the cabin? Annabeth's reputation—"

"You misunderstand. Annabeth isn't coming to the Flying M solely as Sarah's aunt. She's coming as my wife."

Logan's mouth dropped open. "Your wife?"

Wife. He chewed on the word silently in his head with a surge of joy in his heart. For the first time since Jane died,

Hunter's chest didn't ache with every breath he took. His gut didn't feel so hollow.

When had he started to let her go? He knew the answer. The moment he'd pulled Annabeth into his arms and kissed her.

It was time to finish the work he'd begun in prison, time to let go of his past and embrace the future. He had to trust God was in control of his life and stop looking over his shoulder, expecting the worst.

"I'm going to make Annabeth my wife," he confirmed, then added with more force, "as soon as possible."

"I...see." From the knowing look in his brother's eyes, Hunter figured Logan saw the situation accurately.

Now came the hard part.

Annabeth might have agreed to marry him, but now he had to convince her that doing so was a good idea for herself, as well as for Sarah. Words wouldn't be enough. Hunter needed to make a grand gesture, one that would persuade her to become a permanent part of his life. Not solely as Sarah's aunt, but as his wife, in every sense of the word.

He would settle for nothing less.

Chapter Nineteen

A half hour before school let out for the day, Laney entered Annabeth's classroom. "I'd like a private word with you."

Hand poised over the chalkboard, she studied her friend perched in the doorway. "Now?"

Laney nodded.

"But I'm conducting a lesson on algebraic equations."

"Riveting, no doubt." Laney smiled. "But I assure you this won't take long."

"All right." Annabeth set down the piece of chalk in her hand, her mind racing over several possibilities for this unprecedented visit. Had gossip of her connection to Mattie reached Charity House? Even if that was the case, Laney already knew Mattie was Annabeth's mother.

"Review your notes," Annabeth said to the class. "I'll be right back."

Before walking out the door, she dropped a warning glance over the room. A few of the boys shifted guiltily in their seats. The rest of the class pretended grave interest in their math books. *Pretend* being the operative word.

Only Molly Taylor Scott, who loved math even more

than Annabeth, seemed genuinely upset by Laney's interruption.

Shaking her head, Annabeth joined her friend outside. With the sun swallowed up by a band of dark, ominous clouds, the temperature had dropped at least twenty degrees since the morning. The smell of snow hung in the air.

Wrapping her arms tightly around her, Annabeth hunched her shoulders against the cold. A sudden, sharp gust of wind whipped a strand of her hair from its pins. Though she loved the rugged landscape, days like these, when the temperature dropped unexpectedly, reminded Annabeth that living in Colorado came at a cost.

Once they rounded the building and were out of the wind, Laney pulled to a stop. Never one to waste time, she got straight to the point.

"Hunter told me to give you this." She presented a handwritten message scribbled on a piece of paper in bold, masculine strokes.

Stomach quivering, Annabeth stared at the paper in Laney's hand, then looked over at the main house. "Hunter's here?"

"Not anymore. He only stopped by long enough to leave this message for you." Laney pushed the paper into her hand. "He was quite insistent I bring it to you immediately."

Annabeth lowered her gaze and read the words scrawled on the paper. *Meet me at Bennett, Bennett and Brand Law Firm at four o'clock this afternoon.*

Confused, she flipped over the paper, looking for something…more, an explanation for the summons at least. Maybe a word of affection. A quick term of endearment.

Nothing.

Not even a signature.

She felt the first tinges of an indescribable emotion.

Disappointment, perhaps? She bit back a sigh, knowing she was overthinking the matter. From the hastily scrawled words alone, it was clear Hunter had been in a hurry.

The important point was that he wanted to see her. At a law office. In just over an hour.

The timing would be tight.

Regardless, the prospect of seeing him again set her heart quivering with anticipation. She'd spent a sleepless night wondering what their marriage would be like, *if* they married at all. Hunter had left the matter unsettled by giving her a chance to change her mind.

Thus, as Annabeth had tossed and turned through the night, her mind had continually returned to a key point of concern plaguing her. Would Hunter grow to love her with the same devotion with which he'd once loved his wife?

Behind that worry rose another. Would Annabeth and Hunter suit, on an intimate level?

Sadly, she may never know. Not if he followed through with his vow to her mother to keep their marriage in name only.

"Let's save some time, shall we?" Laney placed a hand on her arm, drawing her attention from the paper she'd been staring at with unseeing eyes. "What's going on between you and Hunter?"

Annabeth felt her stomach clench. She wasn't prepared for this conversation. But she needed to tell Laney the truth, in as much as it pertained to her position at Charity House.

"When he takes Sarah to live with him at the Flying M, I'll be…" She let her words trail off, wondering why this was so hard for her to say. Swallowing several times, she opened her mouth and tried again. "That is, when Hunter and Sarah leave Denver, I'll be——"

"Leaving with them," Laney finished for her.

"You don't sound surprised."

"Of course I'm not surprised." Laney shooed that notion away with a short wave. "Marc and I always knew you were only with us on a temporary basis. Truth be told, we've been working on your replacement for some time now."

What? "You and Marc aren't happy with my work?"

"Oh, Annabeth, that's not what I meant. You've been a blessing to us, truly. But you don't belong here at Charity House. Your place is with Sarah." Laney softened her words with a smile. "And with Hunter, as well. Your home is with the two of them, not us."

Home. There was that word again, the one that stirred up such longing and hope. Her heart took a quick, extra thump. She'd thought she'd found a home at Charity House. But no. That wasn't to say she wasn't grateful for her time here, short as it had been.

"I've been very happy at Charity House this past year." Happier than she could ever put into words.

"I'm glad."

"However, you're right. My place is with Sarah and Hunter. Speaking of Hunter. We're getting married." She said this in a quiet, calm voice, as if she was speaking of nothing more complicated than two plus two equals four.

"I'd say congratulations, but…" Laney took hold of Annabeth's hands and studied her face. "You don't look like a happy bride-to-be. Do you not wish to marry Hunter?"

"Oh, I want to marry him." She inhaled a deep breath, and then let it out again, slower and with more feeling. "But I fear he's only marrying me because he's being noble."

"I've seen the way he looks at you." Laney let her hands go. "He cares about you, Annabeth, very deeply."

Yes, he cared about her. But caring wasn't the same as love. Was it enough to build a future on, to raise a family?

The question was moot.

She'd already decided to take a leap of faith and hope that Hunter's feelings would grow stronger over time.

If her faith ever waned, she simply had to remind herself that God was in control. The details were in His hands, not hers. Everything had worked well for her so far. She had to believe the future would fall together, as well.

When she noticed Laney wasn't speaking, Annabeth sighed. "I know that look on your face. You have something more to say."

Laney simply stared at her.

"What? No rant that I'm marrying Hunter for all the wrong reasons?"

"Are you marrying him for all the wrong reasons?"

"No."

"Then why the long face?"

She sighed again, then proceeded to tell her friend about the events of the previous evening, focusing on Camille's untimely arrival and the very real possibility that her connection to Mattie was no longer a secret. "Hunter has agreed to marry me so he can provide me with the Mitchell good name."

"It's a generous reason, to be sure, but that doesn't have to mean it's the only one."

"Oh, Laney." Sudden despair clutched in her heart. "Tell me everything's going to work out for the best."

Laney pulled her into a hug. "Everything's going to work out for the best."

Wrapped in her friend's comforting embrace, Annabeth resisted the urge to cling. Embarrassed by her loss of composure, but unable to regroup, she held on a moment longer.

A mistake.

A loud thud came from inside the classroom, followed by a collective gasp, and then...

Laughter.

Annabeth shook her head. "I better get back inside."

She stepped out of Laney's arms and turned to go.

"Annabeth, wait." Laney caught her by the wrist. "If you need to talk more about Hunter, or your mother, or anything else troubling you, I'm always here."

"I appreciate that."

"I mean it. You aren't alone. I'm with you, and so is the Lord. He already has the particulars of your future worked out. Trust in Him and the rest will come."

Annabeth stared into her friend's earnest gaze. Although she'd said something very similar to herself, hearing the words spoken in her friend's sure voice calmed her worries. "Thank you, Laney. Truly, thank you."

Another thud sounded, this one louder.

"Really, Annabeth." Laney gave her a mock scowl. "Quit dawdling and get back to work."

Joining in her friend's laughter, Annabeth hurried into her classroom, and stopped dead in her tracks.

Molly stood at the front of the class, grinning broadly. She had every student, boys and girls alike, lying on the floor, face up, legs and feet kicking wildly in the air.

"Simon says…" She took a thoughtful pause. "Roll over on all fours and—"

"Get back to your seats this instant." Annabeth pinned Molly to the spot with her best teacher glare. "That means you, too."

A mutinous expression crossed the girl's face. "But, Miss Annabeth, you were taking so long and everyone was getting bored." She smoothed out her expression to one of complete innocence. "I merely thought—"

"I know what you thought." She should punish the girl for her insubordination, but her heart wasn't in it. "We'll discuss this later."

"You're angry." Molly's voice rose with emotion. "When I was only trying to keep everyone calm and—"

"I said we'll discuss this later."

Molly obediently clamped her lips tightly shut. Wise girl.

While the students filed back to their seats, grumbling all the way, Annabeth read Hunter's message again.

Why summon her to a law office? Why such cause for urgency? What had happened between last night and this afternoon?

Eager to find out, she decided attempting to teach algebra to a room full of unruly boys and girls for ten more minutes wasn't worth the effort.

"I've had an unexpected meeting arise that cannot be put off. Gather your things." She raised her voice over the chatter exploding in the room. "Class dismissed."

She didn't need to repeat herself. A flurry of activity accompanied peals of delight. Within seconds, a mass exodus ensued. Slightly dumbfounded, Annabeth stepped behind her desk.

Shuffling her feet slower than the others, Sarah approached the front of the room. "Where are you going, Aunt Annabeth?" Her eyes glittered with intrigue. "Is it a secret?"

"Not at all." Annabeth cracked a smile. The girl did so love her secrets. "I'm heading out to meet your father."

"Can I come?"

"Not this time."

"Why not?" The child's face was so forlorn it made Annabeth's heart ache a little.

"Your father and I have adult business to discuss." She figured this was as good a guess as any.

Sarah huffed out a sigh, wounded and a little angry. She opened her mouth again, but Annabeth wasn't finished.

"Tell you what. After our meeting in town I'll ask your father to come back to Charity House with me."

After a pause to mull this over, Sarah nodded. "I suppose that'll be all right. But you have to promise to bring him back with you, no matter what."

"I can't make that promise. He may already have other plans." Before Sarah could argue the point further, Annabeth continued speaking. "I'll do my best to convince him. Now, walk with me back to the main house. I have to change my clothes. You can help me pick out what to wear."

With Sarah's help, Annabeth decided on a pale blue dress, the color nearly a perfect match with her eyes. A fresh pair of gloves and her best bonnet completed the outfit.

One final kiss to Sarah's cheek and she was off to meet Hunter.

Despite the clothing change, she arrived outside Bennett, Bennett and Brand Law Firm with five minutes to spare. She paused, collecting herself as best she could, considering she had no idea why Hunter had summoned her here.

Thankfully, she hadn't experienced a single scandalized look or hushed whisper as she'd made her way into town, giving her hope that her reputation was still intact.

That hope was dashed the moment she stepped on the front stoop of the fancy brick-and-mortar building housing the law firm. The door swung open with a whoosh. Startled, Annabeth stepped aside to let a pair of well-dressed ladies exit the building.

By their similar facial features and distinct age difference the two had to be mother and daughter. "Good afternoon," she said to them both.

The younger of the two opened her mouth to reply, but

the older one leaned over her and whispered something in her ear.

Annabeth caught only a portion of the words. But there was no mistaking *brothel, madam* and, finally...

Daughter.

"No." The younger woman gasped, her features contorting into a look of horror.

"It's true," the other one said with the confidence of a practiced gossip.

Eyes wide, the girl lowered her gaze over Annabeth. "Are you truly the daughter of Mattie Silks?"

Refusing to feel a slice of shame, Annabeth lifted her chin at a regal angle. "I am."

"Come along, Daisy." The older woman made a disapproving sound in throat. "We don't talk to women like her."

Women like her? As if Annabeth's connection to Mattie made her somehow a lesser person than them.

"You will move out of our way this instant," the older woman demanded.

Annabeth held firm. There was plenty of room for the women to pass without her having to step off the stoop. They were drawing a crowd, she knew, but Annabeth didn't care as much as she would have expected.

This was the very type of confrontation she'd feared most since leaving Boston. But now that it was here, she felt no embarrassment.

Yes, her mother was a notorious madam. But Mattie was still one of God's beloved children. She still deserved His mercy and His love and a chance to change her life.

"My mother has made bad choices in her lifetime." Annabeth whirled on the crowd whispering their own opinions on the matter. "But she is still deserving—"

"Of God's grace as surely as any of you." A ruthless, masculine voice finished the sentence for her.

Recognizing that deep timbre, but unable to see her rescuer, Annabeth lifted on her toes. The crowd parted and Hunter stepped forward. Drawing alongside of her, he wrapped his arm around her waist and smiled.

That smile. It was like a physical blow to her heart.

"Hello, darling." He placed a kiss on her forehead.

"Hello."

He looked over at the two ladies, commanding their attention with nothing more than a raised eyebrow. His dynamic presence had both women blinking up at him, captivated in his stare.

A hush came over the crowd, every single person poised to hear what he said next.

Annabeth would like to know herself.

Although a good dressing-down was certainly in order, Hunter proved himself to be a man of restraint.

"Ladies, if you would be so kind as to step aside, my fiancée—" he emphasized the word by pulling Annabeth closer to him "—has arrived just in time for our appointment. We don't wish to be late, do we, darling?"

Darling. That was the second time he'd used the endearment. The word had never sounded more intimate, or more special. "Punctuality is one of my favorite virtues," she said, her voice a bit shaky.

"Mine, as well."

Voices erupted from the crowd, some shouting at the ladies to move aside, others telling them to hold their ground. Clearly, sides had been chosen.

Hunter took charge before the shouts turned to blows. Without another word, he took Annabeth's arm and guided her around the two women. He didn't give them a very wide berth, that would have been impossible given the limited space, but the message was the same. *We're done here.*

Once safely inside the building, Annabeth glanced back

outside. Mother and daughter had taken their leave, while the crowd had begun to disperse.

Watching the activity outside, it took Annabeth a moment to realize Hunter was tugging her deeper into the building. She pulled him to a stop. When he turned back to face her, she saw the pent-up emotion in his eyes.

His jaw set in a hard line, he darted his gaze to the outside stoop. "I'm sorry you had to endure that just now."

He was angry. On her behalf.

She smiled up at him, feeling warm and touched and very much in love. "All you needed was to ride up on a white horse and the fairy tale would have been complete."

Instead of lightening the mood, her comment had the opposite effect. Hunter's gaze turned grave. "Annabeth." He made her name sound like an apology. "I'm no knight in shining armor."

She reached up and cupped his cheek. "Today you are."

"Let's get something straight right now. I'm not a hero, never have been, never will be." She recognized the pain in his eyes. "I killed a man and went to prison for it and—"

"You're the best man I know." The way he'd pushed through the crowd to get to her and then how he'd stood by her side, defending her honor. "There's no getting around the fact that I'm the daughter of the most infamous madam in town. You just experienced a taste of what the future holds. Still want to marry me?"

"Absolutely." He emphasized the word with a disarming smile. "You know what I bring to the table, too. I have an ugly past. Still want to marry me?"

"Yes, Hunter. I still want to marry you."

Something flashed in his eyes, something new, something real, something that looked a lot like love. "As long as I have breath in my lungs, Annabeth, I will protect you with my life."

"I know." She'd found the place where she belonged. With this man, who thought she was worthy of his protection.

While he hadn't given her touching words of love, she hadn't given him any, either. It was time she surrendered the whole of her heart. "I love you."

Eyes shining with emotion, he took her hand and brought it to his lips. "Annabeth, my darling girl, I—"

"Mr. Mitchell." A tentative voice cut him off midsentence. "Mr. Bennett is ready for you now."

Chapter Twenty

At some point in the trek down the hallway to Reese Bennett's office, Hunter looked down at his hand. It was linked with Annabeth's, their fingers braided together naturally, as if they held hands like this all the time. The most amazing thing wasn't that she was holding on to him. *He* was holding on to her, as tightly as possible, never wanting to let her go.

They were alone, just the two of them in the cavernous hallway, no one to hear them. Yet, he couldn't seem to find his voice.

With the interruption from Bennett's law clerk, Hunter had lost the chance to tell Annabeth what was in his heart. He'd never been good with words, preferring action instead.

All he knew was that he wanted Annabeth in his life, not only because she was good with Sarah. But because he loved her.

It should be simple to say. *I love you.*

But the emotion was so new, so unexpected. In human time, he'd fallen quickly, though it hadn't felt quick. It seemed as if he'd loved her all his life, the emotion unraveling in small degrees through the years.

From their first meeting, when Hunter had barely been off the ranch and Annabeth had been but thirteen, she'd gotten to him. She'd touched the man he'd always been underneath the tough veneer he presented to the world.

Annabeth saw him for who he really was. She knew the good and the bad and loved him, anyway.

In the past few weeks, she'd shown him what unwavering courage looked like, and had taught him the definition of family on a whole new level.

Even outside, she'd remained resolute and loyal to her mother, a woman she could have easily denied in the face of such public humiliation. Annabeth made Hunter want to be a better man. The man he already was in the Lord's eyes.

He glanced down at her, then caught her watching him with those big, beautiful eyes of hers. She didn't voice the silent questions he saw in her gaze, nor did she try to hide them from him, either. That sort of raw honesty was one of the many qualities he loved about her.

He raised her gloved hand to his lips. "I'll explain everything shortly, once we're in Bennett's office."

"I know."

Her confidence in him was another reason he loved her. He was doing the right thing, calling her to this law office today. He prayed she understood the gesture he was about to make.

Maneuvering to the end of the hallway, he knocked on Reese Bennett's office door.

"Enter."

With a flick of his wrist, Hunter opened the door, then allowed Annabeth to enter ahead of him.

"Mr. Mitchell, I—" The lawyer cut off his own words and rose quickly to his feet. "Ah, I didn't realize you were bringing anyone with you today. Miss—" he paused, swept his eyes over Annabeth, cleared his throat "—Smith. It's a pleasure to see you again."

"Hello, Mr. Bennett. And, please, no need to pretend you haven't heard the news. I am Annabeth Silks, not Smith. Silks. My legal name is Annabeth Silks."

To his credit, the lawyer didn't react with anything more than a slight nod of his head.

"Please, have a seat, both of you." He gestured to the matching leather chairs facing his desk.

Once they were settled, the lawyer turned his attention on Hunter. "You requested this appointment, Mr. Mitchell. Am I to assume that you have another legal matter you wish for me to address?"

"I do." He fished inside his jacket, pulled out the land deed Logan had given him and handed it across the desk. "My brother gave this to me this morning and—"

Annabeth interrupted him. "You saw Logan today?"

"I did." He smiled. "I have much to tell you."

"I should say so." She laid a hand on his arm, searching his face, probing deep. He felt as if his very soul was laid bare to her. Whatever she was looking for she must have found because she dropped her hand and smiled. "It went well," she decided. "Your meeting with your brother."

"Better than well. We have begun the process of becoming true brothers again."

"Oh, Hunter," she whispered. "I'm so very happy for you both."

The truth of her words was evident in her solemn, earnest tone. If he'd had any doubt before now, he knew the truth. This woman loved him.

And he loved her.

If he ever failed her...

The thought brought an ache to his stomach, and to his heart. Until now, Hunter had mistakenly believed he'd asked Annabeth to marry him because he was doing her a favor, offering her the protection of his name.

He'd been wrong.

Annabeth was the one doing him the favor. By agreeing to become his wife, by loving him, she was giving him the future he'd always wanted.

"Everything appears to be in order." Bennett set the deed on his desk.

Hunter shook his head. "What's in order?"

"This document." The lawyer placed his finger on the paper and pushed it across the desk. "It's perfectly legal."

His parents would have made sure of that. "Yes, I know."

"If you know, then why did you bring it to me for authentication?"

"I don't need the document authenticated." Hunter leaned forward, realizing he'd been lost in thought and hadn't explained himself yet. "I want to sign over ownership of the land today, so that there will be no misunderstanding in the future."

Eyebrows pulled together, Bennett placed the document back in front of him. "Mr. Mitchell, that's not necessary. The original provision you had me put in your will covers this parcel of land, and any future assets you may acquire through the years."

"You aren't listening, Mr. Bennett. So let me be more clear." Hunter turned to look at Annabeth directly. "I want all two thousand acres listed on that deed to be put in Annabeth's name, not mine."

"What?" She blinked at him in confusion, glancing from him to the lawyer and back to him again. "I...I don't understand. What two thousand acres of land?"

"My parents are giving me a portion of their ranch. And I'm putting the property in your name."

She continued blinking at him.

"I want to take care of you, Annabeth." He took her hand, willing her to understand. "I want to ensure your future is settled no matter what happens between us. I've already made you a cobeneficiary of my estate with Sarah. But I want this piece of land to be yours now, today."

"You want to take care of me." Unhappiness sounded in her voice. "By giving me land that belongs to you."

"That's right." She should be pleased. Why wasn't she pleased?

As if sensing they needed a moment alone, Reese Bennett rose from his chair and made his way to the door. "I'll leave you two to discuss this in private."

The moment the door clicked shut, Annabeth yanked her hand free. "You will not do this, Hunter Mitchell. Your parents are giving you the land. Not me, *you.*"

"Once I explain the situation they will understand why I put the property in your name."

"No, I won't allow you to do this." She jumped to her feet and scowled down at him. "Put the deed in Sarah's name."

"Sarah is still a child."

"She's *your* child."

"And your niece. I want you to come to the Flying M with us, freely, with no demands or expectations." Why was this so hard for her to understand?

"I won't take payment like this." She choked on a sob. "How could you ask it of me? How could you think I would agree to this?"

He'd hurt her. Somehow he'd hurt her when he'd been trying to show her he loved her. He ran her words through his brain, his mind hooking on one word in particular. Payment. "I'm not *paying* you to marry me."

"Aren't you?"

"I'm giving you a gift." He searched for the right words to explain himself, frustrated he couldn't seem to speak plain enough for her. "It's no different than the silver hairbrush."

"How can you think such a thing? This is nothing like the hairbrush. I…I…" She pulled a steadying breath into her lungs and walked regally toward the door, then spun around and glared at him. "I'm not my mother."

"Of course you aren't your mother." He strode across the room to her. "What does Mattie have to do with this?"

"If I take land from you, I'm no better than one of her girls."

That's what she thought? That he was paying for services to be rendered at a later date?

How could she think such a thing? How could she think so little of him?

So little of herself?

Had the encounter out front left a stronger impression on her than he'd first thought?

"Annabeth, you've misunderstood me completely." He gentled his voice. "I'm trying to show you how I feel."

"By giving me land?"

"It was meant to be a grand gesture."

"You don't know me at all, do you?" She didn't hide her disappointment. "You could have just *told* me how you feel."

A knot formed in his throat. "Words didn't seem enough."

The knot turned into a thick ball of regret. He was still working through a way to rectify his mistake when she twisted open the door with a hard yank.

"Annabeth, stop. Listen to me." He hadn't meant to speak so harshly. But he was growing desperate. Exasperation with himself—with her, with them both—was making him careless with his words, and his tone.

She heaved a sigh. "I only needed the words."

She said this in a small, quiet voice, and then walked out, closing the door with a firm snap.

And that was it.

Just like that, she'd walked out on him. As Maria had done all those years ago.

As Jane had, in her own way, when she'd died in the dark alley.

He processed the unexpected pain that came with another woman leaving him, a woman who had become more a part of his heart than any before her.

I only needed the words.

"I love you," he whispered and felt the first stirrings of grief. And not just grief alone, but defeat, too.

It felt like his heart was shattering into pieces.

"She's in love with you," Reese said from the threshold of his office.

Hunter looked up. He hadn't heard the door open again, hadn't known he was no longer alone.

"Don't let your male pride keep you from going after her." A shadow fell across the lawyer's eyes, a look that said he knew what it was like to let love get away. "Follow her. Tell her what she needs to hear."

No, Hunter thought, racing out of the man's office at top speed. He wasn't going to tell Annabeth what she needed to hear. He was going to reveal what was in his heart the right way, with his actions *and* his words.

Annabeth hurried down the darkened hallway of the law firm, her vision blurring with unshed tears. She didn't run, nothing so dramatic as that, but she did move at a clipped pace. She kept her head down, avoiding eye contact as she made her way out of the building into the open street.

The cold March air punched into her lungs, the sharp pain a reminder of her misery. Unexpected snow flurries had begun to fall, clearing the streets as surely as a thunderstorm.

She turned to her left, in the opposite direction of Charity House, and set out at a fast pace.

Ten years. Ten long years she'd spent loving Hunter Mitchell, only to have it end in heartache. She had only herself to blame. She'd put her hope in a man, building him up to a dangerous level in her mind. The Bible warned of such things, of putting any man ahead of the Lord.

What had she been thinking?

She'd allowed herself to believe in a silly fairy tale.

She'd allowed herself to believe Hunter was the only man for her, as if the Lord had planned their match from the beginning of time.

That's how her love for him had felt, as if it had been predestined.

She'd come so close to winning his heart, had actually thought she'd done just that.

How could he love her when he didn't even know her?

I'm trying to show you how I feel.

No, he'd been trying to buy her affection, with two thousand acres of prime ranchland, as if her love had such a high price.

Her feet slowed as the heat of the moment gave way to calmer thinking. Was she being fair to Hunter? Or was she overreacting because of her run-in with that judgmental woman on the law firm's front stoop.

Mind racing, Annabeth turned a sharp corner.

It was meant to be a grand gesture, Hunter had said. And then he'd added, *Words didn't seem enough.*

Her heart thudded to a steady, calmer beat, her steps slowing to meet the new pace. How could she not have seen what he'd been trying to do, what he'd been trying to say with his actions?

Head down, she turned another corner and then stopped as complete understanding dawned at last. And with it, came the shame.

By presenting her with prime ranchland Hunter hadn't been trying to buy her off, he'd been *showing* her how he felt.

And she'd tossed the gesture back in his face.

How could she have been so cruel, so thoughtless?

She had to find him, had to apologize. Lifting her head, she started to retrace her steps, then stopped again and looked around. She was on the street behind Mattie's brothel. It was somehow fitting that she'd sought solace from her mother at a time like this.

Giving into a rueful smile, Annabeth crossed the street. The snow was coming down harder, thick and wet and far too hard to try to head back to Charity House right now.

"Good afternoon, Annabeth."

She spun at the sound of her name spoken in a low, sinister growl. An unfamiliar man approached her. Something in his hard, ruthless gaze had her backpedaling.

"I said, good afternoon, Annabeth."

Her heart thumped double time against her ribs. How could this stranger know her name?

She'd never met him before. She would remember that cold, black-eyed stare inside that flat, mean face.

Was he one of her mother's customers?

That made sense. Except, no, it didn't. She'd never met any of Mattie's customers, one of her mother's strictest rules.

"I see by your confusion you're wondering how I know

you." His face cracked into a smile that revealed dirty, tobacco-stained teeth. "I've been watching you for some time now."

He'd been *watching* her?

"You're Hunter's woman."

How could he know that?

"I'm Cole Kincaid's brother."

She was afraid now, so afraid, for Hunter. If anything happened to her, he would blame himself. He might even seek vengeance on her behalf.

She couldn't let that happen.

Her fear grew white-hot with each breath she took, rolling unsteadily in her stomach and beating a dull ache behind her eyes.

A wave of nausea took hold. She pushed the sensation down and flung herself into a run.

Her pursuer followed hard on her heels, caught her by the arm and dragged her into the alley beside her mother's brothel.

In an attempt to twist out of his hold, Annabeth stumbled twice. Never breaking stride, Cole's brother continued jerking her along with him.

The snow was falling heavier, faster, cutting off visibility beyond a few feet in front of them.

There was no one left on the streets, no one to help her. She lifted up a silent prayer to God.

Fear continued pumping in her veins. Her breath came quick and sharp as she fought to keep the blinding tears at bay.

She needed to keep a clear head.

A swift wrench and she broke free of her attacker's grasp. She made it five full steps before she felt a hand grip her hair.

A sudden yank and she went down. Hard.

Her attacker dragged her back to her feet and then pulled her deeper into the alley. He wedged her up against the building.

She jerked her knee up, kicking him hard.

Howling in pain, he leaned over her with evil intent.

She kicked again, landing blows wherever she could.

He cursed her, and then dug his fingers into her throat. She clawed at him in return, reaching for his eyes.

Catching her hands, he pinned them by her sides. She struggled, but he was too big, too strong and she was too small.

She sucked in a rough breath, suddenly remembering what Mattie had taught her to do if she was ever attacked like this.

Opening her mouth, Annabeth cried out for help at the top of her lungs.

She screamed and screamed and screamed.

He slapped his hand over her mouth. "Shut up."

She bit his palm.

His red-rimmed eyes lit with rage and he called her a filthy name.

Pulling away from his hand, she screamed again.

"I said shut up." He yanked his gun out its holster and pointed it at her head.

She went perfectly still, utterly silent.

Breathing hard, they eyed one another. Jamming the tip harder against her temple, he called her another ugly name.

She shut her eyes, refusing to react.

"Let her go, Rico."

Her eyes flew open. That cold, angry voice belonged to Hunter.

Annabeth nearly collapsed in relief, but she didn't dare look in his direction.

Rico had no such qualms.

With the gun still pressed to her head, he glanced at Hunter and snarled. "You got here quicker than I thought you would. This one must mean something to you."

"Let her go."

"Not a chance." The gun never leaving her temple, Rico spun her around and yanked her back against him.

Using her as a human shield, he shifted until they faced Hunter together. "You think I'd let you get away with killing my brother? That I wouldn't hunt you down? Make you pay?"

"Let her go." This time, Hunter's eyes were deadly calm as he spoke. Whatever he was feeling was carefully masked behind that cold, menacing stare.

He was going to fight for Annabeth's life.

But he didn't have a gun, or any weapon. Not even a knife.

Rico had all the advantage.

"You took the last of my family. Now I'm going to take yours. One member at a time." Rico pulled the hammer back on the gun. "Starting with this little filly here."

Chapter Twenty-One

Hunter checked his balance, sorting through his options at lightning speed. Ice-cold rage pulsed through his blood. He'd only experienced this surge of violence once before. When he'd found Jane dead in an alley similar to this one, lying crumpled and broken in a dark corner.

He pushed the memory away and focused on the present. On Annabeth. The woman he loved now.

Shifting his weight onto the balls of his feet, he moved his glance to Rico's ugly face. The hate was there, in the other man's eyes, smoldering inside the fury.

His past had found him again. In the form of Cole Kincaid's wicked, younger brother, a man known for his fast reflexes and cold, spiteful heart.

"Let her go, Rico." Hunter repeated the words, then moved a step forward. "It's me you want to hurt."

"True. But we both know your weakness is your woman."

Eyes narrowing to two mean slits of hate, Rico used his free hand to yank on Annabeth's hair, tugging until she cried out in pain.

Hunter surged forward.

"Stop right there." Rico jammed the barrel of his gun harder into Annabeth's temple. "Or I'll shoot her dead."

Hunter froze.

Hands rising in the air, palms forward, he forced his brain to work through possible solutions.

Only one came to mind. Infuriate Rico enough to get him to point the gun at Hunter.

The outlaw didn't look well. His physique had gone from lean to gaunt and his skin was a sickly, pasty white. Although three years younger than Hunter, Rico's eyes had the rheumy hue of an old man.

Perhaps his reflexes had slowed with the loss of his health.

"Last I saw you, Rico—" Hunter edged a fraction closer "—you were crossing the border into Mexico, chasing after some senorita who wasn't your wife."

Rico ignored the taunt. "When I heard you were getting out of prison," he hissed, "I decided to come and finish the job my brother failed to do."

Cole Kincaid's brother was here to kill him.

Hunter had known this was a possibility. Though he hadn't seen Rico in years, deep down, he'd sensed the man following him, waiting around the corner, gunning for him. Yet, he'd let his guard down, had allowed himself to grow complacent, convincing himself he'd outrun his past.

"I'm the one you want," he repeated, smoothing all emotion out of the words. Spreading his hands out wide, palms facing forward, he offered up himself. "Come and get me."

"All in good time. First, I'm going to kill your woman." Rico pulled Annabeth tighter against him. "And you'll have the pleasure of watching her die."

The woman he loved was not going to suffer for his mistakes. Not this time.

Not.

This.

Time.

Greater love hath no man than this, that a man lay down his life for his friends.

A moment of peace whispered across his soul. Hunter knew what he had to do.

Regulating his breathing, he edged another step closer and continued goading Rico. "What happened to your little senorita? She kick you out like your wife did?"

Rico growled.

Hunter set his jaw and edged another inch closer. He wanted to rush the outlaw, to end this standoff in a single move.

But that would endanger Annabeth's life.

"Hunter, please." Annabeth's voice sounded desperate. "Stop taunting him."

He ignored the plea and focused on Rico, only Rico.

The eyes that met his were cold and mean. Frantic. The man had nothing to lose. Wanted in six states, Rico had always been more reckless than his brother, more unpredictable. It was a trait that made him especially dangerous in a fight.

Hunter took another step forward.

"No, Hunter, don't." Annabeth's voice lowered to a soothing octave, as if understanding the best way to get through to him was through calmness not panic. "Don't let him turn you into someone you're not."

"You're kidding yourself, little lady." Rico pressed his lips to Annabeth's ear. "He's an outlaw at heart, just like me."

Rico was partially right. Hunter had an ugly past. A past he had to put to rest once and for all.

"I won't let him hurt you, Annabeth," he vowed, eyes

locked with Rico's. He could hear his own breathing scratching in and out of his lungs.

"I'm not going to die on you," she said in a plain, steady voice. "I know how to fall."

"What's that supposed to mean?" Rico demanded as his finger shook over the trigger. "You speaking in some sort of fancy code?"

"Hunter, hear me, I know how to *fall*," she repeated.

What was she trying to tell him?

A split second later, he knew what she meant. His thoughts turned very cool and clear, very precise.

"All right, Annabeth." He adjusted his weight evenly on his feet, gave her one solid nod, and then said, "Fall."

She instantly dropped to her knees and rolled.

The sudden movement caught Rico by surprise. He lost his balance and stumbled backward. The pistol slipped from his hand, landing at his feet. The impact released a bullet from the chamber. It whizzed past Annabeth, digging into the wall above her head.

Hunter flung himself at Rico even as he was aware, brutally aware, that the man was reaching for the fallen weapon, a look of twisted resolve on his face.

"Run, Annabeth."

She scrambled to her feet and dashed toward the street. She moved quickly. But not fast enough. Rico had the gun pointed straight at the back of her head.

Hunter vaulted into the line of fire.

His fingers closed over the gun.

Eyes wild with fury, Rico pulled the trigger.

Hunter weaved to his left. The bullet caught the top of his ear, nothing more than a nick. He continued his pursuit, rounding on Rico with unleashed fury.

This time, the outlaw pointed the weapon at his heart.

Hunter grabbed for the gun, caught hold of the barrel and wrestled the outlaw for control.

Rico's smile turned cold, ice-cold, and he pulled the trigger again. Hunter swerved right.

The bullet hit the ground behind him.

He caught Rico's wrist, wrenched the gun free.

Another shot. Pain exploded in Hunter's chest, but he finally had control of the weapon.

He tossed the pistol to the ground, kicked it out of reach. His vision blurred. Then cleared. Then blurred again.

Working through a cold sweat, he closed his hands over Rico's throat.

The outlaw kicked out, catching one of Hunter's legs.

They went down together.

Rico rolled out from under Hunter, crawling on his hands and knees. He glanced frantically around him, caught sight of his gun and reached out.

Before the outlaw could close his fingers over the weapon, Hunter hauled him to his feet. "Fight me like a man."

Rico sputtered. His face was red from exertion and turning redder by the minute.

Anger morphed into a need to draw blood. It would be so easy to wrap his hands around the man's worthless throat, Hunter thought, to squeeze until he took his last breath.

But that was the old Hunter. The man he was now left vengeance to the Lord, and justice to the system.

Taking Rico by the shoulders, Hunter slammed him against the wall, subduing him with a forearm pressed to his neck.

Slowly, as if coming out of a dream, he became aware of footsteps pounding in the distance, growing closer by the second.

Letting the last shreds of anger slip out of him, Hunter glanced briefly to the street beyond. His vision tinged gray and, for an instant, the world shifted under his feet. A dizzying wave of nausea crashed over him and his mouth went dry.

His grip slipped.

Rico shifted.

But Hunter recovered quick enough to send the outlaw back against the wall.

More footsteps joined the others, several pairs of feet sounded, coming faster, louder, closer.

The world shifted beneath Hunter's feet again. He swallowed, even as he heard his name being called from behind him.

In the next moment, Trey Scott appeared in his peripheral vision. He pried Hunter's arm free. "You can let him go. I've got it from here."

One more shove and then Hunter stepped back.

He watched as Trey cuffed Rico. The seasoned lawman used as little sensitivity as possible without actually inflicting injury. It was a fine art honed through years of practice, and far more consideration than the outlaw deserved, considering he'd tried to hurt Annabeth.

Desperate to find her, needing to assure himself she was indeed safe, Hunter waited until Trey dragged Rico off then swung around and searched for her.

He came face-to-face with a gathering crowd. But no Annabeth. He pushed forward, but moved too fast and lost his balance. He stumbled a few steps to the right, then to his left, knocking into a few bystanders.

Since when did a simple shift in position throw him into a full stagger? And why did his head hurt? Why was his vision turning black?

Pulling in a deep breath, he set out again.

This time the crowd parted and Annabeth came into view.

Seeing him, she quickened her pace. "You're all right. Oh, Hunter, I was so worried. I didn't want to leave you, but I had to get help. Sheriff Scott sped ahead of me and—"

She cut herself off and gasped.

"You've been shot," she rasped out.

In the next instant, her eyes filled with tears, eyes that were no longer locked on his face but his chest.

Baffled, he followed the direction of her gaze, and noted the blood on his shirt. A large, red stain spread across the white linen from his shoulder to his ribs.

He slowly became aware of the pain that burned a path from his shoulder to his brain.

"Hunter. You're swaying. Here, hang on to me." Annabeth reached to him, caught him by the arm, shifted beneath to support his weight.

He hissed in pain, then pushed the sensation to a back corner of his mind. All that mattered was that Annabeth was safe. She was alive.

"Annabeth, my darling." He lifted his hand to her face. "I…"

That's all he got out before he slipped to the ground and then…

Nothing.

"Hunter!" Annabeth dropped to her knees, uncaring that people were gathering around them, pressing in from all sides, stealing their air. "Can you hear me?" Panic threaded through her words. "Say something."

His face was draining of color, turning a sickly shade of green. Putting pressure on his chest wound, she desperately tried to staunch the bleeding. She swung her gaze into the crowd. "Somebody get a doctor."

Nobody moved, except to draw in for a closer look at the man in her arms.

Just then, Mattie appeared at the edge of the crowd. She shoved and pushed and ordered people to step aside. When the command didn't move them fast enough, she shouted, "Get out of my way!"

At last, she made it through the bulk of the crowd. Leaning over Annabeth, she eyed Hunter, her gaze resting on his bloody shirt. "Don't let up on the pressure."

"I know. He's been shot," Annabeth said unnecessarily, her voice thick with rising hysteria.

"Yes, darling, I can see that." Mattie brushed her fingertips across her forehead. "Come, let's get him inside."

She motioned Jack forward.

"No." Annabeth refused to let go of Hunter. "We can't move him. Not until the doctor arrives."

"I've already sent for Shane."

Shane, as in Shane Bartlett, the doctor connected to Charity House, the one who also treated Mattie's soiled doves. Yes, Shane would fix Hunter.

Squeezing back tears, Annabeth dropped a kiss to his lips. "I love you," she whispered.

His eyes fluttered open. "It's going to be all right, my love," he assured her. "Everything's going to be all right."

Those were supposed to be her words. She was supposed to comfort him. Instead, he—the noble, decent, good-hearted *hero*—was attempting to soothe her.

For his sake, she forced herself to remain calm. "I love you," she said again.

"Love you, too." He unleashed a smile, then his eyes closed again.

"Annabeth, darling, move aside so Jack can get Hunter off the ground."

She leaned over him one last time. His face had gone

paler still, completely gray, and his breathing had turned shallow.

"Don't you die on me," she whispered then moved back so Jack and another man could lift Hunter off the ground.

Dr. Shane Bartlett arrived less than five minutes after they got Hunter settled on a large settee in Mattie's private parlor. When it was deemed the bullet had to be removed at once, Shane tried to banish Annabeth from the room.

She refused to go. "What can I do to help?"

"You can get me clean linens and fresh water."

With efficient, capable hands Shane got to work. So did Annabeth. While Shane removed the bullet she provided him with an unending supply of linens and water. There seemed to be a lot of blood. Thankfully, Hunter remained unconscious throughout the surgery, which was probably for the best: the pain had to have been excruciating.

Annabeth prayed for his life, lowering to her knees when her legs gave way. *Lord, please, guide Shane's hands*.

After nearly an hour, Shane stepped back, and began washing the blood from his hands in a basin of fresh water.

"That's it," he said. "That's all I can do. The rest is in God's hands."

Annabeth climbed hastily to her feet. "Is he all right? Will he live?"

Shane rolled his tired gaze to meet hers. "He's young and strong, Miss Annabeth. He should heal just fine, providing he doesn't get an infection, or fever."

She heard what he wasn't saying. "And if he gets either of those?"

"Now, Annabeth, let's not create problems before they even occur." Mattie moved to stand beside her. "Isn't that right, Shane?"

"It's always wise to remain positive," he agreed, then went on to explain how best to care for Hunter in the coming days. "Keep a close eye on him. Change the dressing on his wound every four hours. If you see any redness, or it becomes discolored and warm to the touch, send someone to get me at once. The same goes if the bleeding starts up again."

"I'll not leave his side," Annabeth pledged.

"That's up to you." Shane began gathering his things and placing them in a large leather bag. "Just make sure he isn't left alone for any considerable length of time."

"Annabeth, you cannot stay in this brothel overnight," Mattie said. "Your reputation—"

"Is already ruined," Annabeth finished, wondering why such a thing had ever mattered to her. "Hunter's well-being is more important than what small-minded people say about me."

"If you remain here through the night, won't the people at Charity House wonder where you are? And what about Hunter's little girl?"

Annabeth's hand flew to her throat. How could she have forgotten about Sarah? She'd all but promised the girl that Hunter would come to Charity House later tonight.

How would Sarah take the news of her father's injury? For a brief moment, Annabeth considered withholding the information from her. But she discarded the notion in the next breath.

They couldn't start life as a family keeping secrets from one another, even secrets that hurt.

"Shane, may I ask one last favor of you?"

With a snap, he closed the medical bag. "Of course."

"Would you be so kind as to stop by Charity House and let them know where I am, and why, then ask if someone would be willing to escort Sarah—"

"I'll fetch the girl," Mattie offered.

"You—" Annabeth's mouth fell open "—you…will?"

"Hunter will want her here when he awakens."

Annabeth stared into her mother's eyes, eyes that had gone soft with emotion. "You care about him."

"If you love the man—" Mattie lifted a shoulder in a careless gesture "—then I love him, too."

Annabeth hugged her mother with fierce abandon. There were no words of affection exchanged. That wasn't Mattie's way. She did allow Annabeth to cling to her for ten full seconds before wiggling free.

"Yes, well." Turning her back, Mattie swiped at her cheeks once, twice, then lifted her chin. "The sooner I leave the sooner I can return. Come, Shane, we'll walk out together."

At the door, Mattie looked back over her shoulder. "I'll tell Jack to check on you shortly."

"That'll be fine."

Alone with Hunter, Annabeth hurried to his side. She lowered to her knees and took his hand in hers. Pressing her forehead against his knuckles, she lifted up a prayer of gratitude to the Lord. Hunter was alive. Everything else paled in comparison.

She let loose the yearning and the ache and the hope she'd been barely reining in since he'd been shot. She'd come so close to losing him, all because he'd been willing to sacrifice his life for hers.

"Oh, Lord, bring him complete and enduring healing and a speedy recovery." She placed a kiss on his hand, and then lifted her head.

Hunter was watching her, his eyes full of tenderness. "Don't look so tragic, Annabeth." He touched her wet cheeks. "I'm not dead yet."

She gave him a soggy smile. "You're awake."

He attempted a smile in return, but only managed what

looked like a wince. Tiny lines of pain rimmed his mouth. "My throat's on fire."

"Here, drink this." She poured him a glass of water and helped him take a sip. And another. After the third he placed his head back on the pillow and shut his eyes.

He was fast asleep before she'd set the glass back on the table.

As she watched him slumber, perched on a chair beside the settee, she felt a new kind of peace, an assurance that they were not only going to be good for each other, but good to each other.

A half hour later, his eyes opened again. "You realize you have to marry me now that I took a bullet for you."

She laughed, bolstered by the realization that he was finding humor in the situation already. "When you make a grand gesture you go all out." She combed her fingers through his hair, then cupped his cheek. "I like it."

"I can give you words, too." He turned his head into her palm, pressed a kiss to the tender flesh. "I love you, Annabeth."

She sighed. Fighting for his life, the man was still charming. "Hunter Mitchell, you don't play fair."

"No, I don't." His eyes fluttered shut again. "You should remember that."

He was asleep before she could respond, a convenient trick of his. But at least the smile still played across his lips and his color was returning.

Everything was going to be all right between them. Better than all right, nearly perfect.

About an hour after Mattie left for Charity House, the door flew open with a bang and Sarah rushed into the room. Tears rolled freely down her cheeks. "Where is he?" She looked frantically around the room, her gaze darting around without focus. "Where's my pa?"

Annabeth rose from her perch beside Hunter and was halfway across the room when he answered the question himself.

"Over here." He lifted his head slightly.

Sarah sped to his side, but halted several feet back. She clasped her hands behind her back, as if afraid to get too near. "Pa? You don't look so good."

He beckoned her to him with a half wave.

Sucking in a huge gulp of air, Sarah glanced to Annabeth for confirmation.

"Go on, darling," she urged, her hands gently guiding the girl toward the chair she herself had just vacated. "Sit here and talk to your father."

Eyes wide, her gaze narrowed in on the bandage covering most of his chest and half of his shoulder. "What happened?"

He gave her a sanitized version of the afternoon's events.

"You mean…" Sarah's eyes grew wider. "The bad guy shot you while you were trying to save Aunt Annabeth?"

"That's exactly what happened," Annabeth confirmed.

"Oh, Pa. You're a hero!"

"I'm no hero." The words rasped beneath a long exhale. "I merely did what had to be done."

"Say what you will, Hunter Mitchell." Annabeth moved in closer and peered over Sarah's head. "You'll always be my hero."

"Mine, too," Sarah declared.

"*Mine,* too," Mattie said from behind Annabeth, making all four of them laugh. Hunter a bit more subdued than the rest.

His gaze locking with Annabeth's, he gave her a crooked smile. "Guess all I need is a sunset and a white horse to make the picture complete."

"Plenty of time for those," she said, touched he wanted to give her the fairy tale. How could she not love this man? "Let's get you healed first."

He reached up. Understanding the silent summons, she took his hand in hers. For a long moment, neither said a word. They didn't need to speak. They communicated in their own private way, inside the stare, using a silent language that was all theirs.

"I never asked you properly. And I certainly never used the right words. I love you, Annabeth." His words swept over her, soothing away the last of her doubts. "Will you be my wife?"

Before she could answer, Sarah gasped in delight. "Say yes, Aunt Annabeth."

Taking her eyes off Hunter, she looked over at the child, the very happy child. "You approve?"

"I do, I do." She bounced in the chair. "Say *yes*."

"You heard the girl." Mattie patted Annabeth's arm. "Say yes to the man."

With a happy sigh, Annabeth turned back to Hunter. It mattered that the two most important women in her life supported their marriage.

And yet, she hesitated. She believed Hunter loved her, but did he love her unconditionally and without reservation?

She needed to know his heart.

"The last time we had this discussion, you put restrictions on your offer." She ignored his wince and pressed on. "What sort of marriage do you want with me, Hunter?"

"A real one, the kind the good Lord intended between a man and woman." He held her gaze, communicating his message with an intimate smile on his lips. "There will be no secrets between us, no barriers. With Christ at the center, our marriage will be full of faith, hope, mutual trust and—"

"Love," she added.

"And love." He pressed a kiss to her hand. "Definitely love."

There was only one thing to say to that. "Yes, Hunter. Yes. I want to be your wife, in every way that matters."

Sarah cheered.

Mattie sighed.

Hunter grinned. "I knew you'd come round to my way of thinking."

Seeing that they were of a like mind, Annabeth simply returned his smile. Lost in Hunter's stare, she felt each of their pasts melt away and reveled in the future before them. A future as husband and wife built on a foundation of faith in God, enduring love and family.

Epilogue

On the day of her wedding to Hunter, Annabeth stood outside the chapel situated directly behind Charity House. The sun was making its slow, colorful descent behind the mountain peaks. There was still a lot of daylight left, but the western sky was turning an orangey pink.

Having forgone tradition, Annabeth chose to have her mother give her away. As soon as Mattie joined her outside, they would begin their walk down the aisle.

The guests had already arrived and taken their seats. Much to Annabeth's pleasure, every member of Hunter's family was in attendance. Their presence was proof that they fully supported her union to the returning son.

The Mitchells had even embraced Mattie as one of their own. For weeks now, each one had put their own form of subtle, albeit loving, pressure on the infamous madam to sell her brothel and move to the Flying M.

Their efforts had not been wasted. Mattie had begun negotiations with several potential buyers.

God had blessed Annabeth beyond measure. She couldn't wait to begin her future with the man she loved and the child they shared.

As if sensing her eagerness, Mattie chose that moment to exit the church. With a worried expression on her face, she hurried down the steps. "Hunter is nowhere to be found." Her anxious gaze landed everywhere but on Annabeth. "And I'm afraid Sarah is missing, too."

Despite Mattie's agitation, this news did not alarm Annabeth. Hunter had warned her that he planned to pull Sarah aside before the ceremony for a private father/daughter moment. If Annabeth knew her man—and she liked to think she did—he was presenting the child with another doll for her collection, this one in a wedding dress to commemorate the special day.

"It's all right, Mother. They'll be here shortly."

The sound of pounding horse hooves had her turning to look toward the west.

A jolt of surprise went through her. And then came the joy. It reared up from her toes and settled in her throat.

"Oh, my," she said, her breath stalling in her lungs.

"I say." Mattie shook her head. "That boy certainly knows how to make a grand entrance."

Not a grand entrance, a grand *gesture,* the grandest of them all, because there he was, her man, riding atop a white horse with a coat so pristine it looked too perfect to be real.

Sarah was balanced on the saddle in front of him, smiling broadly, a new doll clutched in her hand.

As if wishing to create the best possible effect, Hunter had timed their entrance perfectly. By the time he reined in his magnificent steed, the sunset had reached spectacular proportions, creating a perfect backdrop for man, horse and child.

"Oh, Hunter," Annabeth whispered. "You magnificent man."

Their gazes collided and she felt the impact all the way to her toes. Her eyes filled.

"You were right, Pa. We did make her cry."

Eyes filling all the more, Annabeth laughed. "Happy tears, Sarah. I'm crying happy tears."

"Those are the very best kind," Sarah decided, then looked over at Mattie who'd become suspiciously quiet. "Look, Pa, Miss Mattie's crying, too."

"Will wonders never cease?"

Appearing highly pleased with himself, Hunter set Sarah carefully on the ground then dismounted behind her. He approached Annabeth with the hint of a grin flirting in his eyes and dancing on the edges of his lips.

"I can't promise the fairy tale everyday of our lives. There will be ups and downs, easy days and hard ones, good times and bad. But, Annabeth, my love " he kissed her square on the mouth "—with the Lord as our guide—" he kissed her again "—I promise to stand by you all the days of our life together."

"I thank God for you, Hunter Mitchell." She lifted on her toes and kissed *him* square on the mouth. "I'll thank Him every morning, noon and night, until the day I die."

Laney popped her head out of the church. "It's time." She eyeballed Hunter. "Come inside and take your place."

He turned to Annabeth, a question in his eyes. "What do you say the four of us make the trek down the aisle together?"

"I can't think of a better way to start off our life as a family."

Arms linked, the four of them entered the church together. The assembled guests drew one, great collective breath and then broke out in applause.

Annabeth couldn't think of a more perfect beginning for her marriage to the man she loved, or a stronger testament to the family they'd already begun.

* * * * *

Dear Reader,

Thank you for choosing *The Outlaw's Redemption,* the sixth book in my Charity House series. If this is your first book in the series, welcome. I hope you enjoyed Hunter and Annabeth's story. If you've been with me before, welcome back!

Many of you requested Hunter's book after he showed up in *The Lawman Claims His Bride.* Thank you for the much-needed nudge. I wasn't sure where his story was headed, but I knew he needed his own happy ending. Like many of you, I adore wounded heroes in need of redemption. When a woman is the catalyst for that journey, well then, I say, more the better.

The most rewarding part about writing a series of connected books is the opportunity to revisit characters that once had a starring role in their own stories. It's always fun to see where their journey has led them and what advice they have to give. One character in particular just wouldn't go away, no matter how often I tried to shove her aside. Mattie Silks. The ornery madam has given many of my characters fits, especially the heroes, but she's also shown a surprisingly tender heart under that hard exterior. Just as Hunter tells her, it's never too late for any of us to change. Isn't it a joy to know God never turns away those who seek Him?

The Charity House series isn't complete. Molly Taylor Scott is all grown-up now, as are Hunter's younger siblings. Those Mitchell men fall fast and for keeps. Their sisters are the same. I'm looking forward to sharing some of their stories with you.

I love hearing from readers. You can contact me

through email at renee@reneeryan.com or at my website, www.reneeryan.com. I'm also on Facebook and Twitter. In the meantime, Happy Reading!

Renee

Questions for Discussion

1. Why does Hunter visit a brothel owned by a notorious madam in the opening scene? What makes this especially difficult for him? Is he wise to try to get answers out of Mattie Silks? What does she have to tell him? Have you ever received startling news from an unexpected source? Explain.

2. Who shows up in the middle of Hunter's discussion with Mattie? Why has she shown up now? What connection does she have with Mattie? Have you ever tried to maintain a secret, only to have a most unlikely source tell you they know the truth? What happened?

3. Why does Annabeth distrust Hunter at first? What in her background makes it hard for her to see the man he is now, rather than the man he once was? Is her judgment of him fair? Why or why not?

4. What motivated Annabeth to return to Denver, when she was happy in Boston? How has her life changed since returning home? How has *she* changed? Have you ever had something good come out of a terrible situation? What was the ultimate outcome?

5. Why does Hunter go to Charity House the next day? Who does he meet there? Is this a happy reunion, or not? How does Annabeth react when Hunter proves to be reasonable? Why do you think she would have preferred a fight?

6. When Hunter first meets young Sarah, was she the way you expected her to be? Do you think her upbringing has made her the girl she is now? If so, how much influence did Laney and Marc Dupree have on her, and how much do you think was innate to her inner character? Did her reaction to Hunter's news take you by surprise? Why or why not?

7. When Hunter takes Annabeth out to lunch to discuss Sarah's future, who shows up? Why does Mattie make such a fuss about Annabeth and Hunter's agreement concerning Sarah? What does she want for Annabeth and why? How does Hunter treat Mattie during this and subsequent altercations? Why do you think he treats her this way?

8. Hunter and Annabeth met years ago, when he was just off the ranch and married to her half sister, Maria. What happened at that first meeting? Does that explain Annabeth's reaction to the hairbrush he gives her now, or is there more to her response? If so, what?

9. When Sarah first meets Hunter, she reacts positively. However, later in the book, her behavior toward him changes. What do you think happened that caused this? What do you think her friends told her? Have you ever been influenced by well-meaning friends in a matter where they didn't have all the information? What happened?

10. What happened when Annabeth made it clear to Mattie that she was going to marry Hunter, regardless of what she thought? Why do you think Mattie reacted

the way she did? What in Mattie's past makes her so distrustful of men like Hunter?

11. What mistake does Hunter make when he takes Annabeth to the lawyer's office with him? Why do you think he did what he did? What does Annabeth really want from him? Why is it so hard for him to give her what she wants?

12. Hunter thinks his past is behind him. What happens to prove him wrong? How does this encounter finally help him give Annabeth what she wants? What happened when he finally said the words she needed to hear?

REQUEST YOUR FREE BOOKS!

2 FREE INSPIRATIONAL NOVELS
PLUS 2
FREE
MYSTERY GIFTS

Love Inspired
HISTORICAL
INSPIRATIONAL HISTORICAL ROMANCE

YES! Please send me 2 FREE Love Inspired® Historical novels and my 2 FREE mystery gifts (gifts are worth about $10). After receiving them, if I don't wish to receive any more books, I can return the shipping statement marked "cancel." If I don't cancel, I will receive 4 brand-new novels every month and be billed just $4.74 per book in the U.S. or $5.24 per book in Canada. That's a saving of at least 21% off the cover price. It's quite a bargain! Shipping and handling is just 50¢ per book in the U.S. and 75¢ per book in Canada.* I understand that accepting the 2 free books and gifts places me under no obligation to buy anything. I can always return a shipment and cancel at any time. Even if I never buy another book, the two free books and gifts are mine to keep forever.

102/302 IDN F5CN

Name	(PLEASE PRINT)

Address	Apt. #

City	State/Prov.	Zip/Postal Code

Signature (if under 18, a parent or guardian must sign)

Mail to the Harlequin® Reader Service:
IN U.S.A.: P.O. Box 1867, Buffalo, NY 14240-1867
IN CANADA: P.O. Box 609, Fort Erie, Ontario L2A 5X3

Want to try two free books from another series?
Call 1-800-873-8635 or visit www.ReaderService.com.

* Terms and prices subject to change without notice. Prices do not include applicable taxes. Sales tax applicable in N.Y. Canadian residents will be charged applicable taxes. Offer not valid in Quebec. This offer is limited to one order per household. Not valid for current subscribers to Love Inspired Historical books. All orders subject to credit approval. Credit or debit balances in a customer's account(s) may be offset by any other outstanding balance owed by or to the customer. Please allow 4 to 6 weeks for delivery. Offer available while quantities last.

Your Privacy—The Harlequin® Reader Service is committed to protecting your privacy. Our Privacy Policy is available online at www.ReaderService.com or upon request from the Harlequin Reader Service.

We make a portion of our mailing list available to reputable third parties that offer products we believe may interest you. If you prefer that we not exchange your name with third parties, or if you wish to clarify or modify your communication preferences, please visit us at www.ReaderService.com/consumerchoice or write to us at Harlequin Reader Service Preference Service, P.O. Box 9062, Buffalo, NY 14269. Include your complete name and address.

LIH13R

"They say he's magic with the long reins—"

"I saw him ride once in an exhibition down by Cheyenne...."

Sarah clutched her schoolbooks until her knuckles turned white. The men of Lost Hollow were no better than little boys, excited over a wild cowboy! Unfortunately, her boss, the chairman of the school board and the reason Oscar White was here, had insisted that as the schoolteacher, she should come along as part of the welcoming committee. And because they'd known each other in Bear Creek.

But she hadn't known Oscar White well and hadn't liked what she had known.

And now she just wanted to get this "welcome" over with. Her thoughts wandered until the train came to a hissing stop at the platform.

The man who strode off with a confident gait bore a resemblance to the Oscar White she'd known, but *this* man was assuredly different. With his Stetson tilted back rakishly to reveal brown eyes, his face no longer bore the slight roundness of youth. No, those lean, craggy features belonged to a man, without question. Broad shoulders easily parted the small crowd on the platform, and he headed straight for their group.

Sarah turned away, alarmed by the pulse pounding frantically in her temples. Why this reaction now, *to this man?*

Through the rhythmic beating in her ears—too fast!—she heard the men exchange greetings, and then Mr. Allen cleared his throat.

"And I believe you already know our schoolteacher…"

Obediently she turned and their gazes collided—his brown eyes curious until he glimpsed her face.

"…Miss Sarah Hansen."

His eyes instantly cooled. He quickly looked back to the other men. "I've got to get my horses from the stock car. I'll catch up with you gentlemen in a moment. Miss Hansen." He tipped his hat before rushing off down the line of train cars.

Sarah found herself watching him and forced her eyes away. Obviously he remembered her, and perhaps what had passed between them seven years ago.

That was just fine with her. She had no use for reckless cowboys. She was looking for a responsible man for a husband….

Don't miss ROPING THE WRANGLER
by Lacy Williams,
on sale August 2013 wherever
Love Inspired Historical books are sold!

The Master Matchmakers

Emma Pyrmont hopes to convince single father
Sir Nicholas Rotherford that there's more to life than calculations
and chemistry. As she draws him closer to his young daughter,
Nicholas sees his daughter—and her nanny—with new eyes.

The Courting Campaign

by

REGINA SCOTT

*Available August 2013 wherever
Love Inspired Historical books are sold.*